Winner of the DC Books Literature
Award & Nooranad Haneef Award

HERBARIUM

SONIA RAFEEK

Translated from the Malayalam original by
MINISTHY S.

THORNBIRD
NIYOGI
BOOKS

Published by
NIYOGI BOOKS
Block D, Building No. 77,
Okhla Industrial Area, Phase-I,
New Delhi-110 020, INDIA
Tel: 011-26818960, +91 7428978881
Email: niyogibooks@gmail.com
Website: www.niyogibooksindia.com

Editor: Zinnia Sengupta, Anwesha Panda
Design: Nadeem Ahmed
Cover design: Apoorva Lalit

ISBN: 978-81-992494-6-2
Publication: 2026

Printed at Niyogi Offset Pvt. Ltd., New Delhi, India

For

The earth which no longer emits fragrance,
The dead trees,
The rivers which have sunk deep,
The children—
Gifted with God's imagination,
To rebuild, recreate everything.

Contents

Translator's Note

In 2016, Sonia Rafeek won the DC Books Award for her debut novel, *Herbarium*. When I encountered the book, I was fascinated by it. The story of Tipu—a little boy who loses his mother—and his deep connection with nature, resonated strongly within me. Tipu's new life at his grandmother's house, wondering at grubs, leaves, ants and flowers, made me revisit my own childhood. Today, our children are mesmerised by the world of electronic gadgets and computers. For nurturing and protecting our beautiful planet, we have to inculcate the love of nature in the young children.

I remember a striking cartoon. Two women and two children. One mother was staring at a cell phone; her daughter did the same. The other was reading a book; her daughter held another. The single bubble on the cartoon, was a question raised by the mother with the mobile: 'How do you get her to read?'

Let us all read more. And get our children to read too. After all, they learn every moment, mimicking us. Books which make them step out of their rooms and pick up a fistful of soil have to be celebrated.

It was a joy working with Sonia Rafeek, a plant pathology specialist. She reposed full faith in me as a translator. *Herbarium*, our labour of love, found a welcoming home at Niyogi Books. I would like to acknowledge my gratitude to Mrs Tultul De Niyogi, Co-Publisher and Shri Nirmal Kanti Bhattacharjee, the Editorial Director, for their warmth and encouragement.

MINISTHY S.

One:
The Garden in My Palm

'One teeny-weeny garden ensconced in the palm of my hand. A pretty brinjal, and next to her, two ladies' fingers with their offspring, who love standing on their heads. Gazing at both, an imperious-looking curry leaf plant. A red spinach, resembling a mad old woman with scraggly hair; the little children spilling over from her mane are the spinach seedlings which have sprouted profusely in the flower pot...The basil, Indian borage, mint and aromatic ginger huddling behind the others, marginalised like second-class citizens. The tomato plant, with its yellow star-flowers, has been beguiling me for a long time. Here, this is the fourth flower she has sloppily shed! If the tulsi grows a finger's length more, a few leaves can be plucked for sautéing in oil.

When the chilli seeds prolonged their germination, I thought of growing cowpeas instead. But when I arrived at dawn, I saw amenably grinning chilli saplings, declaring the ending of their hibernation. My yearning for the cowpeas and frustration with the chillies both ended therein.

I have a fervent desire to bring in every possible flowering plant and let them all blossom in this palm-sized garden of mine! But that longing has been curbed with a few dahlias and petunias. I have a jasmine plant, slightly lethargic; she is nearing budding season, but has a haughty reluctance. When her first bud opens up, I should ask Tipu to sketch the sapling. Let this white jasmine be the first representative of the green world that he sketches! The fragrance of life and its colours should spread across his drawings.'

This was the third or fourth note of Fatima's which inadvertently tumbled into Asif's hands.

He had retrieved one from among old newspapers and tucked it inside his wallet yesterday. The note inside her handbag consisted of a few sentences scribbled on the back of a hospital prescription. This missive was tucked inside the notebook where she jotted down the grocery lists. Folding it tenderly, he slipped it beneath a tea cup.

Asif walked from the sitting room to the balcony, as if moving towards Fatima to discuss a matter. As he opened the door to the balcony, autumn was readying for departure, having hurled a delectable chilly avalanche on his face. He closed his eyes and sauntered back and forth a few times.

It was this garden in the balcony that Fatima had referred in her note as 'the garden in one's palm'. A forest inside their home, all of 10 feet. The basil almost reached his knees and the jasmine was yet to bloom. The mad saplings of the spinach matriarch were already shriveling. Meanwhile, the ladies' fingers and the cowpeas communicated with Asif like characters in a silent movie. The money plant which straddled the railings of the balcony seemed as impassive as before. The curry-leaf had a few new shoots. Most of its yellowed, aging leaves were strewn inside the flower pot.

Ah, the day they had bought that curry-leaf plant! Asif remembered it was a rainy day.

Such rain was unusual in Dubai. The desert sky was resplendent with thunder and lightning. It was Friday, and Asif wasn't willing to sacrifice his afternoon nap for buying a fragile curry-leaf plant. He curled up under his blanket.

'Rain in November is common enough! Why are you acting strange?' Fatima shoved him off the bed.

It was a ritual, an annual November ritual. In the past eight years of their Dubai existence, Fatima and her balcony always geared up for November. It was not just November, though; Fatima toiled throughout the year to sustain her balcony garden. However, despite trying all the tricks in her kitty, soothing the blazing impact of the summer months on the plants was beyond her.

The trip to the nursery at Al Warsan for purchasing a curry-leaf sapling on that rainy day had been a troublesome one. Even a slight drizzle could swallow up the roads in Dubai. And when you were driving during a downpour in a land unaccustomed to rain, the less said the better! The traffic jam, with vehicles brushing against one another, forced them to while away hours inside the car. Asif was now recollecting how he had rebuked her on that journey for utterly wasting a holiday.

Tipu, however, was oblivious to all that melee, comfortable in the back seat. He was lost in the world of some mobile game. Intermittently, his hero fired gunshots in sync with Asif's bitter accusations. And when Asif was silent, the hero continued to run, panting and heaving. It was doubtful whether Tipu had noticed the torrent outside.

Fatima was not responding to Asif's harsh words. She sat silently, holding the curry-leaf plant in her lap. When she put it down for a while, the slushy mud broke through the plastic cover and made the leather footrest damp. When they reached home, Asif had rushed out from the car, grabbed the plant from her hands and vehemently thrown it to the ground.

'Ridiculous! I washed the car just yesterday!' he screamed before walking away, leaving Fatima alone.

From the lift, Asif watched Fatima wiping the mud off the footrest with her dupatta. The memory moistened his eyes now. Once, Fatima had commented that curry-leaves were stubborn plants. Asif could never understand what she had implied by that, neither then nor now.

The tea went cold. A fly slipped inside the flat through the open balcony door. Now Asif would have to usher it outside. Otherwise, unsure of whether it was a guest or invader in this flat-kingdom, it would wander around aimlessly. *Let it suffer*, Asif decided, reasoning that a creature that stepped inside without knowing its way back, was foolhardy. He emptied the cold tea in the sink, and tucked away Fatima's note inside his wallet.

Tipu had gone to play with the kids from the neighbouring flats. What game was it? The same one he used to play all by himself in the flat. Solitary or with pals, he played *Minecraft*, *G.T.A.*, *Star Wars* and the like…Tipu and his friends focused on the games on their tablets, gazing through their thick glasses with the same intensity of scientists discovering the secrets of the universe through their microscopes. Asif wanted to call him home. But he hesitated, since he never had the ability to handle Tipu as effortlessly as Fatima.

Colour pencils and books were scattered on the table. Tipu did not have many toys. He liked sketching, but nowadays, that habit was declining rapidly. Asif spread Tipu's pictures on the table. It was like entering a museum with aliens on display. Tipu's drawings depicted his favorite characters from cartoons and video games. Gigantic monsters, ugly ogres, luxurious cars, guns, planes and more of that ilk. Some had green tongues and blue ears, others possessed 16 fingers and revolving necks; weird bodies made of one creature's head and another's torso! Let alone a lovely colour, Asif's eyes could hardly discern a pleasing picture. Why was the child like this?

The note he had picked up from Fatima's almirah the previous day had been on the same topic.

My Tipu is an artist. Even a straight line he draws is a picture! These lines, circles and triangles have a destiny. The destiny of a moonbeam. It changes the hues of the place it falls upon. A moonbeam is a paintbrush. My Tipu is also a moonbeam.

One day, the beasts, vehicles and buildings in his drawings shall undergo a metamorphosis. Someday, life shall bloom from his colour pencils. Through the vibrant pictures, he shall see this world in a different way. The colours that I see in the moonbeam shall become visible to him too. My Tipu, my moonbeam.

Asif felt a craving for tea yet again. Usually after the house maid's visit, there was a brighter ambience in the kitchen. But the moment Asif stepped inside and shifted even a spoon from its place, the darkness of a battlefield spread through the room. There was a jury pointing at him accusingly from every nook and corner of that kitchen. Fatima brought them all up with gentle care, but not without discipline. Asif was not proficient in the art of endearment. He sighed deeply, sprinkling tea powder into the boiling milk.

The milk changed colour, becoming tea. In Fatima's words, 'the milk hurtled into tea'. Occasionally, she would say many things in that vein. It was Tipu, rather than Asif, who quickly caught onto Fatima's nuances. One could imagine an invisible Wi-Fi network connecting both of them.

Asif had no intention of wasting another cup of tea. He took a sip without waiting for it to cool. 'Ouch!' His tongue was scalded. After that night, when Asif's whole being had been scorched, even the warmth of tea stirred terror in him.

Could Tipu handle that burning? Were there any clear boundaries to what a nine-year-old could see and hear? Asif did not know. But here he was, trying to determine his son's boundaries. Even now, Tipu believed that his Ummudu would return. Or was the child just blabbering?

Asif was yet to understand him properly. Fatima, too.

Two:
Tipu

Tipu was a real smartie pie.

It was he who reassembled Abhishek's drone with the broken wing, making it fly again; he was also the one to repair the headlight of Vinayak's remote-controlled car, making it flash brightly. What he knew, others didn't, and what everyone knew, he didn't. That was Tipu for you!

When baby Tipu began to talk, he added the suffix 'du' to every word. *Paludu* for milk, *Veedudu* for house, *Carudu* for car, *Poochudu* for cat, *Pattudu* for song…and finally *Ummudu* for mother! Fatima had thoroughly relished the sweetness of words when Tipu added the inflection of *du* to them. Consequently, she never attempted to correct him or explain that she was *Umma*, not *Ummudu*. It was rather late when Tipu started calling Asif *Vappu*. By that time, the addendum of *du* had started retreating from his tongue. Now only the *du* within *Ummudu* existed.

Tipu knew that his Ummudu absolutely adored his drawings, and loved to see him playing with colours. Indeed, he often sketched pictures just to make Ummudu happy.

'Look, look…when we reach home, my beloved Tipu will sketch this for Ummudu, okay?' Fatima had once said to him, pointing at the yellow chrysanthemum flowers in the park. He nodded his head, as if fully accepting her suggestion, while circling the park on his bicycle. He never drew the picture, and he fibbed to Fatima that he couldn't recollect the colour of the bloom. 'Huh! Why not admit that you didn't like it? He forgot, it seems!' She gave Tipu a tiny pinch.

When Fatima watered the 10-foot garden in her balcony, added fertilisers and dug the soil, Tipu named that process 'Ummudu's funny games.' There was a gamer in his favourite video game, *Minecraft*, who prowled around a garden with a sword. If he chopped off a tree with that blade, the player obtained 10 smart points. If he made a house using that wood, he could move ahead in the game. Once, provoked by the memory of that video game, Tipu had rushed into the balcony with his cricket bat. Similar to the gamer twirling his sword before hacking the tree, Tipu swung his bat and slashed away; the ladies' finger plant, brimming with flowers, was beheaded in seconds. Fatima was watering the plants at the time. Grabbing the bat from Tipu's hands, she whacked him on his butt. With that, even his rare visits to the balcony had ceased.

Nowadays, Tipu detested Asif stepping out onto the balcony.

'Vappu, where is my eraser? My blue pencil is missing…' With his imaginary complaints, Tipu would persuade Asif to return to his side.

Tipu knew that Ummudu had set off towards the Tilapia Lake in Al Ain. *She would return for sure, maybe after some time…*

When the weekend and the holy festival of Eid had coincided, Asif had felt like going for a trip. An office colleague suggested the Tilapia Lake. Ummudu walking away amidst the sand dunes as the dust storm howled around them, was the last glimpse Tipu had of her.

When Tipu stepped out of the car with Fatima, Asif had cautioned him against it. Fatima agreed, 'You sit inside the car, dearest. There is a cold breeze outside.' He played on his phone for a while, and dozed off. Tipu did not know that while he slumbered, Asif was desperately, unceasingly, calling the police and the fire department.

When Tipu awoke, there was a hue and cry all around. He recognised the fire department vehicles. They were pointing at the little boy standing near the car and muttering amongst themselves. Asif had come rushing, and hugged him tightly. Tipu noticed that Vappu's face looked stricken and his eyes were bloodshot.

In Tipu's video game, if the bike hurtled off the race course and went flying into the air, the biker would typically shudder, climb back on his vehicle and return to the track. It was this bike racer that Tipu remembered when his Vappu came running towards him and lifted him up. He believed that his Vappu's eyes had turned red due to the sand storm.

For the next two days, Tipu stayed at Asif's sister's house. His paternal grandparents were there too. His cousin sister Ryan was there, but he didn't find it exciting to play with her. Meeting her occasionally was rather pleasant, though. After a couple of days, Asif had come to take him back to their flat. To anyone who observed Tipu's behavior, it was as if Fatima's absence hardly mattered to him.

'When will Ummudu get back?' Save for the offhand question flung around intermittently, Tipu seemed very calm. Although Tipu's disposition baffled Asif, the absence of expected, intense repercussions offered him much relief.

No one ever died during a *Minecraft* game.

If a gamer was caught by a monster, one just had to press the 're-spawn' button for granting him a new lease of life. In a matter of minutes, one could get back to playing the game.

No game ended completely; a new one was created every time. When Tipu got bored of one game, Vappu purchased another for him. So what, if one pencil went missing? There were so many packets of pencils awaiting him inside the cupboard! When Tipu's Galaxy Note had crashed the previous week, his father bought him a new tablet just after two days. The almirahs were incessantly being replenished with shirts, trousers, bags and watches. Those would never be empty. And the watches would always be ticking. The absence of his Ummudu was a temporary phenomenon. Like remote-controlled toy cars, whatever stopped running could be brought back to life with new batteries. That was Tipu's theory! Though Asif couldn't comprehend what Tipu's philosophy was exactly, it was comforting the boy in the present circumstances. So Asif did not try to change Tipu's belief.

Asif was also accustomed to churning out chocolate milk shakes, burgers and chicken nuggets for Tipu. Besides that, he had instructed the house maid to prepare whatever snacks Tipu liked. As per Fatima's rules, fast food was allowed entry inside their home only once a week. The rest of the week, Tipu had to eat whatever his Ummudu cooked. She would not even permit him to indulge in chewing gum. Fatima would quip that Tipu's 'imp face' peeped through when he chewed on gum! She had a theory that unlike other food, the aftertaste of chewing gum turned a human being nasty.

For the past week, Tipu had been flooded with KFC and pizza treats. He was delighted with the unrestricted eating spree. Tipu decided that even if Ummudu were to come back, the new practices should be sustained, and systematically saved a few strategies in his mind for the future.

There was a mint plant in Fatima's garden. Once, sniffing at Tipu's mouth as he stood there, ready for school, Ummudu had sharply asked, 'Didn't you brush your teeth today?'

'Yes, of course!' He opened his mouth wide and put his tongue out.

Seizing the opportunity, Fatima plucked two mint leaves and popped them in his mouth.

'Much better than your chewing gum! Go on, chew and swallow...it will smell nice too!'

Tipu was clear about the choice he had to make. The very next moment, he spat it out.

'As if anyone would eat grass! Yuck!'

Tipu swung his school bag onto his shoulder and ran to catch the school bus.

Ummudu and Tipu were buddies. The most friendly mom amongst all his compatriots was his! Fatima would simply ignore Asif's insinuations that the freedom she gave Tipu would end up spoiling him. The boys at school were always complaining about their ever-pestering mothers. Tipu would brag before them, 'My mom is the best in the world.' They were buddies who would fight sporadically, wrangle with each other, but make up with noisy hugs and kisses afterwards. Still, it was vexing for Tipu that Ummudu never joined him in playing video games. And Fatima, too, was peeved that he did not sketch the pictures she wanted to see. Tipu's colour pencils never gave birth to flowers, leaves, trees, birds, earth or rain, but Fatima never tried to impose her preferences either. Her approach was—let Tipu grow up as he pleased, drawing and playing… Or even just playing without drawing!

Three:
Tipu's Ummudu

Fatima was an irrepressible young woman. Someone who would see only light upon closing her eyes and gazing inwards. She was beautiful in her laughter and tears. The lone daughter of a teacher couple, Fatima had grown up in a village. Her life with Asif in Dubai ushered in many changes within her. Fatima could adapt to change, and was never frazzled by the associated ripples. She could acclimatise herself to any environment. An adjustment akin to the shedding of leaves and the incipient budding of trees.

The liberty which Fatima gave to Tipu had been showered on young Fatima by her parents. Fatima was a small circle in the middle of a vast canvas, possessing the freedom to explore the entirety of the naked surface. When they were transferred to Trivandrum, Nabeezath and Salim hadn't been blessed with Fatima yet. It was the headmaster, Rajasekharan Nair, who had arranged a rented accommodation for them near the school. The house, situated inside the compound of his family home—the *tharavadu*—had long been vacant, for almost three to four years. The Lower Primary School at Njarakkadu was within walking distance from the house.

Thiru Nilam—literally 'revered place'—was Rajasekharan Nair's house where he lived with his wife Padmajamma and four children, situated in the middle of acres of land. One could view the rented house of Salim and Nabeezath clearly from Thiru Nilam. Towards the north was a Sarppakavu—the serpent grove—where the snake deities were worshipped.

For Nabeezath, the serpent grove, lush and thriving with unknown trees and herbs, was a fascinating new universe. There were three peacocks which inhabited the surroundings of Thiru Nilam. Whenever the creatures cried, a sadness would seep inside Nabeezath. She would remark that the peacocks were not croaking, but lamenting.

'Look at the burden these wretched things carry, that too only to amuse the spectators…What a destiny!'

Nabeezath was under the impression that they were Padmajamma's pet peacocks. But they were similar to enigmatic full stops—originating from the unknown, reared by no one, never venturing anywhere else. The peacocks' existence was like that of the serpent grove. Bearing their mysterious history, the birds meandered in and around the grove with their melancholy steps.

It was rare to catch a glimpse of Padmajamma. Nabeezath saw her at twilight every day, when she came to light the lamp in the serpent grove. The woman was busy inside her house during the day. When Rajasekharan Nair stepped out for school, Padmajamma could be sighted at the door like a flash of lightning. Nabeezath did not know much about the woman of the house, except that she wore an immaculately starched and ironed *setu-mundu*, the traditional two-piece dress of the Nair women, and adorned her forehead with a dot of *sindoor*. Padmajamma was a slim, fair woman, unaccustomed to smiles or small talk. There were sepia print photographs of her youthful days displayed in the sitting room. In those, Padmajamma looked plump, and had the most enchanting smile on her face. Nabeezath knew that the woman stepped out of her house only for lighting the lamp in the grove.

That day, as usual, Padmajamma arrived to light the twilight lamp. The roosting birds made a mélange of sounds. The lamentations of the peacocks rang out at intervals. The dusk displayed a tenebrific despair, just before pitching into the mysteriousness of utter darkness. When the cries of the peacocks merged with that sadness, an indescribable emotion spread across the serpent grove. Nabeezath walked towards the light, having entered the grove following the peacocks' screams. Not seeing anyone near the raised structure with the lit lamp, she waded through the dense foliage and creepers, and heard a woman's faint voice. It was either a groan or a suppressed sob. Careful not to stir the dried leaves, she edged closer to the sound. Hiding behind a *gulmohar* which had a huge hollow in its trunk, Nabeezath strained her ears.

It was Padmajamma, standing at the foot of an *ashoka* tree in full bloom. She was leaning against the tree and weeping, or was that just Nabeezath's imagination? She moved towards the woman and cleared her throat. When Padmajamma flinched and looked behind, Nabeezath felt confounded, as if she had stumbled upon a forbidden sight. They stood facing each other for a long time. It was the first time that Nabeezath was seeing Padmajamma closely; her hair was unkempt and her eyes were red. Nabeezath had known of only one woman who sat sadly underneath an *ashoka* tree—Sita Devi.

As a perplexed Nabeezath stood there, wondering whether to retrace her steps, the woman queried:

'Why are you here?'

The voice had a pathos which was not congruent with the face.

'Come,' Padmajamma invited Nabeezath to step closer. The twilight darkened. Two *Yakshi*s, lovely female spirits under an *ashoka* tree which was resplendent with red blossoms! It was sad that such a wonderful sight escaped the eyes of artists.

Nabeezath couldn't understand why a woman who possessed a dignified house, children and a family would want to grieve so much? Due to her lack of familiarity with the lady, she desisted from enquiring further.

Yet, that was the day when Padmajamma's heart started melting. There were no fixed places or time schedules for their consequent encounters. The women started talking under the *peepul* tree in the serpent grove; on the verandah of the house; by the kitchen steps, sharing stories which was never heard or spoken about before. They exchanged words and sentences which could have filled up 10 attics, all the while blowing at the embers in the wood stove; harmonising with the tune of the grinding stone; floating with the fragrance of the bar soap at the washing stone.

'I am suffering from vitiligo…seems to have appeared out of the blue… Look at my fingers. The *vaidyan* has warned that it shall spread all over my body. Nowadays, my husband loathes me. Though he knows that my condition is not infectious, the revulsion is so naked… Tries to stay away from me as much as possible…'

Nabeezath understood the reason behind Padmajamma's initial inhibitions. The stark incongruity between the woman in the photograph and the real one of today, had been caused by the villainous vitiligo. Although notorious as a genetic disease, the misfortune had landed exclusively on Padmajamma in her family. When the white pigmentation started eating away the edges of her lips, the lady stopped stepping out even to the serpent grove. As Rajasekharan Nair took pains to avoid her company whenever there were others around, Padmajamma morphed into a creature of the inner rooms.

The children grew up, and the disease spread alongside. By drawing unfinished shapes all over her flesh, the infection enjoyed drawing a *kolam*, the designing ritual, on the woman's body. The intersections, where Padmajamma's skin colour and the discoloration of the disease met, were harshly wreathed in uncertainty, like islands and shorelines. There was no way to decipher whether the islands were travelling towards the vast shores or whether the shores were reaching out to the islands. Eventually, Nabeezath became the only person to visit Padmajamma.

During the days of her pregnancy, when Nabeezath was carrying Fatima, Padmajamma became her mother and sister. Their warm relationship continued until the woman passed away at the age of sixty. Fatima was ten years old when Padmajamma died.

It was Padmajamma who had initiated Fatima to the world of letters. The child addressed her as both *Amma* and *Umma*.

It was after Fatima's birth that Padmajamma started stepping out into the yard and grove again. Fatima never gave her any other option. When Nabeezath left for the school,

Fatima would stick around Padmajamma. Though there was a maid to take care of her, the child preferred to be at Thiru Nilam. Fatima had a name for each of the continents traced by vitiligo on Padmajamma's slender arm. Each one was a house, a home for Padmajamma's four children, with Fatima's residence being on her forehead!

Once, scraping off some henna applied on her palms by her mother during the Eid celebrations, Fatima had pasted a dot on her forehead. Everybody, including Nabeezath, Padmajamma and her friends, teased Fatima profusely on her henna dot as she set out for school. They realised later that the child was imitating Padmajamma's *sindoor* dot in her own way.

Asif's marriage proposal arrived when Fatima had just cleared the medical entrance exams after finishing her 12th standard finals. She had been selected for the nursing course. Asif was an engineer working in Dubai. Although both mother and daughter were in favour of her studying further, Nabeezath had been in a traumatised state when Asif's marriage proposal arrived. Salim's unexpected demise was the cause behind it.

Fatima had been fifteen, studying in the 10th standard, when the accident occurred. Though Salim used to be vigilant in his daily life, a moment's carelessness had cost him his life. When he was returning from a seminar in Calicut, Salim had jumped out even before the train had stopped completely. He was not the sort to be impulsive, but this singular event happened nonetheless, on that day. Mother and daughter became orphaned after his death.

Had Nabeezath been questioned about the significance of nursing studies versus marriage when it came to Fatima's future, she would have argued for higher studies. Yet, in the prevailing circumstances, she had heeded the advice of their relatives, and had given Fatima to Asif. Had Padmajamma been alive, perhaps the wedding would never have happened. It was the one time Nabeezath desperately needed the moral support of someone who truly understood her. But since there was no one to provide that succor, the deciding factor behind her choice became insecurity rather than prudence.

Fatima was happy with Asif. She was compatible with all types of soil and water. She could find roots anywhere on earth, and any breeze could make her wings flutter.

Fatima nurtured a basil plant, at the very least, in the few flats she lived in during their stay in Dubai. Perhaps it was a simulacrum of the serpent grove that she was busy crafting, in the limited space of the balconies. Could she capture the presence of both Padmajamma and Nabeezath through a basil? Asif would feel irritated on hearing her random observations.

'How on earth can you feel the presence of your loved ones through a plant? That too, of a mother who has been long dead and another, who lives back home?' Asif would taunt Fatima.

Asif was a Malayali, born and brought up outside Kerala. Accompanying his banker parents, he had spent his childhood in a piecemeal manner across different parts of India, mostly in boarding schools. Fatima usually restrained herself from boring him by narrating stories of her own childhood days replete with memories of the village, Padmajamma, the serpent grove and the birds. Occasionally on holidays, during bedtime, she would share her stories with Tipu. Though he hardly understood Fatima's motherly feelings for her balcony garden, Tipu enjoyed listening to his Ummudu's childhood tales.

Asif was crazy about vehicles. Consequently, he was intoxicated by the desert safari. They had gone to Lake Tilapia for such an adventure. Typically, they invited their friends to participate in such holiday jaunts. Tipu also found it fun when other kids were around. Fatima's consolation was that with other kids to play with, Tipu wouldn't be immersed in the phone and tablet for at least a few hours. But they hadn't asked anyone else to join them on that particular trip.

After his afternoon nap on a Friday, Asif had asked them both to get ready. Without much preparation, the trio had set out for Al Ain. It was a journey which implicitly trusted Google's guidance—25 km off the Al Ain–Abu Dhabi Truck Road, lay the desert lake of Tilapia.

When they moved through the Truck Road, gazing at the expanse of sand on either side, Fatima commented, 'Look, there is no dust blowing from these sand dunes!'

'Possibly because there is no wind,' Asif responded.

Fatima lowered the glass, and waved her hand in the air outside.

'No, there is a strong wind. It could be that the sand is wet …that's why it does not scatter dust!'

Asif slowly maneuvered his car into the sand. There was a red sign board on the side of the road, warning that swimming was strictly forbidden in the lake. Asif became an Arabian stallion in the mounds of sand. He displayed many tricks by ascending the dunes and diving downwards from the peaks. He had purchased his four-wheeler foreseeing many such trips.

Fatima and Tipu started enjoying the car's dives across the sand, similar to a ship swaying to the tunes of the waves. Tipu clapped his hands, laughing in delight. Yelling with joy, he encouraged his father. He was babbling enthusiastically about a desert racing video game he had once played with a friend. Amidst the sand dunes, Fatima could see a land, resplendent with trees, plants and birds. In the middle of that land, Lake Tilapia lay like an enigma. Beyond that, she caught a glimpse of the Jebal Al Hafeet mountain ranges.

Asif parked his car at some distance from the lake. On the fringes of the lake, there was a luxuriant growth of grass, as tall as a full-grown adult. There were unknown multi-coloured birds searching for prey, pecking among the reeds; some fishing with their heads under the water. A flock of small birds perched in the nearby shrubs. A glimmer of reptilian movement was palpable in the marshy lands beneath.

'Look at the birds in that *ghaf* tree, Tipu! They're all migratory birds…' Fatima pointed out.

'Born and brought up in some other place…yet nonchalant about ending up over here! Regardless of the number of lands they stay in, they never consider themselves immigrants… fascinating!' Although Fatima was musing, her words emerged loud.

Asif grinned at her. 'Exactly like me, right, Fatima? I have stayed in so many places! How many schools, friends, houses… Every place belongs to me. I always chase variety, and I only take what I need. See, that's how I remain immune to everything else in that land. I, too, am a migratory bird, you know?'

After that, Asif proceeded to capture birds in his camera.

The Tilapia waters had a cyan tint, a greenish blue. As Fatima gazed around the environs of the lake, she saw many small, circular ponds amongst the endless sand dunes. Like stray tear drops that had unknowingly trickled from the eyes of a fallen angel, they glistened in the desert.

It was nearing sunset, and the desert started darkening.

'Not a single human being around in all these hours we spent here!' Fatima was baffled.

It was astounding that such a beautiful spot was not crowded on a holiday.

'Alright, let's leave!' Asif packed his camera and entered the car. Tipu was busy playing in the sand. But when Asif started the vehicle, it stalled. It became clear that the rear wheels were mired in the sand. The more Asif pressed the accelerator, the deeper the wheels sank. Although familiar with driving in the desert, Asif had never encountered a situation like this. In a frenzy to escape, the vehicle's front wheels became submerged in the sand as well.

It was twilight, and a wind started howling above the lake. The three of them crouched near the tires and tried to dislodge the sand. Many skeletal remains and bones of various sizes ended up in their hands.

'Ummudu, look, a dinosaur's skeleton!' Tipu held the elongated skeleton of a lizard in his hand.

They continued to unearth remnants of rats and snakes. Fatima asked Tipu to wear his shoes, afraid that a sharp bone splinter would hurt him.

'Even in its skeletal frame, the snake is so creepy!' Fatima remarked.

Light abandoned the desert completely. Apart from the headlights of the car, there wasn't a glimmer of light around. Almost an hour passed since Asif had called the emergency police helpline, yet no help arrived. As more time went by, Asif became more impatient. Nobody among his acquaintances or friends lived nearby. Thinking about seeking help from a vehicle passing through the road, Tipu and Fatima walked forward with a shining torch. They had no idea about the direction in which the road was. The sand dunes towered intimidatingly above them, stopping even the sounds of vehicles from reaching their ears. When they clambered up a dune and managed to descend, there stood another dune ahead!

'Are we playing a game of hurdles, Ummudu?'

Finally, two Arabs were sighted, and they offered help. Although the men tried to tug the vehicle out of the sand pit, it was a futile exercise. After jabbering endlessly in Arabic and gesturing frantically, they left. The wind became stronger. For the first time, they understood that in the winter, the desert could be as freezing as the Alps. When their bare feet touched the ground, it was like stepping on ice. The wind which screamed in their ears was equivalent to a banshee's wailing.

When Fatima and Tipu trudged their way back to Asif, their original path had vanished. The wind played with the dunes, shifting them from one place to another. They found Asif seated inside the vehicle, and many moths hovering around, attracted by the headlights. They all looked like strange creatures, and it was difficult to make out whether they were insects or small birds. Asif was forced to switch off the headlights to drive these intruders away.

'Try calling the emergency number once more,' Fatima suggested, patting awake a lethargic, depressed Asif.

'How many times have I called them! "*We shall reach soon*" is their only reply...The staff must be on leave because of the Eid holidays combining with the weekend. Damn it!'

Asif was enraged.

'You heard what that Arab fellow blabbered, didn't you?'

The Arab had provoked dread with his ominous words. He was berating Asif, questioning why he had come to such a desolate spot with his family. Four Pakistanis had drowned in the lake just the previous month. Deadly scorpions, snakes and lizards slithered under the sand! Then looking at Tipu, the Arab had muttered, 'If those creatures touch him, it will be over in seconds!'

Asif became more and more flustered remembering those words. He started hitting the steering wheel and accusing everybody. Thoroughly incited, he showered Fatima with recriminations too. Tired of seeing Asif's fury, Fatima slipped out of the car and stood outside. Tipu, too, followed suit. The insects had disappeared from the vicinity by then.

Fatima listened keenly. The sound of birds, the plopping sounds of water creatures diving, the hiss of the swaying reeds… Like a symphony in an orchestra, the sounds of animals lapping up the water intertwined with the hum of the wind. She felt like she had entered the serpent grove of Thiru Nilam.

Fatima was used to considering the desert as a metaphor for emptiness, but Tilapia was correcting her preconceptions. She was realising for the first time that a robust ecosystem existed in the desert. Crickets and venomous lizards all lived harmoniously with the birds, fishes, foxes and oryxes…Even if things went awry at times, there was nothing surprising about it; after all, one animal preying on another could not be termed sinful.

Fatima used to explain to Tipu that Tom chased after Jerry not because they were foes. 'Tipu, chicken is food for you, right? For Tom, Jerry is the same!' On hearing that, Tipu would nod at Tom affectionately. Fatima's theory was that the famous duo were just following the laws of nature.

She walked forwards again. Asif, seated inside the car, shouted at her: 'Where are you off to? Come back now! Don't stray near the water…' Fatima waved at Asif as if agreeing with him. Then she turned to Tipu, who was tagging along, and asked him to get back inside the car, 'It is very cold, my dear! Go on…sit with Vappu in the car. Ummudu will be back soon!'

Tipu raced back to Asif. Even while running, he turned back to glance at Ummudu twice or thrice. In his mind, the sight of his Ummudu was imprinted like a motion picture, her bobbing up and down like a dark light, moving further away amid the sand dunes. He played some games on the phone for a while. Then he had fallen asleep.

Fatima walked towards the lake. It was alive with movements and sound; scented with blood and flesh. Suddenly, the spell of the serpent grove seemed to possess Fatima—the sight of the sky as she stood amidst the huge, dense trees; the black mud hidden beneath the dried leaves; the universe that embraced her when she opened her hands wide, eyes tightly shut…

She moved closer to the edge of the lake. Her toe was bruised while brushing past a cactus plant and a drop of blood welled up. It spread into a red circle on the wet sand. Like Padmajamma's big *sindoor* dot that Fatima had once tried to emulate…

The lake was full of fishes, all of them tilapia. Could they see Fatima's face? What did they think she was, observing from under the water? Did they wish she would move her face closer to them for a moment?

When Fatima did not return after a long interval, Asif panicked. He could not leave Tipu alone in the car and go searching for his wife. Supposing he could carry the child and walk, how would he leave the vehicle in the desolate spot? What if someone came searching for them and went back after seeing no one inside? As he sat anxiously, unsure of what to do, he saw a light in the distance. It was the police. Asif requested the cops who were preparing to tow the car, to first search for Fatima. Later, when the police and the fire department found Fatima, she had long become the beloved of the tilapia fish.

When Tipu woke up, it was a raucous scene all around. Asif did not attempt to provide any explanation to his son. Tipu waited for Ummudu to make her way back through the sand dunes.

Four:
The House of Notes

Fatima's notes made her a stranger in Asif's eyes. She had been something else altogether. Inside of her, was an unknown isle inaccessible to him, an isle where no ship reached, no flight landed; now, he was making his way there through her notes.

'Houses are magic lamps where the genies sleep. An Aladdin is needed to usher the genies outside. The number of genies equals the number of houses in a city. When the closed doors and walls of houses are opened wide, the genies step out. It is that stepping out which makes cities burst into bloom.'

Asif hadn't gone to work for the past week, and Tipu was also at home. The walls were gazing at Asif as if nothing untoward had happened. The cot, the chair and the table bore no part in Asif's anguish. Despite living together for such a long time, these objects were insensate to his movements. Perhaps that was why Fatima used to say, '*The house is a cemetery*.' More than the living, there were representatives of lifelessness.

What she had said that day was true.

'This cot was once a part of some tree. Trees, full of green flesh and blood, rooted in earth. Ha, trees...enchanting symbols! Bearing their own biers, they lay dead in our sitting rooms and bedrooms in various forms. If you observe the kitchen, you will find a bigger cemetery. The testimonies of brutal murder sit preening inside the fridge, in the guise of fishes, hens and goats. The dead seeds accumulated inside the bottles on the kitchen racks shall astound us in the form of beans, chickpeas and mustard! There are many corpses in powdered form too. Truly, a graveyard. And I am the keeper of the graves.'

Fatima's notes and the sentences inside them stoked anxiety in Asif. He had never been depressed in his life. Asif was a steed; he yearned to gallop ahead in both life and work. Discomfitures unnerved him, making him wary of life, and he was unable to continue in that state for long. What happened in Tilapia was exactly that. Fatima had disembarked from the vehicle because she could not tolerate his frustration, impatience and the shower of damnations. Besides, many of her favourite attractions lay outside. Her walking away had been similar to Nabeezath's entry into the serpent grove at twilight, attracted by Padmajamma's lamp light.

Now, Asif was busy ransacking the house, searching for Fatima's notes. His curiosity to understand her more was palpable, with every note seemingly bringing her back to life. He searched amongst her clothes, books and jewellery boxes with fervour. Fatima never maintained a diary. She held the view that to jot down every activity in a day was akin to an imposition or writing lines forcibly as punishment back in school. The feelings one experienced during the day were the only noteworthy ones.

The last book she was reading, purchased online, was Lois Ehlert's colourful picture book, *The Leaf Man*. The bookmark slipped out from the page where Fatima had stopped, and fell into Asif's lap. In miniature lettering, on that white, featherlike book mark, was another one of her notes. Extending it under the balcony light, Asif tried to piece the words together.

'My revolution is limited to this balcony. If it has to spread beyond, it has to be through my Tipu. His pictures should come to life. In the veins of the green leaves he is yet to sketch, my revolution shall start pulsing.'

Asif tucked away that note inside a file, like the others.

A while back, Asif's friend Pradeesh, who was based in Kerala, had discussed the setting up of a cargo company with him, over text messages. Pradeesh was planning an enterprise linked with the Vizhinjam Port project. Although Asif hadn't given it much thought then, he felt like following up with Pradeesh now. His Dubai life was making him insecure; all his tactics for handling Tipu were going haywire. Nabeezath,

Fatima's Umma, was in Kerala, and Tipu would be safe with her. Asif's mind was planning an uprooting and Pradeesh's business plan could turn out to be an anchor for the shift. There were nearly two months left before schools opened back home. The summer vacations were on now. Tipu would get sufficient time to adapt to the new environment as well.

Tipu was getting bored, alternating between various television channels. His hand stretched slowly towards Asif's mobile. The TV, the games on the tablet and the mobile phone; Tipu had no means of entertainment apart from these.

Should he submit his resignation? In that one-month notice period, should he send Tipu home? Asif was caught in a flurry of thoughts. He was examining every possible alternative closely in light of the circumstances. But would Tipu stay by himself back home, without his Vappu? One could never predict anything beforehand as far as Tipu was concerned. With a single sentence, he could topple all plans. 'Perhaps, all children were similar,' Asif consoled himself.

He called out to Tipu. The child skipped his way to his father and scrambled into his lap. Tipu pulled at the chewing gum in his mouth and started entwining it in his fingers.

'Open your mouth, Tipu!'

Asif retrieved the gum from his mouth. Tipu's tongue was a deep blue. How many noxious substances did those colours contain!

'Look at my blue tongue! Should I turn it red?' Sticking his tongue out, Tipu tried to rattle Asif.

When he tried to insert a red chewing gum into his mouth, Asif flicked it away. Tipu stared disappointedly at the red sphere which rolled under the table. He glared at Asif as if his Vappu had committed some humungous stupidity.

'What all do you pop into your mouth, eh? From where did you get these?'

'Got it from the grocery shop below.'

Fatima used to catch Tipu red-handed whenever he tried to order chewing gum, chips, soda and the like from the grocery shop downstairs. The child knew that the payment made to the shop was on a monthly basis. So, he assumed that his Ummudu or Vappu would not get wind of it, if he purchased a tiny packet of chips or a bottle of cold drinks. For the past week, he had been busy indulging in such mischiefs.

'I am going to pack you off to Kerala, Tipu. You need to be disciplined.' Asif's tone was severe.

'Okay!' Tipu's response was very flippant.

Even if the skies, clouds and the sun were to veritably surround their home, Tipu would be nonchalant. If the Earth shook or the netherworld lurched upwards, it would leave him unbothered. Fatima wanted him to grow up as a happy-go-lucky boy! *'His nerves should never stretch taut; let him laugh when he wished to; tie himself in knots with mirth and even cry loudly, disturbing the neighbors, if ever he felt miserable... Everything inside him should be fully expressed, and nothing should stagnate within.*' These were the arguments that Fatima put forward to justify the uninhibited freedom that she gave Tipu.

Even though Asif had only briefly hinted at going back home, Tipu was ready the very next morning. He stood with his school bag chock-a-block with his possessions. Asif opened the bag. It was full of Tipu's paraphernalia! Cars, planes, three or four guns, a few playing cards, his tablet Galaxy Note, game CDs and the ilk...

'Is this your luggage?' Asif queried.

Tipu shrugged affirmatively.

It was his first trip home without Fatima. Asif knew that when Tipu reached, a mourning crowd would be waiting to welcome him. How many vehicles would be part of that mournful procession from the airport? He sincerely hoped that the child would not be too shaken.

Many relatives back home were not in agreement with Asif's decision. Some had even showered him with harsh criticism. According to them, Asif's Umma was alive and had the sole right over Tipu. In a matter of a few days, Asif had been branded by society as a major sinner. He had no clue about what they were going to project Fatima as next! Those who had never even acknowledged her existence were now lamenting over her. Asif was immune to such sentimentalism. Nabeezath however, did not deign to give any opinions on the matter. She had never been one for throwing tantrums or being obstinate.

Finally, D-Day arrived and Tipu set out on his journey. The only concern in Asif's mind while entrusting him to the hands of the air hostess was—*The next time I see him, will he be at a distance far beyond my reach*?

There was no trace of panic on Tipu's face, considering that it was his solo trip. How blasé he was about the sudden uprooting! Vaishakan, Asif's colleague at work, shared his views. His daughter was in Class VIII; another happy-go-lucky soul like Tipu. Nothing caused her much concern; she never displayed any intense emotions, nor had strong views on any matter. She was born to live an effortless life.

'Why not? Whatever she wishes for appears in a jiffy! Aren't we their orderlies, butlers, body guards…?' That was Vaishakan's comment about the new generation of kids.

'They are individuals right from the moment of their births! Did you watch the way Tipu strode away? There is nothing he doesn't know about! What is even left for him to know? The world is not hidden from him and lies completely exposed. He was born into a world where there aren't many mysteries left,' Asif responded to Vaishakan. These kids had arrived on the planet at an era where most of the universe's secrets stood revealed; man having mastered solutions to many problems. The world was open wide for their exploits.

Grown-up kids in a grown-up world.

What else was there to say, after watching Tipu clasp the arm of the Nigerian air hostess and walk away, joking and laughing merrily?

Five:
Changing the Nest

Tipu landed in Nabeezath's nest.

He was indifferent to the thronging relatives and neighbors. An elderly woman came near him and tousled his hair, asking, 'Hello, dear one, do you remember me?' Tipu merely glanced at her, and continued to pull his toys out of the bag. Seeing his lack of interest in her, the old lady shuffled away.

Tipu observed that all the folks crowding around had the same facial expression. Most stood with eyes downcast, hands cupping their chins. He asked Nabeezath why all these people looked so desperate! Salim's sister gathered him close and kissed him, murmuring, 'Darling, you have everyone with you …your Umma hasn't gone anywhere.' Tipu wondered whether they were not aware that his Ummudu had gone to Tilapia. He struggled hard to free himself from the woman's flabby arms.

Nabeezath served tea to the visitors. After their repast, everybody went their way. Tipu jumped to the conclusion that all of them had their tea at Nabeezath's home every evening.

Nabeezath gave Tipu a bath. He called her *Rarumma*. She had a unibrow; her thick brows met at the center of her forehead, forming a cradle like shape.

'Look at the eyebrow-cradle on your Nabeezathumma's forehead! *Areero, rareero raeeraro…*' Thus, the Umma with the brow that resembled a cradle, who sang the '*Raree Rareeram*' lullaby, became *Rarumma* for Tipu. It was Fatima who made him call her that.

During his bath, Tipu asked, 'Rarumma, will all the people return tomorrow morning to have their tea?' Nabeezath couldn't make out what he meant at first. Later, she could not stifle her laughter at that memory.

Whenever Tipu came to Kerala for his vacations, he would stay in Nabeezath's house at Njarakkadu, but not for too long. The house would usually be full of relatives and he would play with the children. Tipu hadn't had many opportunities to explore the house properly in the past. Now, he was examining each object with great alacrity.

It was perhaps the first time that Tipu had seen the house so desolate; he checked each room solemnly. He carefully measured the number of his footsteps from one corner of the sitting room to another. Wow! This was as vast as the Dubai flat! One could easily fit in a bedroom, a kitchen and a toilet inside this! The distance between the two walls in the bedroom petrified him a bit. Taken away from the sense of security instilled by narrow walls, and made to face open spaces, the child felt lonely. He wished that the four walls would come closer and huddle around him.

When it was time to sleep, he asked Rarumma, 'Which is the smallest room in the house?'

'Come on, let us sleep in Ummudu's room', Nabeezath replied.

Tipu sprang up, ready to scramble up Rarumma's back. She carried him to Fatima's room. In the narrow room, there was a cot, an almirah, a chair and a table next to the wall. There was no sign of anyone having used it. A fancy clock was hanging on the wall. In Tipu's Dubai flat, there were no clocks with swinging pendulums. If anyone stared at the ball oscillating on a thread for a long time, they would get hynotised. Tipu could not remember which cartoon he had seen it in, but this was a favourite ploy used by conjurors to kidnap kids! He believed that he, too, would become groggy after staring at that clock for too long. He decided to test it out someday, without Rarumma's knowledge. There were four windows, and the two that opened into another room were tightly shut.

Rarumma and Tipu lay down to sleep.

'The bed is freezing, Rarumma. Please switch off the AC.'

'There is no AC here, darling. Come, snuggle against me, your Rarumma shall give you warmth.'

Tipu kept complaining that the bed was cold until he fell asleep. When he insisted on unlocking the closed windows, Rarumma assured him that she would do so the next morning. She warned him that mosquitoes would race into the room if any of the windows were opened at night.

'Then what about the morning?' Tipu expressed his doubts.

'In the morning, the mosquitoes go off to sleep.'

'Ummudu told me that in the night, thieves will come prowling.'

'Hmm…there are no thieves here, dearest!'

'Maybe the mosquitoes are the thieves, hehe!'

Chortling with glee, Tipu hugged Nabeezath tightly. It was then that his eyes fell on the ceiling of the house.

'Rarumma, will the roof collapse and fall on me?'

'No way! The beams and rafters are pretty sturdy, my boy. The roof won't collapse!'

Tipu closed his eyes. He was listening keenly to the outside sounds. There was a mango tree whose branches reached the window; the sounds of night birds perching on it and flapping away were audible. The squeaks of barn mice resounded intermittently. When the wind blew, a *kree kree* sound emanated from the branches of the mango tree—something which Tipu had never heard before. However, Ummudu had once given him a brief introduction to the night sounds in her home. In Dubai, when you closed your eyes, there were no sounds except the rumbling of vehicles. When an ambulance or police car drove by, there was an ear-splitting turbulence.

Just above Tipu's flat, there was a family with a naughty girl. She never slept at night; instead, she played with empty 20-litre bottles meant for fetching mineral water, rolling them across the floor. Tipu, lying beneath the noises, found it very vexing. He even made Vappu complain to the family upstairs. But he remembered Ummudu laughing at that escapade. Apparently, Ummudu recollected the child's mischievous face whenever she heard the bottle's grating sound, and hence could enjoy the ruckus like the music of a drum beat!

Most things that irritated Asif and Tipu, Fatima found funny. It was now that Tipu comprehended why Ummudu could dismiss all of that as silly. She herself was familiar with sleeping with multiple sounds surrounding her at night.

Pondering over many things, Tipu went off to sleep. As promised, Nabeezath opened the windows at dawn. Tipu opened his eyes when the sun kissed his face. Rarumma was not lying next to him. Tipu got up on his knees slowly, and peeped out of the window.

'Ayyo! What a giant tree!'

Tipu was amazed at the size of the thick branches. Nabeezath came in and stood near him.

'Rarumma...if this tree grows more, will it not break our windows and poke inside?'

Nabeezath laughed, 'As if we shall let them! Their place is outside the home.'

Tipu wasn't inclined to totally trust what he heard and stared peevishly at the mango tree. L*ook at that giant waiting to nudge its way inside my room!*

As his toes touched the ground, Tipu gasped 'Ouch! Coo ...lllldd...!' He quickly pulled his legs up. The shiver of cold after stepping on the cold cement floor!

Nabeezath slipped two little slippers on his feet.

After breakfast, she started stacking the almirah with Tipu's clothes, retrieving them from his bag.

'Tipu, your dresses smell so good...a Gulf aroma!'

Nabeezath buried her nose in the clothes.

Tipu pulled the edge of Nabeezath's sari to his nose and took a sniff. 'Rarumma's clothes smell different!'

'What sort of smell?'

'I don't know. The table and the cot smell different too. It's not like Dubai!'

Tipu pressed his nose against the lone chair in that room and inhaled sharply.

'This one has some sort of scent, Rarumma!'

'That is a rattan chair, dear! Have you seen bamboo trees? These are made from those!'

Tipu immediately pointed at the ceiling and queried, 'Is that made from bamboo too?'

'No, that's made from a huge tree; we call it the teak!'

'Does it smell different? Just like my clothes and yours, Rarumma?'

'Ha, ha! Exactly so! Rarumma shall show you all the trees.'

There were two months before the schools opened. Tipu would stay with Nabeezath during this time. Asif had already called four or five times. It was not due to his concern about Tipu; rather, the calls were triggered by the fear invoked by Asif's loneliness. He knew that Tipu would not find the unfamiliar settings discomfiting. After all, which place was strange for him? He made every space his own!

When he sat down for lunch, Tipu piped up: 'Rarumma, I want to have KFC for supper.'

Pointing at a hen pecking and scratching around the dirt, Nabeezath said, 'Look, that is the KFC we have here! Rarumma will serve you two fried legs after catching holding of that one here and setting a knife to it, okay?'

Tipu stared solemnly at the creature.

'Does that chicken belong to you?'

'Chicken? Say *kozhi*! At least call it a hen!'

Tipu had never thought while munching on KFC that 'chicken' actually meant a hen which clucked around scratching the dirt, laid eggs, greedily pecked and swallowed grubs, and fled for its life when it saw a dog! Or perhaps the child wasn't even aware of this reality.

Near their Dubai flat, there was a building under construction. There were a few Bangladeshi construction workers who stayed there, and they kept a couple of hens which could be seen scurrying around the front of the flat complex. Once, they had come chasing after Tipu, who had disembarked from his school bus.

As soon as he reached home, Tipu had panted out his woes to Fatima, 'Ummudu, two chickens chased me on the ground below. They are dangerous!'

Fatima laughed, 'They did that, huh! How can they help chasing you? They must have found out that you are a habitual KFC eater!'

Tipu squabbled with Ummudu after that pertinent observation and did not speak with her for some time. His estrangements, however, had a maximum lifetime of one hour.

Nabeezath took him near the hens and roosters pecking around the yard. Tipu slowly tried to pull back—the ground was full of bird shit. Standing on tiptoes, and hanging on to Nabeezath's hand, Tipu glared at the birds. His toes were tucked in and looked shriveled.

'You're wearing slippers, come on now!' Nabeezath persisted. Yet, Tipu stood at a safe distance. The hens were pecking around and gulping down whatever they found. One rooster was dashing after another which had a grub in its beak. Tipu felt it was a pity that such a great war was being fought over a dirty little worm!

'It is because they gobble up all this muck that their tummies drain…as if they have diarrhea! Yuck!' Tipu was furious.

'Why are you angry? Didn't you telephone me a while ago that Abhishek tried to snatch your doughnut from your tiffin box? It is the same situation here!'

Tipu became deeply contemplative after Rarumma's take on the matter. But there was no change in his decision to eat KFC for dinner. That was mandatory.

Six:
Ammalu

Ammalu was the daughter of Vineet and Sita—the third daughter of Padmajamma. Sita had vitiligo like her mother. The disease, which unveiled itself later on in her mother Padmajamma's life, reared its head early in Sita's. She was almost eight years older than Fatima. When marriage proposals fell on the wayside due to her affliction, serendipitously, Vineet entered her life. If Sita's father was the beloved headmaster of Njarakkadu village, Vineet's father was the lone *thandan*: the coconut climber of the hamlet.

There were no coconut trees around that did not know the man. Shankaran believed that the symbiotic connection between the *thandan* and the coconut tree was equivalent to that of the sea and its breeze. Which other human being ardently embraced a tree with all his limbs before harvesting its fruits? His climbing prowess stayed untrammeled at any time of the day or night, despite any exuberance due to his ingestion of toddy! Shankaran's theory was that coconuts sprouted and the palmyra palms burst into bloom because of the friction between the *thandan*'s body and the tree. The veins of the tree awakened, the narrow nerves widened, the flow of sweet liquid began, the leaves became greener and even the stems became thicker…

Though such chemical changes have never been mentioned in botanical science, Shankaran stood firm in his theory. The less said the better, but there were people who even asked him to bestow them the favour of 'servicing the barren tree' by climbing it! What if the efforts were fruitful? Most reported *Shankaran Seva*, or Shankaran's free service as a very successful venture too! True to the vernacular proverb which sardonically said, 'Shankaran is always atop a coconut tree'—a pithy take about never-changing habits—Shankaran *thandan* was indeed always found at the pinnacle of a coconut tree!

In Vineet and Sita's first meeting, too, some chemical alterations must have taken place. The son, who had grown accustomed to his father's tree-climbing service without mastering the art, had nonetheless become adept at overcoming the thorny hurdles of life. The teachers and kids at school never wasted any opportunity to hail him with that ignominious nickname—*thandanchekkan*, the son of a *thandan*.

Vineet knew, right from his childhood, that trees were not dumb scarecrows providing mangoes, jackfruits, coconuts or areca nuts. Perhaps this clarity dawned on him due to the impact of his father, who proudly showed him the trees which burst into bloom at his touch. The pride, which welled up in the child as his father climbed a coconut tree, was akin to one known by a son watching his President father saluting the flag during the Republic Day parade. Vineet felt the same obsession about the billhook and the *thalappu*, the circular climbing aid, that a cop's son possessed about guns and khaki.

It was about a year and a half since Vineet had secured a lecturer position at the Agricultural College. Before that, he had been doing temporary stints in schools and other part-time work for a comfortable living. His education at the Agricultural College and his job seemed to be a continuum of his childhood experiences. Vineet was among the select few who ended up where they were supposed to. His ending up with Sita, too, occurred in a similar way.

During a panchayat election, Vineet was working as a clerk in the Revenue Department. That was his first job after securing his degree in Agricultural Science. His election duty was at the Njarakkadu panchayat. His job was to apply ink on the forefingers of the voters. Vineet had been bored out of his wits doing that mechanical assignment. He never raised his head to look at anyone; there was no need of that at all. Finally, Sita's finger made its appearance among the fingers which came by his table to get their quota of the ink stain.

The vitiligo's colours had fully spread across Sita's little finger and forefinger, and two continents had appeared on her thumb and ring finger. When Vineet attempted to apply the ink, Sita withdrew her hand, curling it into a tight fist. Vineet looked up at her and she averted her face. The vitiligo which crawled out from the corner of her mouth had covered three fourths of her lower lip. When Vineet tried to ask her something, she sucked her lips in.

'Place your finger here, please!' Vineet said firmly.

Hesitatingly, she let the forefinger emerge from the fist. It brushed against the table like a feather. Vineet's voice gathered gravity, 'I asked you to extend your hand. Can't you see the queue behind you?'

Sita pulled her hand back and stormed out the room in a huff.

Their later encounters were also in public places. The debt of an ink drop grew by leaps and bounds between them. Vineet was a frequent visitor to a library situated near the computer training center where Sita studied. However, it was only after the panchayat election that Vineet realised that a Sita existed, unseen by him until then. Perhaps she, too, had the desire to live her life away from others, like Padmajamma.

Whenever Vineet met Sita, he would tease her about the ink debt, saying that it was an awful predicament to wait with an ink pot, until the next panchayat elections!

One day, tired of his ribbing, Sita came before him with her hands outstretched.

'Go ahead, don't limit yourself to a single drop; dip me wholly in your ink well!'

Vineet burst into hearty laughter, a laugh which turned Sita's vitiligo marks into mush.

In the evenings, he would wait for Sita when she left her classes. The owner of the computer center, Rajesh, was a close friend of Sita's father. When he shut the windows of the room, he would often notice the whispering duo, standing in the shade. Unwilling to believe that any man would fall in love with a vitiligo-afflicted woman, he dismissed the matter offhandedly.

Sita's body was full of vitiligo patches. She was taller than Vineet. Shankaran *thandan* had passed on his slightly dwarfish stature to his son. Vineet reached her height only when he was astride his motorbike. Sita felt embarrassed to walk by his side. Typically, when a tall person walked with a short one, the former felt small—a very crushing feeling!

Sita would slouch, trying to lower herself to Vineet's height. When she used to stand in the last row like a flagpole during school assemblies, she had often wished than a 10 cm-long tube would be hacked off from above her ankles. Did her height mortify her more intensely than the vitiligo? Sita's opinion was that schools should have only circular assemblies to detract unwanted attention!

Vineet was always in the front row of school assemblies and class rooms. Vineet couldn't forget his bus journeys as a student, when he stood with the heavy school bag on his back, unwilling to ask for help from someone taller to heft it into the top rack. And finally, he fell head over heels in love with a veritable coconut tree!

Sita bent her head and looked at Vineet as if slithering down from the second to the third row of a double-lined copy book. To Vineet, her vitiligo marks seemed like oil wells. The oil which welled up on digging these wells was fueling his life. Sita's luminous transformation from a dim hurricane-lamp to a resplendent brass lamp occurred very fast. The marriage was the burdensome culmination of all the agonies which cropped up when a 'low caste Thandan boy' married a 'high caste Nair girl'. Thus, the debt of blue spread as red on Sita's forehead.

Ammalu arrived into their midst rather late. Now, she was eight years old. Having heard of Tipu's arrival, the family visited Nabeezath's home that day. Sita had come earlier as well, on hearing about Fatima, but she had hardly caught a glimpse of Nabeezath. The house was thronging with crowds, as if there was a festival going on. Most people were buzzing with misgivings. Some were blaming Asif; others were recriminating Nabeezath for marrying her daughter off before the girl came of age; then there were a few who were disappointed that Fatima's body wasn't brought back.

Ammalu was a sprightly, spirited little girl, slim and tall. She knew Tipu, having seen him during his vacations. Two thin legs emerged from beneath her pleated white frock, and explored the ground. Her eyes were large, and she blinked frequently. If she focused on anything for long, her eyes would open and shut with lightning speed. Now she was observing Tipu with the same intensity.

Most of Ammalu's education happened through her father, rather than her school. Vineet would teach her something original each day, following the dictum, 'one new day, one new learning!'. Perhaps that was why Ammalu was supercilious about her teachers at school. They did not know why cows ate only grass, nor did they have a clue about how the elephant's trunk grew so big! Did they comprehend why a fish bit the bait, eh? But Ammalu's father, her *Acchan*, knew everything! Ammalu knew lots of secrets unknown to her classmates Ani, Ashik or Tina. Now wasn't that something to be proud about?

'In which class are you studying?' Ammalu ventured. It was obvious that she was more familiar with the first steps of friendship than Tipu.

'Fourth grade…' Tipu responded.

'Grade? I am in Class III,' Ammalu replied, and then paused, 'Ahh, I get it! Classes are called grades over there, right?'

Tipu nodded. They walked around the house. He could testify in less than half an hour that Ammalu had amazing general knowledge. Seated on the verandah, they started playing a game on Tipu's tablet. Ammalu was familiar with *Minecraft*. Vineet's brother had downloaded it for her on the laptop at home. The kids decided that they would enjoy the multiplayer format at Ammalu's house. There was a Wi-Fi connection there. Tipu could log in as 'Steve' from his tablet, and Ammalu as 'Sandra' from the laptop. Ah, what fun it would be! Unanimously voting for the new idea, they high-fived each other.

Ammalu was very close to Nabeezath and her home. After all, Nabeezath was an inseparable part of Thiru Nilam and its surroundings. Ammalu had never seen her grandmother Padmajamma. Her grandfather Rajasekharan Nair now resided in the US. He had been left alone at home after his children got married. Later, his eldest son Janardhanan had taken his father along to the United States. Rajasekharan Nair visited his home once in two to three years. But even during that time, he stayed with Janardhanan in his city house.

When the Thiru Nilam house and property were partitioned, the rented house where Nabeezath stayed was demarcated as Sita's share. After Fatima's marriage, relatives tried to persuade Nabeezath to shift to her maternal house, but she hadn't listened. Nabeezath bought the house from Sita with her Provident Fund money and an additional loan.

Sita and her family stayed in Vineet's family home. Shankaran *thandan* was no longer alive, but his wife Sarojam lived with them. The ripples of blood pressure, diabetes or cholesterol never dared encroach her body, and Sarojam celebrated her old age by making coconut leaf thatches, preparing cattle feed and crafting toys for Ammalu.

Nabeezath was of the opinion that Ammalu took after Padmajamma. Sita persisted that only Nabeezath would be kind enough to bestow such a compliment. She preferred to say that Ammalu took after her father, Vineet being her heart's pride. Nabeezath was always searching for traces of Padmajamma in all her beloved friend's grandchildren. Maybe that's why she had anointed Ammalu with that responsibility, not finding a match elsewhere.

Ammalu had a liking for many things and a habit of collecting whatever she was enchanted with. She loved the smell of nail polish, and would sniff at it closely while the colours dried on her fingernails. Never did she hesitate to smell the nail polish that her mother wore. She collected the empty bottles too. One of her prized possessions was a biscuit container stacked with nail polish bottles with frayed and dried colours on their edges. How many different colours were inside the box!

Another one of her favourite things was round pebbles. Pressing one close to her cheek, she would lisp, 'Wow, it feels so cool!' She would tuck the pebbles into the crook of her elbows and knees. After a while, the pebbles grew warm, and became 'feverish' stones. At times, Ammalu coloured them too. She had lots of other collections too... Barks of trees, tidbits of molten candles, egg shells, empty refills. She was fascinated by the odour of dried ink in the ends of the refill.

Seven:
Superman

Tipu saw Thankayamma on the second day of his arrival. She swept the yard, washed the vessels, helped Nabeezath with her house work and then loitered near the kitchen and the compound till the afternoon. Once her lunch was over, she called it a day. Eating twice a day was more than enough for her. After all, her four-and-a-half-feet body didn't need more! That too, a shriveled, skinny four and half feet!

It was easy for Thankayamma to sweep the ground, as her body was curved and bent like an arch, there wasn't any need for her to crouch further. When she walked, it was as if an invisible broom was attached to her hand; her spine could not have dived deeper into the ground.

Tipu gaped at her sweeping; the woman looked like a weird creature!

'Is this granny a hundred years old?'

Nabeezath smiled, 'Nobody knows her age, not even Thankayamma herself.'

Were there human beings like that? 'If she doesn't know her age, then how does she buy clothes from a shop? Ummudu buys me clothes which have "8–9 years" inscribed behind the collars, from Lulu Hypermarket,' Tipu expressed his confusion. Apart from that, the doctor always asked your age when you visited the hospital. The prescription was written only after that. Tipu found it hard to believe that someone could be unaware of their age. He decided that Thankayamma was a hundred years old.

Thankayamma was not garrulous. But she would be grinning at all times. Her teeth were impeccable, and she would chomp on everything noisily. She stood smiling at Tipu for a long time, but did not say anything. Her dress was a *mundu* and blouse, both squeaking clean.

After finishing off her daily chores, Thankayamma sat below the guava tree. From the knot of her tucked-in *mundu*, she retrieved a *beedi* and started to smoke. Tipu thought that this granny smoked in the same style as that of the Lebanese woman puffing away on her cigarette in their neighboring flat in Dubai. With the cigarette held between her thick lips, the lady would smile in a peculiar fashion. Here, Thankayamma was doing the same! Did all the women across the world smoke in the same manner?

Ummudu had picked a fight with the Lebanese woman once. Since the building was centrally air-conditioned, the smoke wafted from one room and entered other flats. When

Ummudu complained, the woman continued to smile in response, biting into the cigarette.

There was an adventurous story about Thankayamma. Ummudu had narrated that tale to him. In the olden days, Thankayamma used to go to the forests to cut grass. The hacked off grass would be bound into huge stacks which she would carry on her head and sell to households with cattle. The cow at Thiru Nilam, too, used to relish the forest grass sheared by Thankayamma.

Once, when Thankayamma was resting on top of a hill, a python saw her. Its hunger was as monstrous as its body. It came slithering to swallow the woman, and entwined itself around her miniscule form. Then it opened its jaws wide to swallow her head. But Thankayamma was not shaken at all. Smoothly wielding her billhook, the only weapon she possessed, she slashed both sides of the serpent's mouth! The billhook moved along the python's coils, tearing through its tummy. Soon, the serpent loosened its hold on her. Like an old, discarded dress, the python slid down from Thankayamma's body. Except for a fracture in her left leg, the woman was unbruised. Shoving aside the python—flailing around with its head split in two—Thankayamma descended the mountains with her bundles of grass.

Tipu's mind had been indelibly imprinted with the image of the victorious Thankayamma emerging with her billhook from the clutches of the python! In the little boy's imagination, Thankayamma was a superman who whooshed out from the python's mouth with a *shhuuu* sound, brandishing her sword! Thankayamma even had muscles in his fantasy.

But look at this old woman! A pitiable existence, all skin and bones, stooping so badly. All of Tipu's figments of fantasy about Superman collapsed at her actual appearance. Can you imagine such a Superman? Curved like a hook!

That night, Superman Thankayamma played in his mind above all.

'Rarumma, a monster is walking inside my head!'

Nabeezath switched the lights on hastily.

'Ayyo! I can hear a *dum, dum, dum* sound... Save me please, Rarumma,' Tipu shrieked.

'Just hold your breath, and cover your nose and mouth. Don't worry!'

Tipu obeyed, big teardrops racing each other down his rosy, flushed cheeks.

'Look who has emerged from your ears,' Rarumma placed the bug on his palm. Was it this teeny insect that had entered his ears and had been demonically dancing inside his head? He flicked it away angrily.

The insect, which fled out in desperation from the lack of air, filled Tipu's mind with thoughts of Thankayamma again. Both Thankayamma emerging from the python's mouth and the bug which had scampered out of his ears were like Superman. The creature that came tumbling through the dark corridors of Tipu's ears, in search of air, was a smart aleck indeed. If it had died gasping for its breath inside Tipu's ears, he would have been carrying around a dead body forever!

Ummudu had once told him the tale of another such encroacher. When she was 10 years old, Ummudu was checking whether the pipe had water, with her mouth wide open. First, some air hissed by with a *sshhu*, followed by a *kuu* sound. Unexpectedly, a cockroach fell down the pipe, straight into Ummudu's mouth. Before she had realised what had happened, the creature tumbled out of her nose. Tipu conjectured that there was an invisible connection between the mouth and the nose, just like the Wi-Fi connection between Ummudu and himself. When he narrated the story, Rarumma burst into peals of laughter.

'Haha, your Ummudu was such a brat! Such a bag of lies… Just like she used to trick me, she played games with you too, didn't she?' Tipu thought that Rarumma was crying tears of mirth. She wiped her eyes with the edge of her sari.

'Do you know that Ummudu went to Tilapia?'

'Hmm,' Nabeezath gently caressed his hair as Tipu lay on her lap.

'Rarumma, Ummudu has always been naughty, you know? Whenever we visit a shopping mall, Ummudu disappears somewhere. When Vappu calls her on his phone, she will come back running. Once they made an announcement when Ummudu went missing in Festival City...' The child went on enthusiastically.

Nabeezath felt a pang in her heart as she realised just how strongly Tipu held on to his belief in Fatima's return. Could it be one of Tipu's ploys? Wouldn't any child feel alarmed when his mother was absent for such a long time? Why was he behaving in such an inexplicable manner? However, both Asif and Nabeezath let Tipu console himself with his firm hope. There was no point in disturbing him when things were going smoothly. The child's admission in the city school was ready. There were two more months for the classes to begin. Asif would come to take him then. A new home, new friends, new place...Tipu was disposed to enjoying such novelty.

'And time shall slowly move on,' Nabeezath reassured herself.

Eight: Serpent Grove

Tipu was alone at home, with not even Wi-Fi for company. The only solace were the games saved on his tablet. Whenever Ammalu dropped in, he became full of life. Nabeezath installed a decent cable connection only after Tipu's arrival. He enjoyed watching cartoons with Ammalu. She was still miffed with Tipu for laughing when he heard her name for the first time. 'What kind of name is that?' He had chortled in glee, covering his face. Throughout the day, he had sniggered on seeing her. It was only recently that Ammalu had unburdened herself of the embarrassment she underwent that day.

'Oh, I was a little kid then... Now I have grown up!' Tipu tried to explain away many of his peccadilloes as being wrought by his childish immaturity. Those naïvetés included teasing Ammalu over her name.

It was the day that Nabeezath usually visited the Treasury to get her monthly pension. She was considering taking Tipu along with her, when Ammalu came by. Nabeezath entrusted the children in Thankayamma's hands and got ready to go to the town.

Tipu and Ammalu started playing ball in the front yard of Thiru Nilam, and after a while, it became a game of hide and seek. Tipu wasn't too familiar with that one yet, since he hadn't played it much in Dubai. What sort of hiding was possible when there were hardly any hideouts! The flat had just a few spaces to take refuge in: underneath a cot, inside an almirah, or behind a door; there were no other places to hide. Today, he realised that the game could be such riotous fun.

Now Ammalu was counting and Tipu was running around the backyard behind Thiru Nilam, searching for a place to hide in. There was a porch at the back where firewood was stored. Tipu went inside and hid himself. The room had a tiled roof and the beams were full of cobwebs spun luxuriously by spiders. In the corner where Tipu hid, a basket lay upside down. A lizard rolled its eyes at him from underneath. Its body was full of black spots resembling warts. Tipu felt like throwing up. The creature was watching Tipu unblinkingly. With sharp teeth, the lizard would have been a miniature version of the dinosaurs in *Jurassic Park*. The magical shape-shifting creatures, fashioned by Steven Spielberg, flashed in Tipu's imagination!

The lizard's feet were faster than Tipu's and its eyes glinted sharply. It was staring at Tipu, rising warily on its fore legs.

This was not the welcoming gaze aimed at a guest in the house, neither was it the look of a foe; nor an invitation for friendship—there was no trace of concern or pity. The look held wonder, only wonder! Scared of the dinosaur-lizard, Tipu stuck close to the corner of the porch. His limbs froze, and he was struck dumb by terror. When he moved his leg once, the lizard moved in tandem; it was tracking even the batting of Tipu's eyelids. The child scanned the place for a weapon in case of an unexpected attack. No, there was nothing. If only he had a sparkling sword from *Minecraft*!

'Caught you!' Ammalu almost jumped on him.

Tipu's gaze was still on the basket. The lizard had vamoosed during the boisterous arrival of Ammalu. That was it? Tipu felt utterly sheepish.

'I am tired of this hiding game', Tipu pretended to be worn out. Of course he couldn't admit that he was terrified of a lizard, not in the least to a girl.

The children walked through the serpent grove. Kicking the dried leaves, reaching out to the low branches, they walked around, chattering amiably. Mimicking the hens, Tipu started scattering the leaves around with one foot. When he made a *cock a doodle doo* sound, Ammalu started giggling.

They reached the middle of the grove. The place was spread out across half an acre. Banana trees, areca nut palms, taro plants, elephant yams were all being grown in the compound next to theirs. They could see the paddy fields further beyond, but they lay barren without any cultivation. Some of the fields were let out to tenants for farming.

Tipu was gobsmacked at the sight of the huge trees, lush plants and the thick rope-like creepers swaying from the branches. The sky was covered with the canopies of trees. Bemused, he thought: would Mowgli be around somewhere? He was familiar with *Jungle Book*—both the movie and the cartoon. Mowgli wandered around such places in those movies, didn't he?

'I haven't been to these parts much, Tipu. But I think there is no chance that Mowgli would be here,' Ammalu was firm about it. The thick layers of dried leaves, piled over one another, lay smooth and soft like a feather-bed.

Tipu reached out to a *peepul* tree nearby and tried to encircle it with his arms. 'Ow, how fat are these trees! Who feeds them?' He ran his fingers through the trunk. Bringing his face closer, he sniffed at it. 'Is this the smell of the chair at home?'

'Smell of the chair?' Ammalu laughed.

'Yes, Rarumma said it was made from a bamboo tree. Maybe it is this tree?'

Ammalu shrugged in response, 'I have no idea!'

Suddenly a strong wind started blowing. The trees started rustling and shaking. Tipu felt a stab of fear. When the wind quieted, a few yellow leaves dropped on his body.

'Ah, so it was the wind which made the dried-leaf bed over here, wasn't it?'

'Not just leaves, it shakes down flowers and fruits too… not always though!'

'Fruits, which fruits?'

'If you stand under a guava tree, guavas will drop; if it is mango tree, mangoes; if it is a *gulmohar*, then red flowers will shower down…'

'So, if it is a coconut tree, will coconuts drop down?'

'Hahaha, then you will surely be dead!'

They reached the *Sarppathara*, where the snake deities were worshipped. Though Ammalu was seeing it for the first time, she had heard about it. Tipu regarded the snake deities intensely and nodded his head. 'Ah, I have seen this in Dubai. There is a shopping mall called Wafi City. It has been made in the shape of the Egyptian pyramids. There are many paintings on its walls, roof and floors. In those drawings, similar snake-heads are depicted in the crowns of the kings and princesses.'

Ammalu, too, visualised Egypt and a pyramid she had never seen before. Recollecting the picture of a pyramid from some quiz book, she queried, 'Yes, yes, don't they have mummies inside?'

'Who told you? There aren't any mummies in there.'

They walked around the raised platform and carefully examined the surroundings.

'After lighting the lamp, you stand here with folded hands,' Ammalu elucidated.

'Why do you fold your hands?' Tipu asked.

'Dimwit, this is the place where you pray!'

'Do you pray to the snakes so that they don't bite you? They are venomous, we will die if they bite us!'

'I will ask my Amma why we light the lamp. Will tell you tomorrow, okay?' They shed their serpent-related doubts halfway. Sita had strictly warned her to never discuss his mother with Tipu. Consequently, Ammalu evaded the subject whenever any conversation related to mothers was being broached.

Ammalu gathered the black *jamun* fruits strewn on the ground, her frock being the receptacle. Tipu hadn't ever tasted the fruit. Seated beneath the *jamun* tree, she started eating them one by one. Ammalu was wallowing in the achievement of introducing Tipu to a new food item. While she preened, he started blabbering about many fruits which she had never heard of!

'Have you eaten strawberries?'

Ammalu shook her head to indicate 'no'.

'Ummudu makes strawberry milkshake for me when I return from school!' Tipu embarked on a fruit-naming spree, trying to annoy her.

'Avocado? Dragon fruit? Kiwi? Pears? Plum?'

Ammalu felt bewildered.

'Show me your tongue,' she demanded. They relished seeing the colour of the *jamun* spread across their tongues. Tipu was astounded to know that the green, blue and yellow hues made by chewing gum could be obtained from trees. Maybe that was what Ummudu meant by 'natural' colours.

'Ummudu told me that there were peacocks in this place. Have you seen them?'

'No, I have seen peacocks only in the zoo.'

Fatima's childhood tales had peacocks in them. The only time Tipu was away from the world of games and television was bedtime. Tipu remembered being told that the peacock had a tail behind which trailed like a train; it was heavy and the poor creature was stuck with it! Though it was supposed to be an attractive accessory to attract its mate, Fatima argued that this particular display of beauty was an onerous exercise. When the rest of the birds had a gala time flying in the air, this poor fellow had to drag a train behind! Ow, what a fate!

'There are these nomads called Ottar, who trap peacocks hereabouts. They camp on the roadside and their kids tag along; when they beg, my mother gives them food. They are big-time trouble, you know, they steal sometimes!' Ammalu informed him gravely.

'Why do they catch peacocks?' Tipu was hearing about Ottars for the first time.

'They roast and eat the birds, and also brew peacock oil,' Ammalu had gathered these tidbits from Vineet.

'Roast and eat? Like chicken?'

'Hmm,' Ammalu hummed decisively, as if she knew everything.

'Do they eat all birds?'

'Ah, I don't know...but I have heard that Thankayamma eats fried crow!'

'Crow?' Tipu was flabbergasted.

Ammalu started collecting the black plums again. Collecting things was almost like a natural instinct for her.

'Are these Ottar folks beggars?'

Ammalu nodded in confirmation.

'Maybe they eat peacocks since they have nothing else for food,' Tipu tried to placate himself.

One of Fatima's friends had tucked a peacock feather inside her slambook for memory's sake. Most students sought the help of the peacock feather to sentimentalise their separation after Class X. Fatima had squabbled with that friend. What was the need to hoist gratuitous meanings on a peacock tail? It was just a feather. Right from childhood, Fatima detested artifices; especially attempts to associate unnecessary emotions with objects.

The question Tipu raised after hugging the *peepul* tree was still fresh in Ammalu's mind. 'Who was feeding these trees?

Who made them so fat? Just like her mother gave her yellow fish pills to enhance her health, who distributed nutrients to the trees?' She never felt like swallowing the yellow fish pills; they looked so smooth, she would rather add them to her potpourri. When Ammalu stared at her mother through the transparent yellow pill, Sita appeared like a black fish in a yellow pond!

The stepping stones to the *Sarppathara* were ridden with moss. They resembled green velvet cakes. If only one could break off a piece and eat it! There was more such velvet green near the edges of the decrepit well nearby. The serpent grove was totally green. If Tipu had to paint the whole grove, the green pencil in his colour pencil pack would be used up completely. Green was a colour which he rarely used otherwise.

'The trees here are coloured bright. The leaves are deep green,' Tipu brooded.

'So tell me, what is the colour of leaves in Dubai, Tipu? Blue? Ha!' Ammalu teased.

'Green…but not this sort of green…a dull green.'

The park which he used to frequent in Dubai had been full of neem trees. The sand storms of the desert had blasted the leaves to a sandlike hue. There wasn't sufficient rain to wash down the accumulated dust either. They existed as 'dust trees' with their grubby leaves, inwardly suppressing the green. Even a chameleon would have been flustered by those neem trees. The poor creature wouldn't know which colour to change to!

Tipu and Ammalu played with the touch-me-not plants by touching them. They searched for more amidst the grass. Tipu tried spitting on a plant; it immediately took affront.

'This plant is like my classmate Christopher. He whines at the drop of a hat. Then he will sulk for a long time.'

'I know, there is one such girl in my class too, Athira. If anyone gazes at her, she will turn red and then create a brouhaha. One day, I just happened to use her eraser. Ow, what a ruckus she made, complaining that it wasn't perfectly shaped anymore,' Ammalu started giggling.

But Tipu did not smile. He was deep in contemplation.

The day his second term results were announced last year flashed in his memory. It was a Thursday. Fatima had ushered him to the balcony when they reached home. She was bubbling with enthusiasm. The chilli seeds had sprouted after staying dormant for two weeks. Fatima had been depressed, thinking that they were lifeless. Now they had sprung up, auguring hope. When Ummudu and Tipu stood gazing at the tender seedlings, something flashed past their eyes with lightning speed. Something in the colour of Tipu's uniform. It was followed by a weird thud. When they looked below, the Goan boy who lived one floor above them lay with his head cracked in a pool of blood.

The child was the oldest of the Goan family, and studied in class VIII in Tipu's school. He, too, had got his grades that day, losing out on being the topper due to two subjects. In those two question papers, in a question with half or quarter of a mark, some other student might have answered better than him. Because of that crime, here he lay, bleeding to death.

'Why do children become like touch-me-nots?' Ummudu had lamented that day. Though Tipu had first heard about the plant that day, it was only now that he was getting to see it.

That day, Ummudu was furious. Later, whenever the Goan child was mentioned, the term 'touch-me-not' was repeated. After the child's suicide, the family left the flat. The naughty little girl who played by rolling bottles had come afterwards.

'The mangoes have gone bad! Tut, tut!'

Tipu was shaken from his reverie at Ammalu's ruing. She was standing at a distance. Tipu walked towards the foot of the mango tree beneath which she stood. He liked the *crum crum* sound as his feet crunched the dry leaves. To hear the sound again, Tipu raised his foot as high as possible before stepping down. His movements resembled a military parade. Ammalu was looking sadly at the rotten mango on the ground. She must have felt ravenous seeing the swaying cluster of ripe mangoes on the branches.

'Trust the breeze not to blow when one actually wants it to!'

The flies were swarming around the fallen mangoes. Giving competition to the fat buzzing houseflies were teeny-weeny fruit flies.

'What taste will this rotten mango have? Why are they eating such horrible food? Dirty flies!' Tipu found the sight loathsome.

'That is why Amma warns me not to drink water from glasses where flies perch…it upsets your tummy, you know!' said Ammalu, clutching her own tummy. Her posture made it obvious that she had once suffered the wrath of a stomach ache.

On seeing the flies embrace the mango with great passion, Tipu reached a decision. He would never eat a mango again, whether stirred into a Faluda or added to a fruit salad! There was another factor behind that firm resolution. Something provoking had occurred that morning which had turned him off mangoes.

Rarumma had served a ripe mango during breakfast. The main item was *puttu*—the traditional breakfast item of steamed rice cakes. After mixing *puttu, payar* (boiled beans), *pappadam* (fried lentil puffs) and *panchasara* (sugar), she started peeling the mango. To complete the 5 Ps of the *puttu* experience, the only thing left was *pazham*, aka fruit, as per Fatima.

Tipu started eating the small balls of the mixed delight. Rarumma was cutting and slicing a Kottukonam mango exuding great fragrance, possessing striking colour and having an extraordinary sweetness. Of Tipu's two favourite fruits, one was the mango. It was the king of fruits; how could he help adoring it? Whenever Tipu ruminated on a mango, the picture of a Mango King with a crown on his head, hanging from the stem, popped up in his mind. Ummudu had often asked him to sketch the kingly mango. He had never found the time.

Even when he was chomping on the balls of *puttu*, Tipu was unblinkingly staring at the mango. Rarumma would give him mango pieces only after he cleaned his plate. He started swallowing the food fast, causing him to choke and drink water. His greed was something to watch!

Rarumma was dicing the fruit into small pieces after having peeled it. The Kottukonam King's body was shimmering red. Drops of mango nectar dripped down Rarumma's fingers. Tipu's mouth watered at that sight. He felt like the *puttu* on his plate was piling up from moment to moment. Rarumma sliced off four pieces from one half and turned it over in her palm to cut the other half. Her style of flipping the mango was a sight worth watching. Fatima used to tell Tipu that her mother had a special style for bathing infants, turning them around in the *pala*, a curved receptacle fashioned from the palm tree. He remembered that comment when he saw the docility of the mango in Rarumma's hand.

The second half of the mango was sliced too. It was then that the incident happened. There was a small black hole in the middle of the seed, and a fat white grub came wriggling out of it. Its body was slathered in an oily liquid. There was a smattering of dark dust around the hole. Could it be the worm's crap? Yuck! Tipu spat out the round ball of *puttu* which he was about to chew. The white worm which had wriggled out of the mango seed had the length of a pasta tube. Was Tipu going to hate pasta too, in the future?

How desperate the worm was to escape through the hole! It was akin to the situation in an airport after a flight landed. So much pushing and shoving! Tipu's Vappu got furious at the sight of people rushing with their bags to disembark from the plane. In Asif's opinion, those who haggled for prominence in such situations were those who never got opportunities to prove their worth in real life. The frantic haste to get through the door!

The way the grub stretched its neck and looked around in a frenzy was analogous to those racing passengers. But Tipu was afraid that more worms would follow, like the crowd in a plane. However, there was only one worm. The child wondered how the creature managed to drill a hole through the hide, the flesh and the tough seed cover, and curl up inside. Thieves should learn from this worm. Was he from the land of Ali Baba?

'Look Tipu, this fellow gobbled up all the food which this poor mango kept aside for a little sapling inside the seed. What a brat! In a few days, he will transmute into a beetle, a dark beetle with long pincers.' Nabeezath threw away both the mango pieces and the seed. The grub had gnawed the insides of the seed completely. It was empty, like the water bottles the little girl in Dubai rolled around in the flat above theirs.

In the clinic where Tipu had gone to see the doctor when he was feverish, there was a calendar hanging on the wall—a picture of a baby inside its mother's stomach. He had noticed a tube connecting the mother with the child. Something similar to a mobile charging connection. Ummudu had told him that the baby received its food through that tube. Now he had a doubt: could this worm be the baby in the tummy of the mango fruit? The next moment, he discarded that conjecture. Humans beget human babies. None of his classmates had tigers or elephants for their mothers. What a dunce he was! He slapped his forehead in ridicule. Anyway, that was the end of Tipu's love for mangoes.

Ammalu retreated, having unsuccessfully thrown stones at the mango tree. Tipu proclaimed that the mango was not meant for her. By then, Nabeezath had reached the grove, searching for them. Thankayamma had informed her about their whereabouts.

'We were trying to pluck the mangoes.'

Nabeezath felt like the child, initially highly strung, was now slowly relaxing. He did not run away from the hens anymore, and stepped into the compound without any hesitation. There was no doubt that Ammalu had a major role to play in that change.

Asif was arriving from Dubai in ten days' time. He had asked Nabeezath to prepare a list of things that Tipu needed. Asif had also informed her that one of Tipu's friends had come enquiring about him. Tipu did not even bother to find out his name. He was always fascinated by newness. The Dubai episode was over, and now his native land was here! What was the use of remembering the old episodes, eh? Tipu couldn't care less. In every act of his, he made it crystal clear that his was not the existence of the tiny creature called *kuzhiyana*, the ant-lion, which hid itself in the sand.

Tipu started the worm discussion again as they walked back home from the grove.

'How do you think the worm entered the mango seed?'

Ammalu wondered which mango seed he was talking about. And so, Tipu ended up regurgitating the whole wormy story. Ammalu testified that she, too, had been party to many such horrible worm-hunts. Yet, her craze for mangoes remained untouched.

'When the mangoes are tiny, the beetles come and lay eggs on top of them. The small worms which hatch from the eggs drill their way inside the mangoes through the tender skins. Then they bore a hole inside the seed and nestle inside...

It's so yummy and soft inside, like a cushion! The worm grows along with the mango, and it keeps gnawing at the seed. And when someone cuts open the mango, it jumps outside! My Acchan told me all this...' Ammalu's knowledge trove lay open. Tipu could comprehend matters clearly now.

There was a packet which Nabeezath had purchased from the town. Tipu opened it. Wow, a ripe Kottukonam mango! But he hesitated this time around. Nabeezath washed the mango before peeling and dicing it. Ammalu and Tipu sat in anticipation of either a worm or a beetle making an appearance. But all the mangoes were clean and unblemished. There were neither worms nor beetles inside them. On hearing Tipu's suggestion about purchasing mangoes from the same store always, Nabeezath chuckled.

'The worm-infested mango grew in our yard. Look at that tree near the well; it grew on that one. Now this mango, who knows which pesticides it must have been sprayed with? The saga starts at the flowering stage; they keep spraying insecticides until the fruits reach our hands. Tell me, which worm is brave enough to enter those fruits? Each of the mangoes that Rarumma purchased today is actually a bomb, an absolute bomb!'

Nabeezath chucked away the remains of the mango near the foot of the coconut tree. A monologue, wrapped in a sigh, emerged from her, 'I hope the coconut tree will not shrivel up!'

Vineet came to pick Ammalu up; she waved at Tipu, promising that she would come again tomorrow. Tipu called after her, 'Let's play in the grove tomorrow also!' He wasn't done seeing that place and had trailed behind Nabeezath only because he was famished. Tipu was sure that there were many new sights hiding inside the serpent grove.

Adu pambe, adadu pambe, adadu pambe,
Adu pambe, adadu pambe, kavililam pambe...
(Sway, serpent; swing and sway away, serpent.
Serpent of the grove...tender and fragile...)

Fatima used to hum that song. Tipu suspected that it had something to do with the grove. He had no idea how the serpents swayed and swung; would they climb onto a swing? He thought that the snake deities were graceful, like dancers. Perhaps they should be called 'dancing snakes'!

That night, Tipu wanted to open the windows. When Nabeezath forbade him, he knelt on the cot and threw the windows wide open. The room's vastness lay exposed for the tree branches to explore to their heart's content. He told Nabeezath that his bed did not feel as cold as before.

'It has warmed up due to Tipu! Now both you and the bed have equal heat.' Nabeezath closed her eyes with the fulfilment of having revealed a universal truth. Tipu was getting accustomed to the nightly sounds. The day and night murmurs were different here, and even the wind sounded distinct at night.

Nine:
Fever

Ammalu did not come that day. She was breaking her promise of playing with Tipu. He waited till four in the evening. Observing how restless he was, Nabeezath rang Sita up. Apparently, Ammalu was feverish. The fever had started in the night, intensifying in the morning. Vineet had taken her to a doctor before leaving for work. Sita requested Nabeezath to inform Tipu that he shouldn't worry and that his playmate would come back very soon. She also grumbled about how her daughter became cranky when she was ill, refusing to drink water or eat her rice-gruel.

Sita had caught the fever a fortnight ago; it spread to Vineet and now to Ammalu. It was a flu, and almost everyone in the neighborhood was falling victim to it. Nevertheless, Thankayamma seemed immune to any infection, and the fever desisted from entering her home. Nabeezath and Sita were enjoying a good laugh over it. Thankayamma was a superwoman, how would she catch a fever? Thankayamma, who scared away snakes and fevers, was now the real heroine in Tipu's mind.

Tipu thought that when the fever finally left the house, after having visited each family member one by one, everybody would miss it a lot. Nabeezath's heart started beating hard on hearing the word 'missing.' *How would this child, who experienced desolation at the departure of a fever, view the absence of Fatima…?*

In the dejection of not seeing Ammalu, Tipu immersed himself in *Minecraft*. Nabeezath spoke to him when he was rather deep in the game.

'After having tea, we shall go out today…'

Sensing Tipu's loneliness, Nabeezath had hurriedly hatched this plan.

'Where?' Tipu asked, not looking up from his game.

'To Rarumma's sister's house. You know Khadeejumma, don't you?'

In spite of Tipu's efforts to remember, he did not succeed.

'When you came from Dubai, Khadeejumma had come to see you. There are two older brothers, your *ikka*s, in her home for you to play with—Asgar and Anwar. Anwar *ikka* has a fever, but you can play with Asgar.'

Khadeeja was Nabeezath's big sister. Anwar and Asgar were her grandsons. Like Nabeezath said, Anwar was ill, but it was not a simple fever. He had caught the disease at fourteen.

The boy had been a sports champion, and a wild jack tree from Nabeezath's yard had been felled for making an almirah for his trophies.

Anwar had been persistently complaining of leg pain. He would sit up throughout the night, massaging his legs. The pain below his knees grew by leaps and bounds. He would go off to play after school every day, and return home very late. Anwar grew thinner day by day, and was perpetually fatigued. On hearing his grievances, his Appa and Umma warned him, 'Better stop your football and kabaddi; no wonder your limbs always ache!' His parents put a stop to his sports ventures. Yet, the excruciating pain and tiredness remained unchanged.

When they took Anwar to the doctor, he prescribed many tests. In the tests conducted at the Regional Cancer Centre at Trivandrum, the disease was traced. Anwar had bone cancer in his legs. The surgeries did not heal him completely. Sometimes the pain abated, sometimes he shuddered in mortal agony. Now, he moved about in a wheelchair. Nabeezath hadn't seen him for a long time, hence she planned to visit her sister.

They travelled in an autorickshaw. The heave and shake of the three-wheeler was an amusing experience for Tipu. He remembered going to Yas Island in Abu Dhabi. That had been his first visit to an amusement park. There, he had sat in a vehicle similar to the autorickshaw and it had flown up into the sky. Occasionally it would shake, too. In order to simulate the experience of moving around in space, stars and planets had been shimmering around him. Tipu had been over the moon that day!

Tipu stared at the pictures pasted inside the rickshaw. He could see stars, but there weren't any planets. Whenever the auto shook, he would shake twice in tandem. It soon became an amusing game, and he kept shaking in sync with the auto. Rarumma cautioned the driver, 'Go slow, slow!' whenever the vehicle hit a gutter and splashed slushy water around. However, Tipu looked forward to splattering through the next pot-hole. Unanimously, the autorickshaw driver and Rarumma were berating those who made the roads, the holes and the rain. Tipu could not fathom the reasons behind their complaints. What a thrilling ride it was! How on earth could they find fault with it? While speeding at 120 and 140 kilometres per hour on the smooth-as-marble roads of Dubai, he had never experienced such a thrill. What a marvelous adventure it was!

When they disembarked from the rickshaw, Tipu felt miserable. It was like leaving a game halfway through. His disappointment doubled on hearing that the return trip wouldn't be in the autorickshaw. Khadeejumma's son would drop them in his car. Tipu said a heartfelt prayer for him to catch a fever, too. It was Asgar who received the sweets and fruits which Rarumma had taken along. 'Receive' was not the appropriate word, though; it was more of a 'grab' as per Tipu.

There were medals and trophies displayed in the almirah. Anwar came out from the bedroom, seated in a battery-operated wheelchair. When he touched the buttons, the chair rolled in whichever direction he wanted. Instead of his legs, he moved his fingers now. There were framed photographs of him receiving trophies at school. Tipu wondered whether it was the same boy in the wheelchair. What sort of a fever was that? Even when he had been feverish, he'd never been forced to sit in a wheelchair.

When the ladies went to the kitchen, Asgar retrieved a cricket bat from the top of an almirah. Anwar had a cricket ball in his hand. Where had he hidden it till now? Like a magician, he seemed to have materialised it out of thin air, and was now juggling it in both hands. The drawing room was rather long. Anwar moved his wheelchair to the front of one of the bedrooms. Asgar stood in the middle of the room, ready to bat. There, a competitive cricket match was about to start! Anwar's chair moved with amazing speed. Asgar, the batsman, seemed taken aback by the fierce bowling of Anwar in his wheelchair. Watch, here came the second ball… Anwar's speed was formidable, and his facial expression was intimidating. Was he turning into a Shoaib Akhtar in his wheelchair? Even his mannerisms were similar to Akhtar's! Wow, look at the way he moved his arms!

In Tipu's mind, another hero was taking shape—Anwar, the wheeled bowler. The game continued till the glass vase in the sitting room shattered. But before the sound and its effects reached the kitchen, the two brothers vanished from the scene. Tipu was left all alone in the room.

Asgar promised Tipu that once Anwar's legs were cured, they would have a game on the playground. Anwar gifted Tipu his cricket ball when it was time to leave. When Tipu tried to push it into the pocket of his jeans in vain, Nabeezath intervened and deposited the ball inside her handbag. But Tipu took it back and held onto the ball until they reached home.

'When will Anwar *ikka*'s fever go away?'

Anwar's father was driving the car. He did not reply. Tipu was swathed in doubts again.

'Asgar *ikka* told me that once Anwar *ikka* is well, we shall play on the ground.'

'Child, this is not an illness which goes away quickly. Our Maker granted it and hence, it has to be endured,' Anwar's father sounded devastated.

'Yes, yes, we shall go and play with them,' Nabeezath covered Tipu's mouth before he asked the next question. She hissed in his ears not to open his mouth till they reached home. When they reached the destination, his impatience broke through the barriers.

'When will we go and play? When shall *ikka*'s fever leave?'

'Child, he has a big fever, a bad disease… It shall not leave soon.'

'Even I had a big fever. But once you take medicines and miss school for three days, it leaves you!'

'No, my child, Anwar has a painful disease called cancer.'

'Where is the pain? In his legs?'

'Umm…he has big lumps in his leg…and they hurt.'

'But I didn't see any!'

'We can't see those…they are inside…deep inside the bones. Some naughty cells multiply unnecessarily. One becomes two, two becomes four… Doubling in that manner, they turn into a big lump and many such lumps together have made him sick.'

Nabeezath had to elaborate on what 'cells' meant and how big the lumps could turn out to be.

When they watched television, Nabeezath surreptitiously watched Tipu trying to pinch his limbs. Finally, he discovered two swellings in his body. Two spheres which protruded out of his eyelids—his eyeballs! Tipu took a long time before dropping off to sleep that night. Shouldn't one be fat and bulging if their cells kept increasing; why was Anwar *ikka* so thin then? Tipu's doubts kept doubling like cancer cells.

When he was studying in the first grade, Tipu had caught chicken pox. His body ached badly and he had a high fever. There were red blisters on the third day. When the itching and pain became insufferable, Asif had broken off a bunch of neem leaves. He had very adventurously procured them from a villa.

'If you had touched the neem in the park, the cops would have arrested you! In this place, trees are more valuable than humans. Touch them at your own risk!' Fatima had warned Asif.

The neem leaves were full of dust and grime. Ummudu had washed them and dried them with tissue paper before spreading them on Tipu's bed. How cool it had felt to lie on those! Now, he thought that it would feel the same to recline on the dried leaf bed inside the grove. Ummudu had told him that the blisters on his body contained viruses. It was Ummudu who told him that neither viruses nor 'Our Maker' were visible. He concluded that whatever invisible was enormously powerful.

'Rarumma, is chicken pox cancer?'

Nabeezath was on the verge of sleep.

'Not at all, my dear!' She hugged him close to herself.

That night Tipu dreamt of Anwar, cricket, and the playground. There was a chicken pox blister swelling up in Anwar's leg. It grew and grew, enlarging to the size of an orange. There were many tiny cricket balls inside it. Anwar was fast asleep in his wheelchair. The orange-sized blisters grew as big as watermelons. The number of cricket balls inside grew larger. They fought and frolicked with one another. When they hit each other head on, there was an explosive sound. There, that blister was rupturing! All the cricket balls inside shattered all over the place. The balls were rolling on Tipu's body now.

He felt very cold. He had to flick away the cold balls falling on his neck and chest.

When Tipu opened his eyes, it was dawn. Raindrops had splattered on him through the open window, not cricket balls. It was raining outside and thunder rumbled in the skies. Tipu had dreamt that it was the sound of the balls hitting one another! The plump raindrops were poking his body. But Tipu did not feel like getting up. He was enjoying the gentle prodding of the rain.

Ten: Friendship

Ammalu's fever went down. Nonetheless, it entailed two more days of waiting before she could come over to play. It had been raining since the morning. Thankayamma's umbrella was a banana leaf. When Tipu looked over, she was cowering beneath it. The frog in the fairy tale, 'The Frog Prince', had perched at the pond's edge in the same manner. Nabeezath had asked Thankayamma to sit inside the kitchen until the rain abated. But she huddled under her makeshift umbrella, as if the rain would be affronted if Thankayamma, its bosom friend, wasn't getting drenched!

In the evening, when there was a temporary respite, Tipu stepped out into the yard. Throughout the day, he had been immersed in video games. Nabeezath had been forced to take an Internet connection for his sake. When his eyes started stinging due to the continuous gaming, Tipu decided to explore a bit. He strolled in front of Thiru Nilam. It was then that he remembered the dinosaur-lizard. Tipu walked away hastily and entered the grove. The dried leaf bed had been soaked by the rain. Leaves dripped raindrops on him. The touch-me-nots, having amiably compromised with the rain, were staring at him wide-eyed. In the southern corner of the grove, there was a rain tree. Its leaves opened up, splashing a shower of rainwater on Tipu. The leaves had folded after concealing the water and had awakened when the rain had passed. When the little boy was standing underneath, they were blooming once again.

'Ayyo!' Tipu scampered away from the shade of the tree. The banana leaf which Thankayamma had used for protection against the rain, the rain tree leaves which were determined to sprinkle him with droplets of water, the neem leaves which cooled his body during chicken pox, the mint leaves which Ummudu used to freshen his stinking breath, the henna leaves that were made into a paste for colouring Ummudu's hands in her childhood...what a variety of leaves!

When Tipu checked whether there were any *jamun* fruits scattered on the ground, he couldn't find any. The rain had washed them away. A few tiny mangoes were strewn under the mango tree. Well, who needed those anyway? Yet, their naughty looks and glistening skins were so tempting. Tipu crouched on the ground and started gathering them.

A red fire ant was plummeting right into the dried leaf bed. To observe it closely, Tipu gently removed the top layer. What a world met his eyes! Many ants were scurrying along, and some were carrying food in their mouths. No, it wasn't food, but eggs! A procession carrying their own eggs…Fatima had downloaded a picture of this and shown it to him, asking him to sketch it. Tipu had imperiously ignored her suggestion back then.

The ant nests must have become wet in the rain. They were hurrying to transfer the eggs to a safer locality. That naughty rain which had poked him when he lay inside the house early that morning; where else did it pry into? Tipu tried to trace the path of the ants by digging at the leaf bed layers. Realising that it was a futile attempt, he left it halfway through. Tipu understood that it was through the reproductive process that every creature ensured a place on earth for itself. The responsibility with which the ants protected their next generation was astounding.

The child was befriending the ants, dried leaves, rain and rainwater.

Tipu discovered that under the dried leaves was another vast layer of soil, made from the remnants of the older leaves. The leaf particles were fine, like that of the *puttu* he had eaten the previous day. He sympathised with the poor ants who had to survive on the leaf remnants. Ummudu would scatter such dark matter at the roots of the plants in their balcony, saying that it was food for the plants. Fatima had not elaborated that it was humus, organic fertiliser made by the decaying leaves.

Further beneath that dark layer of *puttu*, Tipu discovered yet another layer. When he dug with his bare hands, the boy saw worms. He felt like throwing up. But this one wasn't like the fat grub inside the mango seed. Slim and elongated, with rings around their slimy bodies, these worms wriggled inside the soil and came up again. Had Tipu seen a picture of an earthworm before, he would have recognised it in a jiffy. But as matters stood, the earthworm was a completely strange creature to him.

A few green sprouts peaked amidst the dried leaves. Some were seedlings. They seemed to be flustered after somersaulting out from beneath the earth with tender shoots and a couple of leaves. Bereft of sunlight, the shoots were white in colour. In the matter of two days, they would vigorously shoot their way up through the dried leaf-bed. Tipu gently cleared the way for the seedlings which were yearning to see the sun, by removing the cluster of leaves. He knew they couldn't grow under the soil. All growth was upward.

Tipu created a circle by removing the leaves surrounding him. Now, he was seated inside a different universe altogether! Around him, ants, their eggs, earthworms, other unknown insects, small plants, seedlings and humus created another world. The fact that there was a thriving society under the leaves which he had thoughtlessly trampled upon was an astonishing discovery. Indeed, it warranted a whoop of victory.

'Eureka, Eureka!' In the midst of the new kingdom which he discovered, little Tipu Sultan, the majestic ruler, sat preening.

He noticed another circle in his proximity. Mushrooms standing upright, rubbing shoulders, wearing their round, white caps. Fatima used to make cutlets from edible button mushrooms. Not just cutlets but curry, too, and it tasted exactly like chicken! Tipu was familiar with that species. But one uncertainty lingered in his mind. From where had these white-capped fellows suddenly sprung up? He stepped inside that circle of mushrooms. Angels in white seemed to be prancing around him.

Tipu plucked a mushroom and gazed at it—except for its white cap and a long stem, it had neither flower nor leaf. From under the hat, a black powder stained his fingers. When he turned the hat over and looked closely, he saw many gills; thin, wide sheet-like plates radiating from the stem, with the black powder spilling out from them. He shook the cap and watched the shower of black powder again. It was fun to caress the mushroom cap. It was like touching the tender foreheads of infants. He plucked a few more mushrooms and made his way home.

The velveteen moss on the stepping stones was soaking wet. When he jumped on them, water squirted out. Tipu skipped from one stone to the next. When his footwear started to slip, he stopped the game. When he reached home, Vineet was waiting for him. Tipu's eyes widened and started scanning for Ammalu. But she wasn't there. Vineet had brought a packet for Nabeezath. It was filled with the mushrooms which had sprouted after the last rain.

'Aha, so you brought them too?' Vineet beckoned the child to come closer.

'Lots in the grove. They are standing in a circle, ready to dance.'

'Haha, the fairy dance! They are called fairy rings, you know?'

Vineet seated Tipu in his lap.

'Last year, too, when it had rained, they had popped up at the same spot to dance! But the circle was rather small in comparison. Next year, the circle will be wider.'

'You mean they will stand in the same place next year? But if we make a curry out of them, how will they return?' Tipu wondered.

'Tipu, next year, their kids will arrive! You plucked out their heads, but beneath the earth, they have long legs to travel.'

'Black powder spread over my hands. I will be back after washing them,' Tipu said.

Vineet took the mushrooms from Tipu and showed him the gills.

'These are the seeds of the mushrooms. When these fall on the earth, they germinate. Let me show you a trick! Go, get a white paper and a bottle for me.'

Tipu rushed to his room, pulled a paper from his drawer and rushed back after emptying a cookie container. Vineet spread the white paper on the table. Then he removed the stems of the mushrooms and placed the caps on the paper. He proceeded to cover those with the container. Tipu procured some more bottles from the kitchen. Vineet carefully filled the paper with as many mushrooms as he could.

'It is 6 pm now. Tipu, when do you sleep?'

'At 10:30. I watch *Scooby Doo* at 9 and I sleep only after watching that show!'

'Right, so don't disturb this paper till then. Not even a fly should sit on this table, okay? At ten, remove the bottles. When you lift the mushroom caps, you will see a magic trick!'

Tipu nodded.

As Vineet was leaving, he gravely reminded the child again about his task, 'Ensure that no one disturbs it.' Tipu reaffirmed by bobbing his head again. Vineet promised him that Ammalu would come to play the next day.

Tipu started pondering upon how to while away the time until 10 pm. He strolled past the table twice or thrice. Would a genie emerge from the bottle? Could it be that new mushrooms would sprout? His mind was buzzing with doubts.

The picture of Thankayamma holding the banana leaf over her head raced into his mind. He imagined the old woman with a mushroom cap, standing inside the bottle. He couldn't help but giggle.

Thankayamma's form was appropriate for fitting into a bottle too! He prattled with the Thankayamma inside the bottle; how else was he going to spend the time?

'Thankayamma, why are you standing in the bottle?'

'To escape the rain, dear!' She laughed, her teeth sparkling.

'Did you climb inside the python's nest during another rain?' Tipu gurgled.

'Aye! He was one smart snake, wasn't he? I was singing loudly while cutting the grass; he probably heard the song.' Thankayamma grinned.

Fatima used to sigh that whenever she heard KS Chitra's songs, she felt like eating her up! Tipu assumed that the python felt similarly about Thankayamma.

'There weren't enough teeth inside that snake's mouth, you know! Look, he did not have as many teeth as I have...Huh, how dare he come to eat someone like me? Ha, ha...showed him that my billhook could chop off more than grass, didn't I!'

'When you slashed the serpent's mouth, did it cry?'

'No...It was I who cried, my dear! When I extricated myself from its grip and looked at him from the top of the hill, it was trying to crawl forward, dragging its split head. I felt so sad at that sight. When it tried to climb a rock, it fell and rolled down into the grass. Looking like a twin-headed snake,

it lay stone dead. Ouch, my hairs stand on end recollecting that sight!'

'Do you still have that billhook with you, Thankayamma?'

'Oh, that? Its handle fell off...must be lying around in my hut.' Saying that, Thankayamma placed her mushroom cap on the paper and sat down on her haunches.

Why was Thankayamma shaking the bottle? Oh, that was Rarumma!

Nabeezath was getting the table ready for dinner.

'Rarumma, please stop! Don't put anything on the table.'

He had his dinner on the sofa that night. Even when he watched *Scooby Doo*, he cast a surreptitious glance at the bottle. The clock struck ten, and Tipu ran to lift the bottle. He raised the mushroom caps gently.

'Wow! Rarumma, look at this circle of mushrooms. Like cycle wheels!'

The seeds of the mushrooms had fallen on the white paper, creating a magnificent design. The perfectly distanced rows of gills had spilled their black powder-like seeds and created designs. Tipu took it away for safekeeping. The new 'gift of rain' granted by Vineet was the art of the spore print.

No wonder Ammalu adored her father. Tipu realised that she was probably learning new tricks daily and showing off in front of her friends at school.

Asif reached his native place. His parents were still in Dubai, and they wanted to take care of Tipu. However, Asif thought it better to shift his son from Dubai. That decision had paved way for the 'transplanting' that the child underwent. It was likely that Asif might have wanted a change for himself. He had brought every item of Tipu's wishlist along. Indeed, most objects had been demanded so he could flaunt them before Ammalu: the chewing gum which stained the tongue with bright colours, lollipops, Tipu's favourite, bug-shaped candies and their ilk.

'Vappu, why didn't you bring avocados, kiwis and strawberries like I asked?' Tipu's lips resembled a trembling, red-hued millipede. This was the warning sign of an impending sulking session.

'They would have turned bad during the journey, Tipu.'

'What about some plums?'

'Are you crazy, Tipu? You never gave them a second glance while you were in Dubai. How come you are asking for those now?'

Tipu consoled himself that he would make do with whatever he had to impress Ammalu.

As soon as Asif had reached, he handed over a huge suitcase to Nabeezath. It was full of Fatima's clothes and her knickknacks. Asif had no clue about handling the clothes and shoes of the dead. Would someone else use those? Would they be haunted by fear, guilt or sadness…? Wasn't it stupid to presume that remnants of the dead person remained in those articles? Asif was in a deep dilemma. That was why he had packed up every possession of Fatima and handed it all over to her mother.

Asif was inside a fairy ring; just like the one Tipu had seen inside the serpent grove. And the absence of Fatima was dancing around him like white mushrooms.

'Vappu shall leave for his friend's house in the city after a few days.' Asif wondered whether Tipu had actually heard him.

His decision was to take Tipu along, after joining his new job and arranging their accommodation. Tipu's school would also start by then.

Searching for Fatima's notes had become a game for Asif now. A puzzle, like Tipu's game, Treasure Hunt. He felt that one should indulge in games at every age; the energy provoked by adventures was remarkable. No wonder Tipu took everything so easy. The child's black T-shirt, with the slogan *Trust me, I'm a gamer* in white font, was drying on the washing line outside. It was Tipu's most favourite outfit. Ever since it had been purchased, Tipu would always insist on wearing it when they stepped out. How fast children recognised their own individualities! 'I am this person!', they nonchalantly proclaimed to the world. Indeed, Tipu was a real gamer; a first-rate one.

Asif stood in Fatima's room. Old books, clothes, notebooks filled with her handwriting, stone necklaces, rubber bracelets, rusty candy tins... Four of Fatima's notes ended up in his hands during that search. Fatima entered Asif's life straight from the school compound.

From her Class XI Chemistry text book, Asif obtained the following missive:

Note 1: *Chemistry is very mysterious indeed. It is a Chemical Mystery. It reveals the secrets of the chemicals. Two colours join to create a new one, one thing merges with another, solid turns into liquid, liquid into gas; they play around by transforming into one another.*

Today, we did an alcohol test in the chemistry lab. When two drops of sulphuric acid were dropped into the solution in the test tube, wow...what a fragrance! When we roasted it a bit on the burner, the scent of ripe pineapple filled the surroundings. The utter ease with which the three liquids merged to create the smell of ripened pineapple, jackfruit, mango and banana...Some revelations are absolutely marvellous!

Pipettes, burettes, conical flasks, test tubes—these are such prettily designed instruments. They are also very precise. One should use such instruments in the kitchen too. For concocting a fish curry, add turmeric, chilli powder and coriander powder to a burette and drip the mixture into a flat, traditional earthenware pot. How wonderful it will be to watch Umma cooking in the kitchen like a scientist!

To test whether the proportion of salt is right, one can take a sip with a pipette. Wow, what a sight that will be! The sautéed curd should be stored in a 500 ml glass beaker. Of course, one has to mix it with a glass rod.

To measure the milk needed for making tea, use a measuring cylinder. Payasam, our traditional sweet, should be stored in a flask with a round bottom and slim neck. The semolina's long strands and swellings of sago rice in the payasam shall resemble a flower vase.

Near the sink, we should place a wash bottle for washing our hands. If you press its tummy, water will squirt through the tube. Inside the kitchen rack, one should always have a mortar and pestle for grinding the asaofetida, cardamom and fenugreek.

Since the kitchen is the only part of the house where so many chemical changes occur in the most natural manner, one should anoint it as a chemistry laboratory. It shall be good to keep aside a litmus paper for checking the tartness and hotness of the curries. The lady in the kitchen should wear a white overcoat. If she wears gloves to protect herself while frying fish and toasting crispy pappadam, the woman in the kitchen shall become a true lab technician.

Eleven: Tipu's Tortoise

That day, Thankayamma was very late. Nabeezath grew very annoyed. Could it be that the old woman had been washed away in the downpour? She lived near the river.

'How many times have I asked her to stay here with me? That woman doesn't listen to me; I would have had some company too.' But Thankayamma refused to stay with anyone, not just Nabeezath. She was habituated to eating and sleeping alone. No, it wasn't a habit, it was a preference. Nabeezath kept checking intermittently whether it was drizzling again.

Asif opened Fatima's note about rain and read it. He was clueless about her age when she had scribbled that down. Neither the date nor place was inscribed anywhere in the note.

Note 2: *For the last three days, the schools have been closed. It is raining. Water, water everywhere. Water which the earth cannot hold, water which the earth cannot absorb, water which overflows from the rivers and seas, unending downpours of water.*

How sharp is the rain's memory! It remembers the exact route it took to flow into rivers and brooks. No one knows how old the rain is; it doesn't age, or end up doddering and grey. The rain which falls in my yard is not of my age. Human beings have different perspectives about rain at different stages of their lives, but the rain does not grow old.

There are certain raindrops that remain trapped and powerless to merge with the flowing rain. They stay entrapped in compromises. They are fated to be solitary, bearing the self-loathing of the ostracised. From every snare emerges the frantic panting of the lost, these discarded ones who are unable to flow along with their compatriots. The chiratta (the truncated shell of a dried coconut) filled with rain, is one such container. How rattled I feel when I see that! The chiratta entrapping raindrops becomes a vessel filled to the rim with question marks. If you hack the globe into two, one half would be full of thousands of unanswered questions. That is similar to the ounce of rain caught in that chiratta.

The raindrops caught in the crevices of rocks are also in the same condition. Rocks are likely to be the terrain which receive rain in the harshest manner. The drops shatter their heads against them. The dark crags stare cruelly at the dripping rain. The raindrops are peeved with the rocks too; after all, both the wind and the clouds have been spoiling them rotten.

The tree hollows turn into rain hollows; the tree hollows are the most mysterious dwelling places on earth. They are spaces which hide unpredictable trickeries. How unfortunate is the rain entombed inside a tree hollow! A hideaway where even light is loath to peep into. It is mostly the hollows bereft of birds that trap the rain.

The hollows of the trees which were once replete with chirping and cooing; tiny nests filled with the warmth of birds' eggs. What a desolate look that one-eyed tree hollow has when it becomes empty. The rain inside the tree hollow wails from within darkness, gazing at the light. The hollows persevere, bearing the unborn floods.

There are certain species which have been cast out of kitchens; for example, the attukallu, our grandmothers' grinding stones consisting of the mortar and pestle. When the electric mixer and grinder encroached into their spaces, the poor things were declared pariahs. The rain inside the attukallu will lie still, epitomising the fostering of rejection.

Stagnant water looks unnatural; the frustration of being tied down. The condition of forcing something which has never been static to stay within strict boundaries! Ah, water should run, flow, drip, drop…I hate water surfaces which are paralysed. Perhaps that is the reason why I dislike lagoons. Streams, canals, rivers, all are constantly on the move. But the lagoon lies agape—like an exclamation mark!

The most familiar among this species would be the rain trapped inside roadside gutters. The water in the gutter is pit water; holding the entire accusations of a civilisation within itself. The gutters reproachfully create circles with their forefingers, taking revenge against society and the judicial system. A stationary pool of vendetta!

The fury one feels at the vehicles which splash you with slush during the rainy season as you walk on the roads! Let the unending vengeance carried by the clayey water of the gutter make its mark on every living being who walks through the roads. Let our offices, hotels, hospitals and schools fill with humans splashed with mud drops. Sometimes, such silent shouts are necessary for eye-opening moments. Let the slush-revolution continue forever!

And finally, the rain in my cupped palms! That is a rain which is trapped in me. Something which can be thought of as my love, my memory, precious to me. I shall never let that trapped rain flow. Shall I carry it along even when I die? No, after transferring it to the cupped palms of someone most beloved, I shall depart. Trapped rains are like lonely deaths and uninhabited islands. Even so, they too, possess an enchanting, soothing love. A love which will seep within, if you just dip a finger inside.'

Asif folded the note and put it back in its place.

The rain in the note was pouring down outside. Who was Fatima? Asif simply could not fathom…She was Tipu's mother,

Asif's wife and Nabeezath's daughter. Yet, Fatima was none of those, she was something else. She was stirring inside Asif even now. Fatima was in Tipu, albeit in a different guise; she was also giving company to Nabeezath, always present by her side.

Tipu was gazing at the path, waiting for Thankayamma's arrival. By 10 am, he could see two figures approaching from a distance. A big arch and a small arch. The big one was dragging the small one with the help of a coir rope.

'No wonder this old woman took such a long time to come today! I wasted my time worrying.'

Nabeezath became incensed at Thankayamma's homecoming and went inside the kitchen in a huff. She had started sweeping the front yard, and threw away the broom in annoyance when she left.

Tipu was seeing a tortoise for the first time; the little arch was crawling obediently under Thankayamma's control. He had seen a tortoise only in fables before, when the hare and the tortoise raced each other!

Tipu imagined Thankayamma as a hare. Though it was the most unsuitable simile, he just felt like visualising her in that form. Thankayamma the hare was asleep under a tree. The tortoise reached the tree and slowly crawled its way to the finishing line without awakening the hare. When the tortoise crossed the hare for the first time, he scored ten points. In the next round, he would score an additional 10 points. So if the tortoise crossed the tree ten times without waking up Thankayamma the hare, its total score would be 10×10=100! Tipu imagined the potential of a brand-new video game. What was inscribed on his T-shirt was true: 'Trust me, I am a gamer.' He was a gamer through and through.

The hare and the tortoise reached the gate. Tipu sat on his haunches and observed the tortoise keenly.

'This is your Umma's tortoise, you know', Thankayamma explained.

'Ummudu's tortoise?' Tipu gurgled in wonder.

'I caught this tortoise for your mother, my *Pathu mol.* I took him away when she left. A little bit of grass or a few cockroaches are enough for him. He gives me no trouble but does not die either. He will not die even after I conk off!' Thankayamma grinned broadly.

Tipu touched the tortoise's shell with slight repugnance.

'Aww! It's like touching a cricket ball!'

Having touched it once, Tipu understood that the creature wasn't dangerous. He began to caress it.

'Will you give it to me?'

'Of course, I dragged it all this distance just to give it to you!' Thankayamma walked towards the kitchen.

Perhaps fatigued due to all that crawling, the tortoise was motionless now. He was immobile, as if having declared a strike. When Tipu plucked some leaves, the tortoise turned its head away. Tipu was stroking its hard shell, and the creature stared at the boy, stretching its neck. Tipu understood that the tortoise was aware of everything. That gaze, however, was not like that of the dinosaur-lizard which had looked at him from the back porch of Thiru Nilam.

He had often wished for a pet puppy in his Dubai flat. All these desires had been redirected into video games. Tipu tried to lift the tortoise into his arms; it was very heavy. Stretching its tiny head, the tortoise was searching for something. It was also looking at Tipu with its big eyes. When it opened its mouth, a stink emanated from it.

Tipu decided that two mint leaves would serve this fellow well! What if he went for a ride on the creature's shell? He could go to Ammalu's house and give her a shock! But it would take a long time, perhaps until evening, to reach her house on a tortoise's back.

When the sunlight spread, the tortoise crawled its way to the shade.

'Rarumma, should we not put it in water?'

Thankayamma was the one to reply, 'Let it wander around. Fill a basin with water for it. He likes that…give it lot of water to drink.'

Nabeezath finally opened her mouth, 'Now you will take away all our vessels for bathing the creature! Thankayamma, don't you have anything better to do? Fatima used to follow this thing around for years. Ever since she saw this creature, she didn't even care for her exams. After Tipu plays with it for a few days, get it away from here. I wouldn't have minded had it been an affectionate creature…'

Thankayamma shook with laughter. As she relished the rice gruel, she gleefully watched Tipu, who was caressing the tortoise. The creature resembled a human infant, with its four legs spread wide. Even the look in its eyes was childlike. Tipu started crawling on all fours along with the tortoise. Nabeezath looked daggers at Thankayamma as his pajamas and palms became muddied.

Fatima's note about tortoises was hiding in a nook, away from everybody's gaze. She had written it with red ink, over the printed letters of an old story book. It was the story of a princess called Blondie and a tortoise.

Poor Blondie was treated cruelly by her stepmother and stepsisters. She was abandoned in a forest by the evil stepmother, but she made some good friends there. Fatima could easily recite all the poems that Blondie wrote from memory, stuck in a magic fortress inside the wilderness. Many wicked spirits had tried to harm her while she was trying to get away from there. Finally, a gigantic tortoise had come forward to help her escape.

'Come, sit on my back. If you stay silent, I shall take you out of the forest. You should step down only when I stop moving.'

Seated on top of the tortoise, Blondie sighed, 'Oh! How long this journey seems to be! Indeed, how long this journey has been! Have you seen a tortoise walk? They are very, very slow.'

Finally, after six months, the tortoise reached the gates of the kingdom. There was a picture of Blondie astride the tortoise in that book. The beautiful Blondie dressed in a white gown, seated on top of the huge, green shell of the creature. Her long tresses were scattered all over the shell.

Her tortoise note was in the same book. Since it was scribbled over the printed pages, it was difficult to decipher. But for those used to her handwriting, it was easy to read.

Blondie's huge tortoise tempts me so much. The deer and the cat are tricking her with their falsehoods as she languishes inside the magic fortress. What they promise will never come to pass; she is not going to meet her father again. She whiled away the days by writing notes, like me. Blondie never writes about incidents which have taken place, her notes always point out at what is about to happen. The parrot which assured her that it would come singing to save her, went back on its word too. Of all the animals that she saw in the forest and the fortress, it was the tortoise, the slowest among them all, which came to her rescue. The parrot, deer, cat, frog…none of these creatures helped her.

'If you sit silently on my back without weeping and with patience, I shall take you back to the kingdom; but you should not step down even if you feel like it,' the tortoise told her. The tortoise knew that nobody would have such a gargantuan amount of patience. What was left to be endured, considering that she had to travel with a tortoise?

I have a tortoise too. His name is Anku. Thankayamma must have got it from the Ottars. I am guessing that she managed to steal him as the nomads were readying to roast the creature. Thankayamma never reveals such secrets. Even the 'Legend of the Snake' became popular because of the gossiping women who had gone to cut grass that day. It is best to be skeptical about the percentage of truth and falsehood in that particular tale! Thankayamma finds puppies and kittens trailing behind her, as if hypnotised by the magical spell cast by a wicked witch. I wonder when will she come to my gate with an elephant following her?

If you observe the imprints left behind by Anku the tortoise, they resemble railway tracks. A lazy train which weaves its own tracks! Even if I die, he will stay alive. Why is he living on and on like this? Animals have no recourse to taking their own lives either. They are constrained to live until their deaths occur.

Yesterday, I smuggled Anku inside my room without drawing Umma's attention. He has no distinct smell about him, unlike mice, cats or dogs. A useless, flavourless creature! I caught a snail inching forward on the wall and tried to feed Anku. One idle creature eating another idle creature. He smacked his lips while eating it; akin to little kids savouring ice cream.

Tortoises, snails, clams: all possess shells, and all three are slow-natured. Could it be that the security of the shells makes them lazy?

Anku's breathing is very noisy, like an asthma patient. It is as if he is sucking all the oxygen in the atmosphere through his throat and sending it straight to his tummy...

Anyway, I have no intention of losing him. Maybe my children will play with him too. Just consider that remarkable lifespan.'

The storybook was lying in the assortment of wastepaper packets and rusted vessels meant to be sold to the scrap-dealer. Perhaps it would travel somewhere in the scrap dealer's sack, like Blondie on top of the tortoise.

Tipu's wait for showing his tortoise to Ammalu extended till the evening. Since Nabeezath refused to let Anku inside the house, Tipu stayed in the front yard throughout the day. It was dark by the time Vineet and Ammalu arrived.

'Will it bite?' Ammalu asked.

'Nobody has ever died of a tortoise bite till now, children,' Asif was the one who replied.

'This creature was around during Fatima's schooldays. She used to call it either Anku or Appu.' Nabeezath had introduced Asif to the tortoise. Tipu and Ammalu were busy flipping the creature onto its back, curious to see beneath the shell.

'Why are you torturing the poor thing?' Asif asked. He seemed to have developed a soft corner for the creature after hearing that it was once Fatima's pet.

'He isn't as simple as he seems. The fellow has astounded even Charles Darwin. Darwin had a pet tortoise called Harriet. He got it from the Galapagos Islands. Even after the demise of Darwin and the deaths of his children and grandchildren, the tortoise continued to live. They say that it lived for almost 175 years,' Vineet enlightened Tipu with some of his tortoise know-how.

'Why doesn't it die?' Ammalu raised a query.

'Maybe because it is so slow in every activity, it lives so long,' Tipu answered.

'Everything crawls at a snail's pace for him, right? Like we celebrate our birthdays every year, maybe he celebrates his every four years! Since his birthday comes every four years, he ages slowly,' Ammalu suggested a solution.

'Since he walks very slowly, he will need lots of time for doing everything. So, he has no other way than to live very long.' Both of them were now assured of the answer.

'I have skater shoes purchased from Dubai in my bag. They have two wheels underneath; shall we try them on him?' Tipu's idea provoked a bout of giggles in Ammalu. She couldn't help but laugh at the thought of Anku skating away in his skating shoes through the city traffic. All he needed was a pair of tinted sunglasses to leave an unforgettable impression on the passersby. Dress him in Adidas sportswear too!

On his tablet, Tipu was exploring ways to take care of a tortoise: its habitat, food, behaviours, quirks; it was his own independent research project. It was then that he saw a tortoise poem. It was D.H. Lawrence's "Tortoise Family Connections". He wrote it down on the back of the spore-printed paper.

On he goes, the little one,
Bud of the universe,
Pediment of life.
Setting off somewhere, apparently.
Whither away, brisk egg?
His mother deposited him on the soil as if he were no more than droppings,

And now he scuffles tinily past her as if she were an old rusty tin.

A mere obstacle,

He veers round the slow great mound of her.

Tortoises always foresee obstacles.

It is no use my saying to him in an emotional voice:

"This is your Mother, she laid you when you were an egg."

He does not even trouble to answer: "Woman, what have I to do with thee?"

He wearily looks the other way,

And she even more wearily looks another way still,

Each with the utmost apathy,

Incognizant,

Unaware,

Nothing.

As for papa,

He snaps when I offer him his offspring,

Just as he snaps when I poke a bit of stick at him,

Because he is irascible this morning, an irascible tortoise

Being touched with love, and devoid of fatherliness.

Father and mother,

And three little brothers,

And all rambling aimless,

like little perambulating pebbles scattered in the garden,

Not knowing each other from bits of earth or old tins.

Except that papa and mama are old acquaintances, of course,
But family feeling there is none, not even the beginnings.
Fatherless, motherless, brotherless, sisterless
Little tortoise.

The little tortoise which had hatched from the droppings-like eggs of his mother felt no emotional attachment to her. On reading the poem, Tipu felt that there were some similarities between the stoic little tortoise and himself. The tortoise who never searches for a friend does not realise that he is alone. Solitude is his birthright.

Tipu discovered many more tortoise poems written by D.H. Lawrence online. He saved all of them on his tablet. He named the folder containing the tortoise poems, *Anku's Treasure Box.*

Twelve: Sketches

Anku the tortoise, pulled by a thread around its neck, soon became an integral part of Tipu's sojourns. Right after, Asif proceeded to the city. He had to join work the very next day. When he packed his bags, Asif did not forget to take Fatima's notes along.

The first note he tucked inside the bag was the one retrieved from Fatima's notebook, something commemorating her Class X school-leaving rites.

Note 3: *I have been studying alphabets for the last 10 years. Hindi, Malayalam, English: I learned to read and write their letters. Presumably, this is the great knowledge that I have obtained from this place. Now I have to search for opportunities to use it. In Science and Mathematics, whatever one learns is seen, heard and applied on a day-to-day basis. By studying Science, one can appreciate the mysteries of nature and explore how the present-day world came into being. Mathematics teaches us that there are step-by-step ways and shortcuts to solve complex problems.*

Only Language stays a new subject, to be mastered without the help of pre-existing clues.

Take the case of Hindi, where a carelessly drawn line, the vowel diacritic on the left or right changes the entire meaning of the word. There is an ulakka—our very own long pestle used for grinding grains—a sort of longish line imposed on top of every Hindi word and due to its weight, the alphabets cannot twist to either side even a little. What a hapless state indeed! Umma says that everything has its own fate line. Hindi is the only language fortunate enough to draw its own fate lines on its forehead.

Of all the languages that I've seen, Malayalam is the most robust. It has very few slim alphabets. It is snidely remarked that the Malayali gorges on cooked rice and hence his tummy bulges. Could it be that we feed our vowels and consonants with the same rice? The chillaksharam—the special consonants—are no lesser bodies; even they are subject to the battle of the bulge. They are veritable compatriots of Soori Namboodirippadu—that flabby villain in our first perfect novel Indulekha. English alphabets are the most disciplined. If one were to make them stand in a school assembly, they would be striking! After all, they are the discoveries of the white man; discipline would be an inherent feature.

In this world, there are as many languages as there are birds, animals and insects. Just because we cannot understand the language of the plants doesn't imply that they don't have one.

They, too, have sturdy alphabets. A language they use to spring up when it rains and fade away at sunset. Plants converse with the sun, soil and rain. Can anyone argue that the touch-me-not has no language of its own? How clearly it makes its stance evident before us all.

How did the carpenters come to being? The first to carve out a home from the trees were the woodpeckers. Human beings simply continue to use that language. Who taught us music if not the birds?

School was a place of joy for me. Simply because I shall not be there, the school does not cease to exist. It will remain there. Tomorrow, when everyone cries on the last day of school, maybe I shall weep too, although I dislike my crying self.

Tipu tied the other end of Anku's rope to a white ebony tree. At a little distance, Thankayamma was scratching around like the chickens did. Anyone would suspect that she was a hen, seeing her stooped figure and searching style!

'What are you searching for?'

Thankayamma did not look up on hearing Tipu's question, but responded promptly.

'Am plucking the *kayyonni* for sauteing with oil.'

'I shall help, Thankayamma.'

Tipu stared at the *kayyonni* plants, the 'false daisies' which Thankayamma held in her hand. He started searching for the plants using his binoculars. Whenever he caught one through the eyes of the binoculars, he would sit on his haunches, uproot the plant and hand it over to Thankayamma.

Some false daisies were stubborn when it came to leaving the soil. When Tipu pulled them up, they grasped the earth will equal strength, resisting. Often, only the upper half ended up in his hands, and the portion of the plant still rooted obstinately in the earth would glare at him vengefully.

'Enough, enough', Thankayamma called out.

But Tipu was in no mood to listen. The search for the false daisy was becoming a thrilling exercise. Especially since it was a technical process using his binoculars.

'Ouch! Ants have bitten me, Thankayamma!' Tipu wailed, scratching his hands frantically. His hands had become red and swollen by then.

'Ha ha…*choriyannam* bit the boy searching for *kayyonni*!' Thankayamma chortled in glee, infuriating Tipu. He threw the climbing nettle plant far away in anger.

'What a nasty plant! If my Anku had eaten it, its mouth would have been itching so badly by now!'

Thankayamma started her return journey from the grove, carrying the collection of false daisies.

'Come, let's go home.'

'I shall come later.'

Thankayamma, the arch, slowly turned.

'Listen, there are some colour pencils and a drawing book on my table. Can you please fetch those for me?' Tipu hollered after Thankayamma's retreating back.

When the arch disappeared from his view, Tipu ambled towards Anku the tortoise. The white flowers of the tree were scattered on his shell, making a lovely sight.

'Aha! Look at that design! It is clear that you were immobile till I came. Or else how could so many flowers have fallen on your back? You lazy thing!' Tipu nudged the tortoise affectionately using his big toe. By that time, Thankayamma returned with his book and colours.

'You may leave,' Tipu issued his order authoritatively. Assuming that something secretive was up, Thankayamma withdrew her arch from the vicinity.

Under an *elanji* tree, next to the cluster of climbing nettles, Tipu settled down. Balancing his drawing book on his right knee, he started sketching the plant. After completing his drawing, he prominently drew a skull and two cross bones with a red sketchpen and wrote 'Danger' beneath it. Climbing nettle is a warning sign! He must have felt the need for a red warning signboard here, similar to the one that he had seen near the Tilapia Lake, cautioning people against swimming in it. Knowingly or unknowingly, the first representative of the green universe that Tipu sketched turned out to be a climbing nettle.

Tipu was exorcising the spirits of all the guns, racing cars, monsters and aliens that he had sketched so far by sketching the nettle. To prevent them from encroaching into his creativity, he built a fence of climbing nettle, demarcating the boundaries.

He started colouring his second picture: Anku the tortoise with his head held high, and a shell covered with white ebony flowers. Two legs extended from either side of its neck, looking like Diwali sparklers. Anku was looking up at the flowery tree. Tipu's caption for this read—'Even a tortoise can flower.'

The third drawing was of serpents and the *sarppathara*, the raised platform for the snake deities. There were trees crowding the platform, with monstrous creepers entwining with the dangling branches. Pharaohs wearing snake-crowns were swinging on them, all topsy-turvy. The clothing and ornaments of the Pharaohs were similar to the depictions Tipu had seen at Rafi Mall. Underneath the picture was the catchphrase: *From pyramids to groves.*

The fourth picture was decorated with mushrooms. Tipu, looking at a circle of mushrooms through his binoculars. That drawing took up half the paper, and the other half was its description, explaining what Tipu was observing through his binoculars. It wasn't mushrooms, but spore prints, like tyre marks on a white paper. The caption was, 'The insight.'

The fifth had a long python under the *jamun* tree, its tongue flicking out. Ammalu was extending a black plum to the python (maybe she was trying to colour the python's tongue). Thankayamma was running towards them from afar, with her billhook lodged between her teeth. She was no longer a hunchback in the drawing. Ammalu's face had a naughty expression, while Thankayamma looked fierce. The title of the drawing was: 'The colour of fear.'

Thus, in a single day, Tipu sketched many pictures of the snake grove. They had arrived after a wait of many long years.

Nabeezath started teaching the Malayalam alphabet to Tipu. Every day, they spent an hour learning the language. Tipu started to scrawl 'A, Aa, E, Ee' on top of Anku's shell using a sketch pen.

'Oh, how could you? You're hurting the poor creature!' Nabeezath was outraged.

'What's wrong? You said that the tortoise lives for a very long time. My alphabets will remain on its shell without getting erased!'

'Do you think this is your blackboard? Are any of your scribbles still there? The ink has percolated down its body. I hope it does not die!'

After hearing Nabeezath, Tipu became agitated. He rushed to fetch some water, and washed Anku's shell clean.

These were the peculiar ways in which the bond between Nabeezath and Tipu strengthened.

While thinking of the close bonding of his son and his grandmother, Asif ended up in Fatima's childhood days. That singular note came into his hands from a very secret hiding place. It had been tucked away into a corner under the table cover, folded six times, almost ready to be thrown away. When he opened it, he discovered that it was a letter meant for Nabeezath. Fatima had written it when she was in Class XII.

To my Umma,

Umma, you really like me a lot. My feelings for you are the same exactly.

My Umma is not like other mothers at all. There is no sneaking behind my back to unravel my secrets, nor any interruptions to disturb my fun. But I keep many secrets from you, Umma. I need to confess it all. Hereby I am accounting for those one by one.

1. *I don't do namaaz at all times, unlike what you taught me. Also, I tend to pray rather too little. To openly proclaim all my selfishness to Allah is an embarrassing proposition. Somehow, great fears and avaricious desires do not affect*

me. Maybe that is the reason why I often tend to forget to pray. But I believe in the force inside myself, that is my God.

2. *I love Umma more than Vappa. Of course Vappa is kind, does everything for me, loves me dearly. But I doubt that I will cry when he dies.*
3. *I never eat the mutton from Khadeejumma's house shared as part of the sacrificial feast. Usually I throw it away, fibbing that I will eat it inside my room. I cannot consume sacrificial remains.*
4. *I have smoked Thankayamma's beedi. Many, many times in fact. Though I never had any doubt that Thankayamma would snitch on me, I used to steal few coins from your purse, Umma, for tipping her.*
5. *I was the thief who stole the 'Queen of the Night' plant from Khadeejumma's house. Out of everyone's sight, I sneaked inside the serpent grove and planted it there. I wished that it would bloom only for me. At midnight, I had gone all alone to the grove to watch the blooming of the queen. You must remember how a thief crept inside the house through the open door. Of course, I ended up telling you that I suffered from sleep-walking and Umma, you took me to the doctor too. I buried all the medicines which he prescribed inside the serpent grove.*
6. *Umma, though you sent me to a girl's school, I have always preferred the company of boys. Every day after school,*

I used to chat with the son of Shanta Teacher. But that doesn't mean that I ever accepted any of the letters that he offered.

It does not end here... I have many more big secrets to reveal. First, you should read this note. I am placing it inside your bag. You shall see it when you take out your lunchbox today afternoon. (Do not tell Shanta Teacher about her son.)

Asif couldn't help grinning. He read it twice.

Nowadays, Tipu was always busy sketching. Whatever struck him as interesting, he would try to capture in his drawings. Walls, and even the plates, became his canvas. His tablet, games and cartoons were relegated to the side. After indulging the tortoise, the grove, Ammalu and his sketches, there was hardly any time in Tipu's day for other activities.

Sunday was the day Vineet, Sita and Ammalu used to enjoy a trip to the city. Since Tipu's KFC craze was pretty well known, they took him along once.

'Tipu, you are a real fan of KFC, is that so?' Vineet asked.

'Yes, I love it. But Rarumma's chicken fry is also very tasty. I like that too. Rarumma is going to learn how to make KFC. Yesterday, she made some doughnuts; though they tasted different from ours, I found them very good.'

Nabeezath's doughnut was an item which was a worldwide exclusive! She would fry up some *vada*, a fried snack made of lentils, and pour chocolate syrup on top—her own version of local doughnuts. By adding a little masala, stirred tomatoes and onions to *idiyappam* made of rice flour in a special mold, she would cook up a storm of noodles!

Thankayamma and the neighbors were dumbstruck at the way Nabeezath 'modernised' the local snacks. The tale wasn't over yet…Cutting the round *idli* in half, she would make a filling with chicken, tomato sauce, coriander leaves and onions to make a stunning 'burger'! Finger-length potato slices freshly fried into 'French fries', a dish of 'pasta' churned up from cuttle fish cut into tubelike shapes…Nabeezath's continental menu was long and ingenious.

'What else do you like?' Vineet gently engaged Tipu in conversation.

'He likes tortoises,' Ammalu laughed.

'Also video games, right, Tipu?' Sita looked at him with a teasing smile. He did not reply. When all of them became silent, he spoke softly, 'I like sketching.'

'Oh, is that so? You sketch?' Vineet was pleasantly surprised.

'His drawing book is full of sketches—the plants in the grove, the *jamun* tree, the mango tree, Thankayamma, Anku the tortoise, snakes…all of them are there! Yesterday, he drew the ants beneath the dried leaves too.' Ammalu was bubbling with enthusiasm. Bragging about how talented her friends were, was an activity which gave her enormous satisfaction.

'Wow, I would like to see your sketches, Tipu,' Vineet said.

Tipu nodded.

'Shall I show you some sights which none of your friends can draw?' Vineet asked.

Tipu and Ammalu looked wonderingly at each other's faces.

'A micro-universe which the naked eye cannot see! None of your pals would have seen these colours or shapes. What about it then? Shall we try?'

'Where is that place? Is it Alice in Wonderland?'

Vineet's car took a detour from the KFC target, and took a different path. It was moving towards the Microbiology Department at the Agricultural College. It had been one and half years since Vineet had started to work there.

It was a holiday, and the whole campus was desolate. Spinning the key to the microbiology laboratory lab on his finger, Vineet hummed, 'Here, here lies the Wonderland of Alice!'

Sita's face took on a sullen expression, as if she had been stung by wasps. The microscope, lab and instruments inside were no friends of hers, and she was averse to them.

'You all go and watch Alice and Anna! I am going to the farm to see cows and hens. At least one's eyes will have something good to watch,' miffed, Sita walked away towards the Veterinary Department. How many sights were waiting out there in the lab? What earth-shaking discovery was going to be made through that one-eyed microscope? Where was the fun in drilling a way to hidden sights? Sita's face grew petulant.

Ammalu and Tipu stood inside the lab, flabbergasted, like two guinea pigs subjected to experimentation. There were many vials of different coloured liquids stacked in the lab. Tipu convinced Ammalu that those were 'energy drinks' meant for soothing scientists who were fatigued from the lab work. Seating both the guinea pigs on two high stools, Vineet left the room. The wooden stool was too high for them to touch the ground, and it revolved on its stand. Pretending to be astronauts, the children enjoyed twirling around their 'rocket seats'.

Ammalu the astronaut toppled down from the spaceship, at the very start of the journey. Tipu started teasing her, laughing loudly, 'What sort of an astronaut are you, when you cannot even travel on a stool? You dunce, you can't even travel in a plane! Ammalu Madam will fall down when the plane takes off and roll her way to the cockpit! Ha ha!'

Obstinately, Ammalu started spinning around again on her stool. She calmed down only after she was faster than Tipu.

There was a long table on which many round vessels were spread out. Some liquids had congealed inside the containers. A moss-like growth flashing a medley of colours could be seen on top, sticking onto the liquids. The mosses in the vessels were green, black, yellow and ash in colour.

Ammalu nudged Tipu, 'Whatever is that? Shall we open the lids and take a peek?'

'No, no, not for kids. Don't you see?' Tipu forbade her sternly.

In the corner of the table were many big microscopes. There were few mysteries which could not be fathomed through their long necks.

Vineet entered the lab with many leaves in his hand. 'Come on, tell me the names of these leaves.'

Banana leaves, chilli leaves, coconut leaves, ladies' finger leaves…there was a mélange of everything. Vineet spread them out on the table.

'All these leaves are faded. Look at the chilli leaf; it is all dried up. Black stripes on its petiole,' Ammalu was the one to discover this.

'This banana leaf has brown circles on it, and there is a smattering of yellow around those,' Tipu wasn't too far behind.

'The same yellow is there in the leaves of the rice plant too.'

'Isn't there a similar colour change in the coconut leaf too?' Vineet queried.

'Yes, indeed.'

'But the ladies' finger leaf is so pretty. The veins are all yellow and the rest of the leaf is green. We should plant such a colourful plant in our yard too.' Ammalu love the art inside the ladies' finger leaf.

'Huh! No way! We don't need ladies' finger plants with such leaves. Don't you guys get exhausted due to fever? Blanched, after losing the healthy red flush on your cheeks? This leaf is also feverish. Like Ammalu who caught viral fever, this ladies' finger leaf is suffering from viral fever too. Viruses are boisterously floating through all these yellowed veins!' Vineet explained.

'Can't see anything! Tipu, you should've brought your binoculars!'

'Good heavens! Even if you gaze through that microscope kept there, you won't be able to see viruses. Binoculars indeed!' Vineet laughed playfully. When she heard that the nasty viruses would not stop until they sucked the ladies' finger leaf dry, Ammalu's initial affinity grew cold. She discarded the leaf on the table.

'All these leaves are diseased. This is their hospital ward and I am their doctor. First, we should understand what disease they are suffering from. Only then can we prescribe medicines for them. Did the pediatrician in Dubai prescribe the same medicines for both cough and diarrhea?'

Tipu recollected the colours of the medicines and the sizes of the vials. No, they were different from each other. Vineet snipped away the diseased portions from the leaves, and placed them on the liquid in the round container.

'It contains the nutrients meant for these microscopic creatures in the leaves. All the food they need is here.'

'Why are we letting them grow?' Ammalu asked.

'Shouldn't we know who they are? The rate of their growth shall reveal how fast the disease will spread in the plant. To understand the villain causing the disease, we need another trick.'

Vineet kept the container away safely, and lifted a microscope from its place.

'This fellow will tell us who is brewing all the troubles inside the leaf!'

Tipu and Ammalu had seen the fungus growth inside the round containers when they stepped inside the laboratory. Selecting one fungus, Vineet reached their side. Placing the pristine white fungus, fluffy like the Indian milkweed, under the microscope, he beckoned Ammalu and Tipu to watch the marvel.

It was Tipu who looked through the microscope first. Covering one eye with his hand, he keenly observed the creature hiding inside the milkweed.

'Wow, how wonderful! Is that a creature? It does not move!'

He saw lemon-shaped bubbles hanging on blue-coloured threads. Vineet said that there were many seeds inside each. When the lemon-bubbles burst, the seeds were scattered far and wide, and the viruses reached new abodes. From one plant to another, from a fistful of soil to a hilly heap of earth, from a drop of water to a gushing stream. Like the dingy shops crowding each other on both sides of a bustling market street, intertwining their thin limbs, they created many colonies. When any stranger entered their dwelling places, they swayed in tandem, resisting en masse. The entire colony showered their blessings on the newly scattered lemon-bubbles for bringing up a robust new generation of viruses!

Tipu and Ammalu were taking turns to observe.

Vineet changed the milkweed fungus and placed another one.

'Take a look!'

This time, Ammalu was the first to take a peek.

What if the drumsticks dangling from the slender branches of the drumstick tree were to be dipped in that popular brand of fabric whitener, Ujala Blue? That was the sight Ammalu saw. There were crescent moons at their ends, looking as if they would fall. She saw a series of crescent moons. But when Tipu took over the microscope, he did not see Ammalu's moons. He thought that that they were sickles. Each sickle was divided into four by marks. He joked that it was Thankayamma's billhook.

Comprising of a mother, father and children, these small families invaded plants. They were monsters which could choke the supply of water and food and kill the plants inch by inch. Tipu had never expected them to look so stunning. Ammalu was gobsmacked at the thought of thousands of sickles hiding inside a small circular patch on a leaf.

External sights were a fraction of the unseen empires. This insight enthused Tipu. The fungus-residents in a sliver of leaf were innumerable; so, if one counted the total number of fungi and bacteria in the world, they would outnumber the total number of human beings, animals and other insects so easily!

Was that all? They were such sneaky thieves. In order to reveal their presence, the hapless leaf had to turn yellow, or droop and fade, or at least develop a spot. Even then, were they easily visible? If not for the microscopes, they would remain in hiding forever, fighting a guerilla warfare with the world using lemon-bubbles and sickles.

When Vineet spoke of the green mold which grew in spoiled bread, Tipu felt that this was something that could affect his own body. Bread and cheese were regular ingredients of Tipu's Dubai breakfasts. Consequently, any catastrophe that befell the bread was of interest to him.

'Sometimes, it looks black, and Amma throws the bread away,' Ammalu chirped.

Under the microscope, the dark mold on the bread looked a splendiferous plant in bloom. When Ammalu creatively quipped that it was a flower vase which had developed roots beneath its stems, Tipu opposed.

'No, it is shaped like a bulb...so many lightbulbs tied up at the end of a wire... Look at the marbles inside the bulbs, maybe those are seeds! What do they eat by the way?'

'Wherever they reach, they reign supreme. Just like your Rarumma prepares pasta and doughnuts for you, Tipu, these fellows gorge on the food readied by the plants, converting them into dishes which they relish,' Vineet explained.

As the children watched, a bulb burst into bloom, scattering seeds. Ammalu yearned to gather a few of those.

The next item Vineet displayed was the green mold which grew in bread. A huge bouquet at the end of long stems, the seeds looked like beaded pearls. They were also moving sporadically. Ammalu felt like touching the fascinating bouquet of pearls. Inside each pearl was a life; a huge society which thrived on bread, as if it was earth. Just like the greenery on soil, the viruses made the bread their all-encompassing home.

In the bread slices which Sita kept aside for Ammalu, the viruses made their homes and bred their families without seeking anybody's permission. Indeed, what place wouldn't these viruses make their own? If the homeless beggars who slept in front of the shops on the roadsides had half the raw courage of viruses, there would be mass evictions from the luxurious houses in the city! Vineet wished to elucidate further, but the children were too young to comprehend what he meant. For that, they needed to grow older.

'Didn't your Ummudu apply ointment when you hurt your knees after falling from your bicycle?'

Vineet's question was out of the blue.

'I got an injection, too, when I slipped off the steps,' Ammalu chronicled her own experiences.

'Do you know that penicillin, which is applied on wounds, was developed from a fungus like the one you saw on the bread? The *Penicillium* fungus has the power to kill bacteria. You will read about a scientist called Alexander Fleming in your Science textbooks. He discovered the medicine through a goof up! One evening, he forgot to shut the windows of his lab, and the next day he saw a growth in all the glass containers where he bred bacteria. Fleming was irritated that he hadn't shut the windows, due to which all his bacteria colonies seemed to have been infested with some sort of weedlike growth. Suddenly, it struck Fleming that the growth had eaten halfway into the colonies of bacteria! Moreover, the bacteria seemed to be terrified of the new invader, and hesitated to spread near it. They were huddling away on the other side of the glass container. It was as if Veerappan, the notorious forest marauder, had entered the forest! For Fleming, it was his Eureka moment, what he had long been searching for. It was the time of the Second World War and millions of soldiers had lost their lives because of infected wounds. The world did not have medicines to heal such wounds. It was then that a fungus came flying inside through an open window, threatening the bacteria!'

'Mmm…the way that penicillin made its entry is impressive!' Ammalu evaluated.

'Of course, and penicillin became the world's first antibiotic. If not for it, most of us would have been dead a long time ago!'

Tipu wished that some of the green mold could heal the wheelchair-bound Anwar too.

Vineet showed them different varieties of fungi and bacteria. A world which they did not know, a world which they never saw, a world of strange creations! For the first time, there was an awakening inside Tipu that along with the observable world around, many microscopic worlds were being nurtured, and their growth and decay had direct impact on human lives.

The realisation that there was a universe inside a leaf enlarged Tipu's vistas of thought. The fact that he had been ignorant of this truth was not surprising. Previously, he had been living in a world where people were indifferent to those living in the neighbouring houses. Now, new colours and forms took shape inside the child's imagination. In the colonies of the microorganisms, exact geometrical figures like the circle, triangle and square from the Mathematics textbook became visible. Astounding designs, perfect shapes, all formed without any measures, unaided by any artist's brush strokes! The universe inside a ladies' finger leaf—the home and village of the viruses, as well as the playground and school of the kid viruses. How many 'mini universes' thrived around him!

Tipu drew many pictures that day. True to what Vineet had said, these were pictures that none of Tipu's friends had ever drawn. The sketch of the outer surface of a banana leaf revealed blooming fungi. In the place of the huge *peepul* inside the serpent grove, there was a coloured portrayal of the long, thin creatures that Tipu had seen through the microscope. They were growing in a cluster, *peepul*-high! When the wind billowed, they brushed against one another like bamboo shoots.

In another drawing, there was a boy looking into a microscope. His head was the globe, and his body was depicted as a tree trunk. Ammalu couldn't decipher the meaning of many of Tipu's pictures. Consequently, she was no longer inclined to brag about his pictures in front of others.

But whenever Vineet met him, he advised Tipu to continue with his sketches. Vineet started enquiring about the possibility of exhibiting Tipu's drawings. Perhaps he felt that the interventions that nature had made within a child, like Tipu, should be known to the world. It was also the most delightful news about Tipu to reach Asif's ears. How quickly Tipu had realised Fatima's dreams for him!

Once, Fatima had commented about the Bangladeshi person who came to clean their flat, 'What sort of a life do these fellows lead? They have no visas or passports. They are stacked like mackerel in a dingy flat and somehow carry on with their lives!' An alien who had descended into our world from another; the one who swept our flats, cleaned the cobwebs and washed the toilets. The way they drew energy from the earth by sending their roots deep inside was very different. In one note, Fatima had written that only the sun, moon, wind and the sand were the same for them as the rest of the world. Tantamount to the bacteria growing in a container, the Bangladeshi person and his ilk had a world of their own; invisible, though it did not require the help of a microscope to observe.

Tipu had witnessed a world never before seen after removing the dried leaf layers in the grove. The world of the grub inside the mango seed had been another surprise, and the mushrooms playing Thiruvathira—the traditional folk dance where dancers stood in a circle creating cycle designs…

all were new worlds! And wonder of wonders, the universe of organisms exposed by the microscope!

Thankayamma announced that the grove had become a lively place after the children had ventured inside. Nobody dared to enter it before, and she was astounded to see the children pluck fruits from the trees and relishing them.

'What's wrong with touching the plants in the serpent grove? Ammalu and I ate the *jamuns*,' Tipu said.

Nabeezath, who was listening in, scolded them.

'Good for you that there is nobody in the house. If this girl's grandmother Padmajamma were alive, she would have caught you both by the ears and tossed you afar! I was never allowed to even pick up a dry leaf, you know?' Nabeezath warned.

'Nothing happened to us after eating the guavas and *jamuns*!'

'Tipu, it's not that anything is going to happen! These myths are just little lies. The grove is a forest, right? The forest belongs to the house. So human beings spread such tales to ensure it is protected,' Nabeezath said.

Tipu's sojourns were solitary nowadays. He would never fail to carry a drawing book with him. The serpent grove had transformed into the art studio of Tipu the artist. It was forbidden to take anything from the grove; no picking of mangoes, no plucking of guavas, no gathering of *jamun*s either! But he could transmit the beauty of the grove to his pictures, couldn't he? Or was that taboo, too? Thankayamma said that was hardly likely.

Tipu had seen her pluck false daisies and other medicinal herbs from the place. The belief was that the plants of the grove were doubly effective as cures. Ammalu quipped that if Anku ever fell sick, all he needed was to feed on the grass inside the serpent grove.

'The grove is not a grove. It is a set of colour pencils. My art-kit has just twelve colours. But the grove has more than those; although the shades of green are more in number. To catch the hue of the *jamun*s staining our tongue, I searched high and low among my crayons and water colour set! But I couldn't find it. The grove is a huge colouring box.' When Tipu gestured 'huge', his hands were busy drawing big circles in the air.

'Why don't you say that the grove is a canvas?' Nabeezath corrected him.

'No, no, a canvas has only the colours that we select. But we don't choose the colours seen in the serpent grove, do we?'

Nabeezath agreed with that observation. The topic of the canvas inspired Tipu to think of another idea. He was busy contemplating how to implement it. He couldn't discuss these ideas with Ammalu; she would get peeved, and even start scowling.

Tipu entered the grove with a yellow poster paper. Depositing the sheet on the raised platform of the snake deities, he started searching for different leaves and fruits, unaware that he was stepping into a hitherto unfamiliar world of art and design. Tipu brought whatever he could gather to the platform. Then he mixed some mud and water and poured it inside a truncated coconut shell...*jamun* fruits, asparagus, hibiscus flowers, teak leaves, small mangoes oozing sap, ladies' finger leaves, pollen from flowers, *gulmohar* flowers... the multicoloured pencils of the grove! The chart paper was spread on the platform; Tipu wished to use Anku the tortoise as a paper weight, but he was enjoying a wonderful dip in a puddle nearby.

Tipu grinded and pounded the leaves, flowers and roots and squeezed out their juices. He filled many coconut shells and cups made out of wide taro leaves. Dipping his finger in colour, he started sketching on the paper. The first colour was of the *jamun* fruit. A small green stem with its top portion crushed formed his makeshift paintbrush. Tipu intended to depict a laboratory with the grove's colours; a replica of the microbiology lab which Vineet had shown him, captured with the array of colours.

The floor and walls of the lab were slush coloured, and the microscope became leaf-stained green. Tipu gave the colour of the roots to the long work table and the swiveling chairs. There were flat vessels in which microbes grew aplenty; he painted fungi with *jamun* hues, pollen tints, and hibiscus colours. It was as if a grove was encroaching inside a lab! How better to describe the intermingling of the laboratory and nature? Tipu did not show the picture to anyone. He hid it inside the desk where Fatima's books were stacked.

Ammalu's obsession with collection was now traveling in a different direction. She was hoarding leaves now. Not just leaves, those that were gnawed by worms. She even had a term for the worm infestation on the leaves: *puzhukkala* aka 'the art of the grubs'.

'Look at the mildewed leaf of the crown flower plant. Hasn't the worm eaten it in an alphabet-design?'

In the next, she saw a heart pattern. 'See, the love of the grub! It fell in love with the leaf!' She chortled.

A pumpkin leaf eaten away by beetles, leaving behind just the veins. 'The skeleton of the leaf, ting tong…it was swarming with beetles! Couldn't the nasty gluttons have gulped down the skeleton too, huh!'

'Aye! It looks pretty. Ammalu, you were the one to say that it is a *kala*, a *puzhukkala*! Any art is pleasing, right? Anyway, the worms eat those; let them eat artfully. Consider it the worm's talent.' Tipu's opinion made Ammalu ponder over the matter.

'Doesn't your Rarumma nitpick when you leave unfinished rice on your plate? Doesn't she warn you to leave only the fish bones behind when eating fish? I am sure the mothers of these worms, too, are very strict!'

On the leaves of the long runner beans that Ammalu showed him, the caterpillars obviously practiced their alphabets. There were 'ka' and 'ma' designs; *grub-letter*s, Tipu felt, were as pretty as *grub-colours*!

'After the greedy caterpillar chomps till his tummy is on the verge of bursting, he curls up in his swinging cocoon and goes off to sleep! Then he needs neither water nor leaf. When it wakes up, he becomes a gorgeous butterfly! One day, I shall go to sleep under a blanket too, like him! I'll refuse to wake up even if my parents call me. Nor shall I eat anything. I will go on sleeping for very long. And finally, on waking up, I shall remove the blanket and make my grand entry! A princess more beautiful than Cinderella, you wait and watch!'

Ammalu's fantasies!

Tipu was highly amused. These girls were always thinking of only one thing—how to become beautiful at any cost! That too 'ultimate beauties', like Cinderella and Sleeping Beauty.

Ammalu's collection was replete with many leaves manifesting the artworks of worms and beetles. But she was clueless about how to safeguard them. By the time she reached home, they had usually shriveled and shrunk.

'This collection is not going to work, Miss Cinderella... better leave it,' Tipu warned Ammalu.

'I shall immerse these in water, then they won't fade!'

'Stupid Cinderella! Are these mosquitoes, to lay eggs in water? The leaves will decay.'

'Oho! When we went with Acchan to his college, we saw that pond full of leaves. It was full of lotus flowers too. Nothing was decayed!'

'Ayyo, silly Cinderella, didn't Vineet Uncle tell us that those plants had roots underneath? What did you see there, really?' Tipu teased.

That was more than enough to rile Ammalu. She turned on her heels and marched home, followed by Tipu. Ammalu's stomping was enough to turn the Earth upside down. As soon as she reached her house, she entered her room and shut the door.

'What happened? Picked a fight? Just ignore her, Tipu! She will come out very soon. Can any mouse hide for long when its stomach starts to growl with hunger?'

Sita went inside the kitchen with an all-knowing attitude, having seen it all when it came to her daughter's tantrums.

Tipu slowly climbed upstairs. It was the first time that he was exploring Ammalu's house properly. Usually, they played in Ammalu's room or the courtyard. There was a big hall where the stairs ended, and two small rooms on either side.

Now, Tipu was standing in a place which belonged exclusively to Vineet; his most favorite place, but deemed by Sita as a scrap station. Everything was ancient, but was stored systematically. Though the only household accessories were a steel almirah, table and a cot, the room seemed complete. The dinosaur lizards and spiders that Tipu had seen in Thiru-Nilam were absent in that room. Hence, he did not feel timid though he was alone.

There was an hourglass on the table. Tipu inverted it at once. From the triangular bulb on the top, there was a *shurr shurr* trickle of sand. But the bottom bulb was not full. Would a minute get over so soon? Oh, the sides of the sand clock were cracked. Sand was strewn across the table, spilling through the gaps. Beware, this was the room where time developed a crack!

Tipu gathered the 'scattered time' on the table into his palm. He had heard about this trick of measuring time with a fistful of sand. But this was the first time he had caught a glimpse of it. The background picture on his laptop as it booted up was that of an hourglass. *If he could shape a clock from a fistful of sand from the Tilapia beach, he would have retrieved the exact moment that Fatima had gone missing.* Tipu replaced the hourglass in its original position.

He sat down, and pulled a square box from beneath the cot towards him. It resembled a small suitcase. On the blue paper stuck on it above Vineet's name, the words 'Insect Box' were inscribed. When Tipu pulled up the top lid, an excruciatingly pungent smell penetrated his nose. The child scooted backwards on his bottom. Along with the smells of mothballs and chloroform, there drifted a stink of putrid flesh.

There was a thick layer of thermocol inside the box. On it was an array of pinned insects—moths, butterflies, bugs and weevils. Tipu tentatively touched the wing of a blue butterfly. The pin pierced the chest of that butterfly, with its wings spread beautifully on either side. The moment he touched the wing, it collapsed!

The dead bodies of insects were crucified, and there were snippets containing the name of each insect above its head. Tipu tried to read the names but he failed; was it even English? One thing became clear to him; these were named just like human beings. Everyone had a name divided into two! Just like his own name, Tipu Asif, there was a butterfly called '*Papilio demoleus*'! No one could escape their family name and surname anywhere!

One of the beetles he was most terrified of, was in there, stone dead. Tipu took it in his hand and examined it carefully.

There he was, a black beetle with a flat, wide face; he played by rolling dung. Tipu remembered that it was Thankayamma who had introduced him to it. At first, he had been mistaken that the beetle was playing; by making a *laddoo*-like round sweet out of dung! The only lucky beetle among his comrades who could become a football champion!

Keeping the box aside, Tipu was now immersed in flicking the pages of a dust-laden file. Like the insect box, 'Vineet Shankar' was written on the file too. The name of the file was 'Herbarium'. The scent wafting from it reminded Tipu of the Ayurvedic medicines which Nabeezath consumed. He started turning the pages. It was like an album containing dried leaves, stems, flowers and buds. On the right side of every page was an introduction of each plant in Vineet's handwriting. A short writeup comprising the name of the plant, its family, place of origin and date. The leaves were pasted so firmly that they seemed to be still attached to the plant. They seemed faded though.

An idea took shape in Tipu's mind. Holding the Herbarium close to his chest, he ran downstairs. Ammalu's door was open. It was obvious that she was expecting Tipu to walk in and offer a compromise. Though the door was open, she was lying on her tummy on the cot. Sulk-mode was still intact! Tipu ran into the room, scrambling onto the cot, and started shaking Ammalu's shoulders.

'Ammalu, there is a surprise for you!'

As if not interested in the least, she raised her head.

'Where are your worm-eaten leaves?'

'They faded away.' Ammalu's face had faded too.

'We will pluck them again from the grove and paste them like this in a file! We will name the file 'Caterpillarium'!'

Ammalu sat up and started flipping through the file.

'This belongs to my Acchan. Why do you think he made it?'

'Look below, he has written the names of the plants; maybe he wanted to study?'

'No way. He could refer to any book for that, couldn't he?'

'Haven't you seen the dinosaur movies? *Jurassic Park* and such? Don't they show a dinosaur museum in it? They stored the teeth and bones of dead dinosaurs there, right? It was because they kept those safely that we could see them years later!'

'Hmm…fossils, I know! So, is this Herbarium a museum of plants? Will these plants die like dinosaurs, after some years?'

In Tipu's imagination, there emerged a world brought to life by Ammalu's words. A day when all the plants, trees and mushrooms of the grove would disappear… Plant museums like dinosaur museums! Inside the glass interiors, there would be roots, bark and dried leaves of the plants. Oh, and a few human beings gazing at the plant corpses with astoundment!

He felt afraid.

Thirteen: Dream

Two dreams entered Tipu's sleep that night. There was a common strand connecting them both. After waking up from the first, Tipu had reluctantly moved to the second dream.

Dream 1: He was on the platform of the snake deities inside the grove. Instead of the deities, Tipu's game CDs were the new gods. Through the hole in the middle of his favourite *Minecraft* CD, a head protruded. It was glaring at Tipu. A brown face, closely cropped hair and green teeth. Instead of ears, there were some objects resembling slippers dangling from its head. The tip of its tongue was punctured. Tipu was dressed like Mowgli, swinging from a creeper. Tipu's gamer name was 'Steve Rocks' in this scene, so the weird creature knew Tipu as Steve Rocks.

'Steve Rocks, I have been waiting for you. I am your playmate, Cool John. Have you forgotten me?'

Tipu jumped down from the swaying creeper.

'Okay, Cool John. Why don't you select another gamer to play with? I am not interested.'

'Steve Rocks, that will not work out. I have shared all my resources with you. Unless I get all of it back, I shall not go away. You have to play with me.'

'No, I quit!' Tipu turned on his heels.

'Stop, Steve Rocks! Didn't you accept all the conditions of the game? Now you cannot escape. Or else you shall die! After your death, all your resources shall become mine. Your energy levels and points shall be transferred to me. Now my battery is about to run out. You better die soon and save me!'

Tipu was moving away, ignoring him. Cool John's tongue slithered after him. Now, Tipu was running, panting heavily. Tipu was weaving his way through the trees in the grove, and the horrid tongue was chasing him. Finally, the tongue caught up with Tipu and coiled around him. Tipu yelled hoarsely, 'Give me power!' Immediately, sickle shaped fungus-seeds sprouted from his fingers. They looked like sharpened nails. Tipu mauled Cool John's face and it turned bloody. With his sickle-shaped nails, Tipu relentlessly attacked Cool John's face. When his enemy's face became wounded, Tipu shouted at the top of his voice, 'I got the power of fungus!' Cool John's blood clotted on Tipu's nails. Tipu jolted awake, his body feeling like it was drowning in his foe's blood.

Dream 2: A vast playground. Tipu and Ammalu were walking hand in hand. All around them were towering buildings. A dog leapt on them, barking loudly. Ammalu searched for a stone to throw at it, but there were none around. She retrieved coloured pebbles from her bag and started throwing them at the dog. The dog immediately transformed into a statue. Leaving the playground behind, they climbed onto a road. Vehicles were rushing past, and human beings were carrying oxygen cylinders on their backs. Tubes connected the cylinders with people's noses. The children were seeing people attached to the life-giving gas for the first time.

'Kids, are you still wandering around? The shop will soon close; hurry up and buy what you need!' A sound resounded, as if emerging from the bottom of the sea.

'Which shop?'

'The shop selling oxygen.'

It was then that they noticed—there were no trees or plants around them, no sign of green anywhere. Something curled up near Tipu's feet. When he looked, it was a touch-me-not plant. It was peeping out from underneath the ground, only three leaves showing above ground. When he cast a backward glance, the plant hurriedly withdrew itself under the soil.

Suddenly a tunnel appeared in front of them. It went down to the depths of earth. They stepped inside it. All around them were amazing sights. Trees were hanging upside down! They were flourishing under the earth with the same glory.

'Ayyo! Does that mean only humans and animals live on earth now? Are the trees growing under the soul?'

'Didn't you find out that we are all going extinct?' The touch-me-not asked, shaking its nettles.

'No, none of us knew! How could you leave us alone and hide over here?' Ammalu's face filled with misery.

'Ah, poor kids! You seem to know so much, hence it is difficult for us to accept that you were not aware of this news. Your gaze is always at Mars and the moon, right? We had given you enough warnings, but nobody heeded us! Huh!' It was a *peepul* who smirked at them, its lips twisted contemptuously.

A dahlia nodded in agreement. After waiting for the *peepul* to pause, it began: 'Birds migrate, humans shift to better places, animals leave forests and enter human habitations, but we are immobile, forced to stand in one spot even during greatest of hardships. Those like me hide as tubers under the soil. When an accommodating climate arrives, we resurrect. Our migration is measured not in kilometres but in days.'

Ammalu and Tipu walked forward. There was a vast ground where pumpkin creepers spread lusciously. They squirmed through the plump vines, and Ammalu got trapped under those. Springing into action to save her, Tipu also became entwined with the creepers. They coiled round the children and made a huge ball. A huge globe of green! The creepers started spinning the globe at great speed. The globe broke off from the pumpkin plant and flew out of the tunnel.

Tipu rolled off the cot. Nabeezath, lying on the nearby cot, woke up with a start. She made him lie next to her. In the darkness, Tipu gazed at his fingers. They were moist. Was it Cool John's blood?' No, it was not just the fingers which were wet; his whole body was moist!

'Tut! Did you piss in your sleep?' Nabeezath teased Tipu. Getting him into fresh clothes, she put him to sleep again. The child ruminated over both his dreams. In the first, he had sliced the enemy's tongue; in the second, the pumpkin creeper.

Anyway, Tipu was assured that the common bridge connecting his dual dreams was the grove. Due to his explorations inside the serpent grove, he hardly had time for computer games. Perhaps that was the reason Cool John, the co-gamer, had come calling for him in the first dream.

Tipu had already seen the plants in Vineet's Herbarium inside the serpent grove. He was horror-struck by a scenario where all plants would be relegated as dried specimens stuck on pages. 'What if the grove disappeared under the earth as I witnessed in that dream? What if the *jamun*, mango, Indian *bael*, *peepul*, banyan and the guava started growing under the earth?' Maybe that was the foundation of the second dream. He hugged Rarumma tightly. Her arms gathered him close. A love-coil, without the smugness of the pumpkin creepers and the wicked tongue.

Fourteen: Herbarium

Vineet's Herbarium was now in Tipu's hands.

Compared to Sita, Vineet's world was 10 times bigger. That large world of his comprised many microscopic worlds. The tiny worlds which he could see in a drop of water, a pinch of earth, or a breath of air, were inaccessible to Sita. She would jest that using the time Vineet wasted in conversing with the microorganisms, she would rather train 10 parrots to chat with her! Vineet would respond that those used to communicating exclusively with creatures who followed 'an eye for an eye' philosophy, would never understand him.

There were many more Herbarium files that Vineet had. Unseen and useless weeds, medicinal plants that were sought only when diseases went ravaging, ornamental plants which got their due attention only on blooming, ancient trees which existed only for building nests... Vineet's Herbarium collections were varied. There was no need to wonder about

Ammalu's afffinity for collecting things. Evidently, it was Vineet's own contribution.

Could it be that Vineet had foreseen a catastrophe, where the green emissaries would be reduced to the pages of a Herbarium, saved as keepsake? Was it why he had safeguarded these leaves through the passage of all these years? Vineet was protecting these files like precious albums preserving memories of all the plants on the earth.

In Vineet's mind, akin to films meant for keeping the memories of the dinosaurs alive, a movie was playing in memory of the plants. It might be an urgent need in the imminent future. *Herbum Sediments* would be the film's name; an eulogy to the remnants of the earth's foliage. The film would speak about the burial attire of the plants. The clothes that enshrouded them on their final days would have nothing else but the smear of decay.

In the archeological museum 'Herbarium' which Vineet would build in the future, each plant would be displayed with its special features highlighted. For illustrative purposes, consider the touch-me-not plant. It needed to be laid on the postmortem table before being ushered into the pages of the Herbarium. Its place would be among those who died with bodies that were bound tight. Indeed, it would necessitate an exorcism to loosen up that dead body with its leaves tightly shut in order to glue it onto the pages of the Herbarium.

Siam weed, Ceylon slitwort, nut grass and the climbing nettle were indifferently denigrated as weeds. Vineet's favourite among the Herbarium files was one where these 'weeds' were preserved. The Ceylon slitwort could be called a weed or a herb at the same moment. An entire society was oblivious that the plant locally called *thumba* was a mere weed, during the ten days of Onam. During that time, the *thumba* flower was mandatorily used for various celebrations. After the festivities, it was once again downgraded to a 'weed'.

The 'communist *pacha*' aka the Siam weed, was passionate in colour and spread. It had grown as lushly as communism! They sprouted like slogans, from the vastness of coconut groves and the laps of the spinach clusters.

The touch-me-nots were denigrated as weeds typically. In Vineet's view, they were living motion pictures. Like a CD which moved at the flicking of a switch, these plants were natural movies, where their leaves closed one after the other at a gentle touch. One could try putting a hair on a touch-me-not leaf before it closed. Would it be present when the leaf opened again? Analogous to human beings who wore rings made of elephant tail hair to keep fear at bay, would that plant become intrepid after wearing a human hair? Would it stop shrinking away, terrified by a mere touch, afterwards?

Like flesh inseparable from bones, the leaves, stems and flowers were glued onto the pages... After the passage of centuries, the skeletons in the Herbariums would crumble into dust. The dried greens would turn into ashes if one so much as shook the Herbarium file too hard. Gathering the fragments together and stuffing them inside a small pitcher, covering its mouth with a red fabric, one should deposit it on the attic, for preserving the precious ashes of the ancestors!

According to Vineet, the Herbarium was something which deserved such precious preservation.

Fifteen: Companionship

The Herbarium became Tipu's constant companion. He compared every tree in the grove with the Herbarium file and learned their names. The boy discovered many plants in the grove which had been unnoticed before.

Today, Tipu was travelling to the hospital with Nabeezath. He had taken the Herbarium along, wrapped in a cover, holding it close to his chest. Nabeezath periodically experienced these bouts of exhaustion. She wouldn't heed instructions to get her fluctuating blood pressure checked regularly. After the news about Fatima, the illness had strengthened and her immunity had weakened. Since Tipu's arrival, Nabeezath had totally ignored her symptoms.

In the hospital, the nurse started checking Nabeezath's blood pressure. Tipu was seated on the chair meant for visitors. There was a boy of his own age next to him. His wheezing was like the outpouring of a pipelike instrument. The wind over Tilapia Lake also had such a tune to it. Tipu was observing the boy keenly to find out which part of his body that singular sound was emerging from. Neck, stomach or nose? Where was the origin?

'Asthma! He was wheezing all through the night,' the boy's mother was speaking to another woman. 'Watching him flailing around for breath is an unbearable sight.'

Tipu contemplated on the previous night's dream. He recollected the images of the people carrying oxygen cylinders. This boy also deserved one! If everyone who struggled to breathe started this pipe-like wheezing, the whole world would be flooded with this tune.

The nurse called the boy away and started the nebuliser machine. Through a mask connected to an instrument covering three-fourths of his face, he was inhaling medicated steam. Tipu asked the boy's mother why she did not purchase an oxygen cylinder, like the ones that astronauts who went to the moon wore on their backs.

'He cannot breathe properly, dear. The phlegm has clogged his nasal tubes, the doctor said.'

Some could not breathe, while others inhaled more air than was needed. 'Will the oxygen available on earth get exhausted if everybody started breathing in a competitive spirit? Is that why a few people succumbed to asthma. Shouldn't there be some discipline to breathing, too?' Tipu wondered.

When Nabeezath went to pay the bills, Tipu started scrutinising the names of each department. Orthopedic,

Pediatric, Dental, Gynaecology…he knew that each specialised in different body parts, though he was unaware of the exact details. Tipu thought of Vineet's laboratory. He had given them an introduction by saying that when plants were sick, they were brought there; just like human beings went to hospitals.

Plants had neither families nor friends, neither fathers nor mothers, so who would bring them to hospitals when they fell sick? The lab would have to go to their houses. When the phlegm choked the boy's lungs and made him wheeze, Tipu himself felt suffocated. When the fungi congealed in the leaves and stems of the plants, wouldn't they feel strangulated too? Who would listen to their desperate whistling when they yearned for life-giving air? Tipu decided to press his ears against the chest of each tree the next time he explored the grove. He would find out whether the bugle sounds of chest congestion could be heard.

There was a rush in front of the bill counter. There were no signs of Nabeezath's quick return. Tipu pulled out the Herbarium and showed it to the asthmatic boy. His name was Jobin.

'This is like the album in my house. It has pictures of dead members of the family,' Jobin observed.

'Oho…does that mean there is another album for the living members? Why didn't you feel that this reminds you of the living? Tell me, why didn't you say that?' Tipu was put off by the 'dead people's album' simile.

'I mean this is old and dried up, also dead! Just see.' Jobin elucidated.

'Yes, dead and dried up. True.' But Tipu thought that Jobin had forgotten that there were living specimens too.

'We shall meet again,' he said.

The children parted.

How on earth would they meet again? Tipu felt embarrassed about having said something so silly. He hadn't noted down Jobin's phone number, had no clue about his address, or any idea about his school or class. Within a month after his arrival, Tipu had become adept at these meaningless formalities exchanged by local people. There was a time when saying 'we shall meet again' to people one would never see again would befuddle him, but now he was accustomed to it.

When they reached home, Thankayamma was there. She was grinding some leaves and squeezing out some juice. 'Stomach ache! If I offer that woman some pills for controlling gas problems, she would rather die than take them!' Nabeezath griped. Tipu ran to fetch his Herbarium and started comparing Thankayamma's leaves with the pictures.

'Aloe vera, I plucked it from the neighbouring compound; just need a few drops of this. I hate pills!' Thankayamma explained.

Tipu's Herbarium did not contain aloe vera. The leaves of the rambutan fruit that Ammalu had got for him were also not present in the file.

Tipu decided to start a new game. His Herbarium had a hundred different leaves inside. Whenever he encountered any plant not included in the Herbarium, he would pluck out a portion consisting of the leaf, stem, flower and fruit together. Then he would get it ready for pasting in the Herbarium, scrupulously following Vineet's instructions. Spreading the leaves inside a book, he would place something heavy on top of it. He brought hefty books such as the encyclopedia from Nabeezath's shelf for this job. When he reached for the Qur'an, Nabeezath had to forbid him.

When the leaves dried, Tipu glued them onto the Herbarium file. He had created beautiful borders on the pages for this purpose. There was a rectangle on the right side to note down the details of the plant. Tipu could only jot down the place of collection and the date. The rest of the space he left blank, hoping to get Vineet's guidance.

In Vineet's Herbarium, Tipu tick-marked the plants he could find in the grove, and made a cross mark above those that he couldn't. This marking assignment was carried out by Ammalu and him, with the little girl discovering most of the plants. They found 65 of the plants in the Herbarium inside the grove and there were 35 with a cross mark. Furthermore, they also took on the task of discovering the 'Missing 35' outside the serpent grove.

Since then, wherever they went, both children kept a lookout for these 35 plants. Irrespective of whether it was a hospital, cinema theatre, restaurant or even a house of mourning, their eyes would scan around for the lost 35.

Even Anku found himself ignored by Tipu nowadays. Nabeezath, who planned to get the tortoise removed from the house, had found an opportune moment. Nonetheless, her efforts were foiled. Regardless of his multiple activities, Tipu refused to let go of Anku! He toppled Nabeezath's ploy, and started dragging Anku along with him throughout the day. A nine-year-old with the Herbarium in one hand and a tortoise tied to a rope in the other: Tipu, Anku and the Herbarium were like vignettes from some forgotten fairy tale.

Of the Missing 35, the kids discovered one or two. If Anku had seen the Herbarium, he would have most likely recognised all of them easily. He had been around when Vineet had prepared that Herbarium; he might have even chomped on these missing plants then!

The days passed by. Tipu and Ammalu could not decipher the enigma of the 35. It struck Tipu that he could take a strategy or two from the forgotten video games he possessed. He and Ammalu designed a new game—*HerbaRush.*

Sixteen: HerbaRush

HerbaRush was 'set' in the area where Tipu and Ammalu lived. There were only two players in that game—Tipu and Ammalu. For convenience, Tipu could be referred to as Rusher T and Ammalu as Rusher A.

HerbaRush did not have the same background as the games that Tipu used to play on his tablet and laptop. This particular game was abounding with forests, meadows, villages and towns. All the paths and objects familiar to the duo were part of it.

The game progressed in three levels. The goal of the game was to discover the missing 35 plants shown in the Herbarium. There was a citation about each plant containing its picture and name. That was called 'HerbaSink'. Each player had a 'Keeper'. Every plant the player found had to be handed over to the Keeper. That is, when Tipu discovered a missing plant, he would race at maximum speed towards his Keeper and entrust the plant to him. The Keeper would safeguard the plant in the 'Herbarium Press' or the 'HerbaPress', the place where the leaves were 'pressed' and stored.

Who was Tipu's Keeper? Who else, but Anku the tortoise! When Tipu gave Anku a plant, he would keep it in the HerbaPress and shut it with a resounding thump! The leaves would stay flat inside the press without curling up. The moment a plant reached the Keeper, its picture would get deleted from the Herbasink. That removed the possibility of Ammalu retrieving another specimen of the same plant. If both gamers brought the same plant, the one who reached his or her Keeper first would get the points. Not only that, but the other gamer would get negative points too!

Ammalu's Keeper was a hornbill. The tortoise and the hornbill, two species which were slowly disappearing from the face of the earth; the best mascots to play as Keepers! Let them keep the 35 retrieved plants safe. The hornbill with its yellow beak would wait for Ammalu. When she ran towards it with her plant, it would soar high. Then the Herbarium Press would open. Once the plant was deposited, it would shut close with a thump. The bird would descend and take its place again on the press.

Both the Keepers had to be extremely alert at all times. They had to ensure that neither gamer stole from the other. The hornbill was waiting to snatch the plants away from Anku in the blink of an eye! So the tortoise had to be always seated on top of the press.

As the game began, one could sight Tipu and Ammalu standing in front of a long racing track. Behind them were their two Keepers guarding the HerbaPress. There was a giant scoreboard in their back; it displayed the HerbaSink with flashing pictures of the plants, appearing and disappearing in a jiffy. The kids' names on the scoreboard were Rusher T and Rusher A.

The game was beginning. Both the gamers were ready to run. Rusher T was dressed in a blue jersey and shorts. Rusher A was decked up in a green jersey and frock.

Level 1

1, 2, 3—the wager began. Both gamers were running as fast as they could. Tipu ran inside a forest; a grove-like forest. When he saw the plants inside the forest, the images of the missing thirty-five species flashed in his mind. When he found a matching plant, it would get confirmed after a quick comparison with the original.

A shrub lay ahead of Tipu now. Pulling out a sword, the sharpest weapon in his armour, he hacked at it thrice, *crish, crish, crish*. He was bounding forward. Suddenly he felt his feet sinking. Tipu struggled to pull his legs free. It was a swamp. He needed knee-length gumboots to move ahead. From his knapsack, he retrieved a stylish pair of boots. As he moved ahead in his boots over that marshy land, he saw a clump of weeds in front of him. One plant with reddish brown spikelets was peeping at him. There were fans of flat, narrow leaves emerging from the swamp, like twigs. Yes, it was Hoorah Grass aka *Fimbristylis*! One among the Missing 35!

As soon as he reached out to pluck the plant, darkness fell. He could not see anything. As per the rules of the game, the Rushers had to stop searching for plants after sunset. Tipu returned, frustrated at having lost a stroke of good luck. He felt sleepy. In the fear that there would be wild animals in the forest, he entered a cave. To find out if some other animals were inside, he flashed his torch around. Except for some bats which were hanging on the cave walls, he could see nothing. When the darkness thickened, the bats would leave and the cave would belong to Tipu alone. Removing his boots, Tipu lay down to sleep. His slumber was disturbed due to the various sounds of wild animals. When the bats returned to roost as the dawn broke, Tipu awakened. His timer showed it was 5:30 am. He could not wear his boots again, since the rules forbid reusing any object.

Tipu moved out of the cave, ruminating on possible strategies for claiming the *Fimbristylis* without wading into the swamp. He raced towards the swamp as morning arrived. 'Ayyo! Where did it go?' He had seen it yesterday but now it was gone!

Flustered, Tipu scoured the clayey swamp with a thick piece of wood. He saw boot prints around. There, a sudden rustle amongst the leaves. Tipu rushed forward. It was Ammalu. She was running at a hundred miles with the *Fimbristylis*. Tipu chased her for some time and then gave up. It was of no use. There shouldn't be tussles among the gamers. What mattered was who claimed the plant first, not who had seen it first. Thus, Ammalu won the first round, and scored 1000 points. The *Fimbristylis* went to the hornbill's guardianship and a plant was deleted from the HerbaSink.

Ammalu's investigations were meticulous. She was a veteran of collecting things, after all! She was more enthused than ever, having claimed the first plant. Her explorations reached the grove. Ammalu was sure that Tipu wouldn't be there; he was last seen near the swamp in the forest. She did not notice that Tipu was wandering near the platform of the snake deities.

Ammalu noticed the Devil's Pepper, the *sarpagandhi*, growing close to the ground near the *peepul* tree. Breaking off a portion with flowers, she ran towards the Keeper. The hornbill ascended into the air, the plant was deposited and there was a thumping sound as the HerbaPress shut tight. Another 1000 points for Ammalu.

Tipu was incensed, and started climbing the mountain next to the serpent grove. It was a determined scaling of the heights. Ammalu would not be able to climb the sheer drop. He had all the equipment needed for his climb, and was intermittently looking behind him to check Ammalu's whereabouts. No, she wasn't following him. Tipu reached the summit. He was relieved. Now he was resolute about searching the area and retrieving at least 10 plants!

There, in the crevices of the rock, a plant with heart-shaped leaves and white flowers! The blooms reminded him of orchids. It was the pretty *Nervilia aragoana*. Tipu had identified the short-statured herb at the very first glance. Finally, when he clambered down, he was hoisting the plants in his hands like victory flags: the *Strobilanthus kunthiana* or *nilakurinji*; the wild nutmeg; the red sandalwood; and the *sahachara* aka the *Nilgirianthus ciliatus*. Ammalu was nowhere to be seen.

It was time for the end of Level 1. The timer boomed. The collections had to be compared for the calculation of points now. Out of the 35 herbs which were on the brink of extinction, 10 had landed in Anku's custody, the credit going to Tipu. Ammalu had gathered 15 in all. Thus, Ammalu won the first level by 5 plants. But whatever happened to the 10 missing plants?

Level 2

Both competitors were ready to handle the challenges of the second level. After ensuring that the plants had been dried properly, sticking them neatly on the sheets to create a beautiful Herbarium file constituted the second level of the game. Tipu was hellbent on winning this round.

He lifted Anku out of the way and started sticking the plants. They had dried nicely. Tipu became engrossed in gluing each one on the sheet. Two of Ammalu's plants had not dried as yet, and were still raw. Still, she went ahead with the task. Another two started crumbling as soon as she touched them, due to over-drying. 'Oh no, what shall I do now?' she exclaimed and started sticking the crumbled bits together using gum. The paper turned messy. Then Ammalu tried sketching the leaves to replace the lost ones. The buzzer rang out; Ammalu's act was against the rules! It could even lead to a penalty and cancel her existing score.

Tipu was done preparing the Herbarium file with his 10 plants. Ammalu could stick only eight specimens of her original 15. Three minutes remained for the level to end. Ammalu's sticking glue had finished. She appealed to Tipu for lending her some. The hornbill went to him with the appeal, and returning with the glue, started helping her stick the pictures. It clutched the tube in its claws and tried to open the cap with its curved beak. Oops! The sharpness of its beak made the whole tube of gum leak to the ground! What was to be done now? After sticking eight plants, Ammalu could do nothing except for wait for the timer to announce the end. Thus, Tipu ended up winning Level 2.

Level 3

In this level, both gamers had to race each other. But there was a twist in the tale; it was their representatives who actually had to race! The one who managed to submit the Herbarium file at the foot of the *ashoka* tree in the grove first was the winner. Both the Keepers were tasked with the assignment. Of course Ammalu's confidence for this level was boundless. Her Keeper was a hornbill which could fly. Tipu's Keeper was a tortoise! He would lose against other land animals, too, let alone a bird.

Tipu was remembering the famous fable of the hare and the tortoise. The hare slept, the tortoise didn't. But there was no chance that the hornbill would go off to sleep! Especially since it knew the old tale. Both players tied their Herbarium files on top of their respective Keepers. When he saw Anku crawling slowly with the burden on his back, Tipu felt really sad. By the time Anku took a turn, the hornbill would swoop down on the *ashoka* tree. If Tipu had to win, the tree would have to walk towards him! He consoled himself with the fact that although it would reach the destination late, he could create a Herbarium with more plants than Ammalu. He believed that there was a victory in that aspect.

The buzzer rang. Both the Keepers started moving. As the tortoise slowly ambled forward, the hornbill made a croaking sound and rose rapidly into the air. This time,

Anku the tortoise felt sleepy. While he was planning to rest, it started raining unexpectedly. It was no drizzle; this was a heavy downpour. Anku put the Herbarium down and stepped on it, covering the file with his body and his hard shell. Safeguarding the 10 almost-extinct species of plants under his shell, Anku slipped into a blissful slumber. The raindrops splattering on his back seemed to be humming a lullaby for him.

Let's see what the hornbill was up to then! It was supposed to have reached the destination by now. But could it stay focused when it was raining? With an unending thirst, it opened its beak to the rain. The only source of water for the hornbill was fruits; it hardly ever drank water. The hornbill could not resist opening its beak in the generous downpour. He did not care that the Herbarium tied on his back was getting wet.

The Herbarium became moist and the glue started leaking and sticking onto his wings. Ammalu's instructions were to spread his wings and protect the Herbarium in case of rain. The hornbill seemed to have forgotten all of that. By the time the rain abated, he tried to open his wings in vain. Try as he might, his sticky wings refused to spread open. The hornbill undertook an arduous journey on his claws, and carried the soaking wet Herbarium to the foot of the *ashoka* tree. However, the Herbarium had become sodden by then.

On the other hand, Anku woke up fresh after a sound rest. The Herbarium was dry and ready beneath him. Though he needed the aid of a few implements to load the Herbarium onto his back again, the game easily provided such resources. He started lumbering towards his destination. Anku could now appreciate the hare's state of mind rather well! The hornbill must have won the race. There was no doubt about that.

By the time Anku reached the grove, it was quite dark. The hornbill was present there, as anticipated. But he was whining miserably. When the situation became clear, Anku felt like grinning. The tortoise had won the race yet again! He chuckled, thinking that his clan was born to win. Tortoises would win in the race of life too.

Ammalu could not bear seeing her despondent hornbill, its head cast down in defeat. Anku the tortoise celebrated Tipu's victory by chewing on a fat snail which crawled down the tree. Tipu won *HerbaRush*, and Ammalu lost.

However, in the case of the 10 missing plants which neither child could find, the whole world was the loser.

Seventeen: The Starting of the Massacre

Herbarush was just an imaginary game, but in reality, what transpired was very similar to it. With Tipu's 10 plants, Ammalu's 15 and the missing 10, their searches continued. Tipu often wondered whether he should put up a 'Missing' notice with details of all the plants on the internet. But who would even care a dime, whoever had the time for such a news?

It was around that time when Rajasekharan Nair and his son Janardhanan came home from the US. Nabeezath still maintained her awe and respect for Rajasekharan Nair considering that he was the Headmaster during her school teacher days. But Sita was rather indifferent towards both her father and elder brother. After her marriage with Vineet, she had never felt the need for another loving companionship either.

Ever since her brother had taken Rajasekharan Nair to USA, Sita had hardly chatted with her father. Even during an occasional, formal phone call, it was Janardhanan and his wife who talked with her. Janardhanan never encouraged her attempts to converse with their father, behaving as if she was trying to steal away someone who belonged exclusively to him. Janardhanan's wife was an American; and when she picked up the call, Sita would silently cut the call due to the compulsion to speak in English. Whenever her brother and family came to India, Sita paid them a formal visit or two. Janardhanan had two sons—Aaron and Noel. Aaron was from his first marriage.

According to Sita, her father had never been too comfortable with her as his daughter. It was possible that the thought of having a vitiligo-affected daughter and marrying her off troubled him to no end. Besides, he had also kept a distance from his wife Padmajamma after the effects of the vitiligo started taking root in her. Sita believed that her father was happy with his son and American daughter-in-law.

Nobody in the village was aware of when Janardhanan had married Julia. She was a music teacher. Both the children were being brought up by her. Sita never tried to pry the details of how she was bringing up Aaron, Janardhan's son from his first marriage. Except for smiling indifferently when Julia chatted away, Sita had never talked to her. But in Janardhanan's words, Julia was far shyer than Sita. A shy American lady! Sita couldn't digest that easily. She felt unnerved on seeing Julia's blue eyes. Her blonde locks made her feel inferior. Sita presumed that

Julia would be queasy at the sight of her well-oiled, long hair. Aaron, however, had pitch-black hair like his father.

Julia wrote poems and had a blog, too. Vineet liked Julia's poetry. Though Sita tried to read her poems, she found herself restless. All her life, she had carried countless psychological burdens, and these wretched vitiligo marks hadn't helped her outgrow her inhibitions. Sita was always curled up inside the restrictive circles drawn by her disease.

Janardhanan's first wife had left them when Aaron was three years old. Julia was the child's music teacher. The teacher–student relationship had finally blossomed into a family bond. Aaron was very keen on music. It was likely that his deep need for Julia's attention and love was a causal factor in that interest. Janardhanan must have been delighted that Aaron's interest in music led him to a companion. He had never expected to have a family again, but it had happened. Vineet had gathered all those tidbits from Julia's blog. In the blog was a poem, recited jointly by Julia and Aaron.

When Noel was born, Aaron had been eight. Julia filled the lives of the children with poetry and songs. Vineet's opinion was that Julia's dignified nature had led to Rajasekharan Nair's decision to settle with them in the US. Yet the family members never exhibited any closeness with Julia. If language was the formidable barrier for Sita, for Vineet, it was his lack of closeness with his brother-in-law.

Ammalu liked the toffees, cakes and cookies offered by her cousins a lot. But she would hide behind Sita if asked to step up to them. She was not a child who would get intimidated by skin colour. Indeed, she was quite familiar with the multitudes of colours on her mother's skin. Aaron knew a little bit of Malayalam. Ammalu would scoff at it, however. 'His Malayalam is like noodles dipped in sambhar,' she would jibe.

Julia's poems had forests, wild creatures, wildfire and wild men in them. Some poems displayed the signs of the fiery rhetoric espoused during street dramas. Vineet had discovered that Julia's poem 'Jungle Vibes' had a very close resemblance to Malayalam poet D. Vinayachandran's poem "*Kaadu*" (The Forest). He had recited that poem for Sita that day.

'Njanenthu peridum kattile
Karanonmarrkenthu peridum...'
'What shall I name them;
Ancestors of the forest?
If I start with the alphabets
The trees, shrubs shall be created again
In infinite repetitions,
Rocks and stones, eternal...
What shall I name them;
Friends of the forest?
Visible are the unseen colours
Audible are the unheard sounds...'

There were many depictions of the forest in Julia's blog. Most were photographs of her sojourns. From Vineet's perspective, such trips to nature reserves were the pastimes of those who had to survive amidst the rat race of a fast-moving city life. But he did not know that Julia carried a forest inside her, though she was a city dweller. Neither could he decipher the poem in her blog which hinted that the wilderness within was more enchanting than the forest outside.

Julia believed that those who knew forests were proficient in a language unknown to mankind. But Kerala's forests had never charmed her. She often complained that they were getting swallowed by houses. She disliked the forests at Munnar, Mattuppetti and Gavi, which were highlighted for attracting tourists. Her main task, while trekking through the forests, was to gather the discarded plastic covers. Julia lamented that plastic cohabited with Keralites in the state.

The only exception were the trips to the deep forests of Wayanad. There was a forest co-existing with each house out there, but the rate of increase in the greenery was not as high as that of the percolation of houses. She had written in her blog that never before had she seen such foolishness of destroying forests to make way for development. However, the joys from Julia's Wayanad trips did not last for long. After travelling through what they believed to be uninhabited forests, Julia and her group had been shocked to see a resort being built in the far reaches of the forest once. Acres of forest land had been destroyed for the buildings. That journey had disappointed her deeply. She had returned after warning everyone that 'the encroachment into natural habitats will face an equal and opposite reaction that would be devastating'. Julia had not ventured into forests in her visits to Kerala after that incident.

Janardhanan's trip to Kerala had a certain purpose this time, which was why the vacation was almost four weeks long. When the family properties were partitioned, Thiru-Nilam and the surroundings had been earmarked for him. Usually, whenever he arrived, he would pay a casual visit to his family home, and open it for the sake of formality. He would stay in his city home. Had he entrusted Thiru-Nilam's keys with his sister Sita, she would have kept it neat and tidy. But Rajasekharan Nair had never had any sentiments about these things and hardly cared about the house being locked up.

Of the four offspring of Rajasekharan Nair, Janardhanan was the eldest. The other two brothers were in Singapore. Sita was the youngest, and after her marriage, she was almost an outcast. Both father and son were planning to sell off their 60 cents of land, including the serpent grove. It was as if they were determined to sever all their attachments to the village after their current visit. Nobody was there to wait for them to come back, neither did they ever wait to see anyone—so what was the use of their native land?

The news that both the serpent grove and the house were getting sold off reached Sita too. Neither her brother or father had disclosed it to her, instead it was the broker, Sudhi, who revealed the information. Though a lot of people came to take a look at the property, only the nouveau riche could afford such a plot. Thus, Sudhi was diligently pursuing the Gulf returnees and wealthy contractors of the Excise Department. Finally, as expected, Thiru-Nilam and the serpent grove became engulfed by oil money. Rashid Ali, who had returned after shutting down his business in Kuwait, was the buyer. Apart from the bungalow where he resided, Rashid Ali had two flats in the city. Nobody knew what other properties he had, outside the town.

Rashid Ali, who worked as a driver for an Arab, had visited his native place only four times in the last 15 years. On his first trip home, the man had shifted his impoverished parents to a decent accommodation. Rashid Ali had procured a visa for his sister Ramsina, too. The next time he visited, he had extended an invitation for his parents to accompany him to the Gulf.

Rashid Ali had taken his sister to his Arab employer's house to work as a maid. If she took care of the Arab's children carefully, dinars would start pouring heavily. His *Arbab*, his beloved master, was so benevolent! The hue and cry about

Rashid Ali's kind benefactor was popular in the whole village. But nobody ever saw Ramsina again. All the letters that arrived were in Rashid Ali's handwriting. How could Ramsina write anything when the Arab's kids were clinging to her back, eh? She was so precious to them! Umma and Uppa grew more prosperous and flabbier with the money drafts which reached them regularly. After shifting their residence to the new bungalow, they changed their personalities too. Like parents who proudly brag about their child being an IAS officer, they started singing songs of praise: 'Both our son and daughter are in the Gulf. The Arab cannot live without Rashid Ali, and his children simply adore Ramsina.'

Rashid Ali returned after 15 long years; accompanied by an Arab girl in *purdah*. Everyone believed him when he said she was his wife. There were whiffs of rumours that he had eloped with the Arab's third wife, while another theory was that the girl was a Pakistani on a false passport. Be that as it may, he had arranged all possible facilities for his Arab wife in his new house. There was a chef from Calicut who was a specialist in Arab dishes. Nobody had ever seen Rashid Ali's wife; some caught a glimpse of her arm, others heard the jingling of her ornaments, and many saw her footprints on the yard.

No one knew of Ramsina's whereabouts; she remained the quintessential embodiment of a 'maid' in their minds. The only two people who knew that she would never return were

Rashid Ali and his Arab wife. In reality, Ramsina was no maid but the *biwi* of the blind 80-year-old Arab.

When the Arab expressed his desire to marry a very young girl, Rashid Ali had remembered his sister. He had sold off Ramsina and transmitted the oil money from the Arab's treasury to his native land. His justification was that Ramsina had no use for any bridegroom from the village. What if she had married some *ustad*, muezzin, fisherman or manual laborer, eh? She would have given birth to four or five children, suffered the wrath of poverty and endured abuse at her husband's hands. It was a better business deal that Rashid Ali had struck. The first person to implement a barter system in their land, by offering a Malayali girl in exchange for an Arab one, was Rashid Ali.

It was this Rashid Ali who was going to purchase the serpent grove. Gossip was rife that he would build another bungalow there, or a cinema theatre. On the day Janardhanan took a hefty advance from Rashid Ali and settled the deal, he threw a grand party at his house. Both Nabeezath and Vineet were invited to participate in the revelry. Though they were not aware of the reason behind the sudden celebration, Janardhanan announced the 'good news' at the very start.

Both Tipu and Ammalu were there too. It was the first time they were meeting after their Herbarium adventure had been derailed by the 10 missing plants. The children were sitting in Julia's room. In the party held in the vast garden, Rashid Ali and his family, lots of prominent villagers and relatives were all present. Tipu and Ammalu had entered the house, bored of the party. The corridors were thronging with visitors and they had sought Julia's room as a respite. Rashid Ali's wife was having her food, seated on the corner of the cot. She would not mingle with other men or laugh or chat with anyone. Julia had opened her room for the woman's convenience.

The woman was seated with her back towards the door and was gobbling down some food. She would raise the *burkha* with one hand, grab a fistful of food, and pull the *burkha* down. Once the frantic chewing and chomping subsided, the hand would rise again with the next lot of food. The *burkha* would be opened yet again and then close shortly after. The children stared at that phenomenon for some time. Though it was not an uncommon sight for Tipu, it was wondrous for Ammalu. She remembered seeing an elephant during the temple festival. It would use its trunk to separate the bananas from the bunch, holding the bunch down firmly with its foot, then use its trunk to manoeuvre the bananas towards its mouth. When the food was lifted up, its mouth would open out like a basket! While it munched lazily, its trunk would be doing many monkey tricks. Rashid Ali's *biwi*, dressed in a dark dress covering her from top to toe, resembled an elephant. Her dexterous hand was like a trunk which extended to procure the food from the plate… Ammalu relished the fantasy for a while.

All the objects in Julia's rooms were intriguing, and unfamiliar to the kids. There was a round table with two chairs near the window. Tipu explained that it was there so she could enjoy the sights outside while sipping her morning coffee. They could see a beautiful garden and a fountain through the window. Ammalu wondered what was so special about it all. Tipu could not understand most of the paintings hung on the walls.

He was familiar with the 'smiling yet not' Mona Lisa. Tipu had a teacher like that at his school. She was always smiling, but the molars were like fangs, and looked as if someone had hacked at them! It was better when she did not smile. There was something wrong with the Mona Lisa in the picture too, or else why wouldn't she smile even a little? One day, his teacher should be decked up in similar clothes and made into a smiling Mona Lisa! Perhaps a caption would be pithy: *At last, Mona Lisa smiled and it proved to be fatal.*

Apart from a dressing table and mirror, a small cupboard and bed lamp to the right of the cot, there wasn't much furniture in the room. Just the bare necessities for a bedroom, where one only went to sleep.

'Tipu, what shall we do about those 10 plants?' Ammalu raised her grievances.

'Shall we request Julia Aunty to check in America?'

'True, she knows forests well.'

'But these are plants of our land, would they be available in America?'

Tipu felt that it was a pertinent question. He pondered for a while.

'Like birds move from place to place, perhaps plants migrate too? Although they can't fly, maybe they have some tricks for moving between places?'

In Tipu's *Minecraft* game, there was a level when the gamer reached an isolated island. The famished gamer would deposit the seeds in his pocket on the earth and pour a 'growth hormone' over them. Suddenly, a tree would sprout and its fruits would grow round and juicy. He had saved the seeds of a fruit eaten a long time back and they had arrived to help him in a timely manner. The gamer had not consumed the seeds when he had felt hungry, and saved it for the future. Tipu thought it to be an inspiring deed.

The child was assured that the 10 missing plants of Njarakkadu would sprout again in some part of the globe. Nobody could go missing forever. There was an eternal circle of transformation occurring in the world and that was why he expected his Ummudu to return.

Ammalu had once approached Tipu with a new game. A Ouija board game. Apparently, Sita had taught her how to play. Sita and her friends used to play the game as well. Vineet had scolded her, saying that it was inappropriate for a mother to teach such an ominous game to her daughter.

Sita took this game—where one could call back the souls of the dead to the board—very seriously. They would spread squares filled with English alphabets and numbers in a circular shape on the ground. Next, in the middle of the circle, they would place a one-rupee coin and light a small, mostly melted candle on top of it. A steel glass would cover the whole thing. All the players would then place their forefingers on top of the glass and murmur in unison, 'O kind spirit, please come, please come!' Although inviting ghosts into the house was a dangerous step, Sita trusted that bad spirits would not be invoked and only the good would make their way to her home. If there was a spirit in the vicinity, the glass would suddenly spring to life! It would start answering every question they posed. The spirit inside the glass would travel in a circle and touch the alphabets or letters to form replies. If anyone around was skeptical, the spirit would take offense and retreat; no amount of invocation could placate it again.

Sita narrated an incident to Ammalu of a child's spirit visiting the Ouija board. He had died when he was just six. Upon asking how it happened, he had replied that it was due to a bike accident. The child told them the names of his parents and the place of the accident by touching the letters of the Ouija board. He spelled out the date as well. Sita and her friends had dismissed it as a naughty spirit. But next day's news shocked them to the core. Sita still remembered how her friend Sheela had secretly passed the newspaper to her with trembling hands during the English class. Sita had almost collapsed after reading the details of the family which had died in a bike accident. Her friend's face had clouded over. It was the same child's spirit that had appeared on their Ouija board; the time and place of the accident and all the other details were exact! They whispered among themselves so restlessly that the teacher had harshly asked them to move out of the room. Sita's belief in the Ouija board had been enforced by that event.

More and more spirits visited her Ouija board. Once, the ghost of an insane woman had paid a visit, and the glass tumbler started rolling madly inside the circle. It was an aimless, frantic rush. A crazy woman who was crushed to death by a speeding vehicle while she was resting near a shop foyer. The glass moved fast when the mad spirit took over and sped around, scattering all the letters. When it moved beyond the Ouija board and started rolling under the cot and furniture, Sita and her friends had realised the imminent danger. They sat terrified on the bed, hugging one another tightly. Finally, when the tumbler hit the wall and turned upside down, the mad rush finally stopped. They dared not play that game ever again.

Tipu and Ammalu had tried to play the Ouija board game too. Ammalu offered to invoke Tipu's Ummudu that day.

'Why call Ummudu? She will not come, only the dead answer the call!' On hearing Tipu's response, Ammalu abstained from the game. Sita had forbidden her from discussing Fatima with Tipu. But Tipu decided to play that game one day. The spirit he planned to invite remained mysterious and hidden. Maybe he would call the 10 missing plants, ask them where they had vanished suddenly, enquire after their wellbeing, plead with them to come back…

'What's the time now? I am so sleepy.' Ammalu always felt sleepy at 8 pm. Her biological clock had been designed in that manner. The party was still going great guns downstairs. Tipu looked around for a clock. It struck him then that he had not seen one in the house. There wasn't a clock even in the drawing room. Rashid Ali's *biwi* was murmuring over the *tasbih*, her prayer beads, which she was counting on her fingers. Tipu thought he would check with her. He was familiar with some Arabic after all! Clock was called *saeat*. Maybe it was the same for time?

Julia entered the room. Ammalu leaned against the chair and started dozing off. 'Hello,' Julia smiled pleasantly at the children. The kids returned the wish while the Arab woman remained silent. Julia had a tray with glasses of fruit juice in her hands, and she extended it to Tipu. Each child took a glass. Julia enquired whether they liked her room. It was the first time that such a mischievous smile was gracing her face.

'Yes, it's a well-kept room,' Tipu answered. But he complained that there was no clock in the room.

'Not just in this room but nowhere in this house will you see one!' Julia placed the tray on a coffee table and sat down beside them. After asking the groggy Ammalu to sleep on the bed, she asked Tipu to come closer. She asked him if he was wondering about the reason behind the 'clock-less' state of the house. When he gazed into Julia's blue eyes, Tipu remembered the picture of Snow White depicted on Ammalu's pencil box.

Julia was a petite woman. If she was dressed in white and wore glass shoes, she could have been exhibited in the showcase as Cinderella.

The absence of clocks was linked to certain physical peculiarities about Julia. She had noticed at a young age that none of the clocks in her house kept time. All the expensive watches that her father used to buy for her stopped working within 10 days. She had been subjected to many recriminations due to this fact. It was only during her adolescence that she could comprehend the wayward nature that time exhibited with her. Her watch and the clock which she used were always off-time. Sometimes, they would stop altogether, or else show the wrong time; running either fast or slow. The class prefect always had to correct the clock in their school room. Slowly, she discarded the habit of wearing a watch. In the school where she was teaching, the clock was nailed on the wall opposite to her seat in the teachers' room. It was either five minutes fast or slow. Finally, Julia stopped looking at it. Tipu was hearing about such a phenomenon for the first time. Was Julia infested with spirits?

It wasn't just clocks and watches; Julia's quirk manifested itself in any battery-operated appliance. She never used anybody's computer. During an emergency, she had once borrowed her colleague's laptop but after she had typed out a line, it had rebelled and conked off. She felt like an innocent woman condemned to the gallows during such occurrences. The same story repeated with torches and remote controls. This was her big secret. Perhaps, because she feared being mocked as a weird creature or being ghost-ridden, she had abstained from sharing it with anyone else. Yet, Julia revealed her secret to Tipu.

As a person who was attuned to electromagnetic waves, it was no wonder that she could resonate with the same energy radiating from Tipu. Experts call this phenomenon by various names, but Julia had quite reconciled with it now. In Tipu's mind, Julia—the one who could move the needle of a clock with her eyes—was elevated to superhuman status! He wondered whether he should tell her about the 10 missing plants of the Herbarium. But he did not have it with him. Then he decided to simply ask Julia.

'Julia Aunty, have you seen a Herbarium? Do you know what it is?' Tipu wished that she would answer in the negative. Only then he could stun her with the surprise. But he was soon disappointed to know that Julia was very familiar with the term. When Julia expressed her wonder at how well he spoke English compared with the other children, Tipu narrated to her how his life had been before Kerala. Julia had not known that Tipu was the Gulf-returnee kid. Janardhanan had told her about the incident at Tilapia Lake and how Fatima's child had returned to the village. She now recognised Tipu. He started telling her about the Herbarium project and the trees in the serpent grove.

Julia had heard about the grove, and had seen it once. She wished to visit the place before it was sold off. Though Tipu was aware of the business deal, he had not shown much interest in it. Regardless of whether the ownership changed hands legally, the grove would remain the same, and they could visit and play there as usual. Besides, he did not believe in permanent disappearances. But after talking to Julia, Tipu understood that matters were different here. Julia told him that Rashid Ali planned to construct a new building in the area where the house and grove were situated.

'A building can come up anywhere. But can you create a grove? What is the need for such a gigantic building? For constructing houses? Or is it a shopping mall? Has he come to build another Burj Khalifa in India?' Tipu was infuriated.

'Angry young man, you seem to adore that place!' Julia exclaimed in surprise at his fury. She was determined to find the reason for such an emotional reaction. Julia promised to stroll around the grove with Tipu the next day and then they parted ways. When Tipu walked to the gate after the party, he glared at Rashid Ali; he wanted to clamber up the man's chest and pull at his hair. If only he had Thankayamma's billhook with him! He would have inserted it inside Rashid Ali's mouth and slashed in one go! That would be the end of his grove-devastation and his monstrous building plans.

Tipu felt miserable thinking of the small mushroom caps struggling to come up from beneath Rashid Ali's huge new building. Next year, there would be no angel dance of the mushrooms! They would get trapped under the earth forever. The universe under the dried leaves of the grove would be crushed into smithereens. The ants and their eggs would be smashed to bits. There would never be a next generation. That gave Tipu a rough idea about what had happened to the

10 missing plants. Their seeds must have been crushed under some buildings like Rashid Ali's. Perhaps that was how they became extinct from the Earth.

Would the seeds that were getting ready to germinate under the dried leaves start growing downwards? Would they be able to create a new world there? As he had dreamed, would the fellowship of the plants decide to stay far away from mankind? Tipu thought that the time was ripe for such an event. Where would the earthworms live if not in the earth? The first warning about Rashid Ali's new mansion had to be delivered to the earthworms. They would need time to crawl out of that area and find a new dwelling space.

The laidback, sleepy attitude of the touch-me-not plants shall not help them now! When the shovels hit their roots, their leaves would droop, as if to say 'I cannot watch any of this!', but then it would pave way for their eternal slumber.

The climbing nettle would not be able to cause itching any more; those who were coming to pillage were unafraid of such irritations. None of their defense mechanisms would work with the raiders.

The *peepul*, *jamun*, teak, rosewood, *ashoka*, giant milkweed and their ilk reigned with grandeur like great statesmen. But when the chainsaw struck, they would fall headlong on the earth. The fall of the great was dreadful. Pitiful and horrible.

Anku's food stall would have to be shifted from the serpent grove to somewhere else. Since enough grass and leaves were not available near the house, he would have no access to his favourite snacks. Someone would have to pluck his food for him and deposit it in a vessel. Maybe he would need a dining table and plate like Tipu.

Not just the serpent grove, but Thiru-Nilam would also be demolished. The spiders and dinosaur lizards would vanish. Though that was a cause of relief for him, contemplating that it would be akin to murder, Tipu felt unhappy. He dragged his feet on his journey home, as if carrying a heavy burden. He did not answer Rarumma's questions. Nabeezath knew what the matter was—the affiliation of every generation with the grove, starting from Padmajamma, was known to her. Of course, a small fraction of Fatima's affinity was bound to reflect in Tipu. The same anxiety Fatima would have felt, on hearing about the grove's impending destruction, was being expressed by Tipu. Fatima had been sensitive to the fading of every *nishagandhi* flower—the queen of the night flower. It was apparent that Tipu had his mother's nature.

When Fatima was in school, Nabeezath would braid her hair into two long pig tails and tie them with red ribbons. But the girl preferred leaving her hair loose and free. Though this was strictly forbidden at school, she wouldn't miss any opportunity to do so. Fatima enjoyed the carefree feeling when her tresses fell about on her face and shoulders. All the red ribbons in Nabeezath's stock had slowly started disappearing. In the morning, when it was time for doing her hair, there would be no ribbons available and the girl would play dumb. Finally, the mystery of the missing ribbons had been solved in the form of a long, red, ribbon-garland unearthed in the serpent grove. Fatima had tied all the ribbons to a long swinging creeper dangling from the *peepul* tree. The 'red creeper' swaying in the breeze looked as if the tree had spat out blood!

Nabeezath had become suspicious after that incident. Fatima had some more secrets hidden away in that grove! Many of her deep confidences were safe with Thankayamma. But the old woman would grin craftily and never divulge even a teeny bit despite the harshest of inquisitions. Sometimes, Fatima would go to the grove to study, especially before her examinations. Once she had fallen asleep under a cluster of *ashoka* trees! What a girl!

Nabeezath was tortured by the changes happening in Tipu. He was transforming more and more into Fatima with every passing day. Every act of his was a journey to Fatima. The presence she was trying to forget, was yet again imposing into Nabeezath's life.

Eighteen: Dwelling in the Grove

Julia arrived at their house with Aaron. He was a calm child. Tipu and Aaron were meeting each other for the first time. Tipu had talked only to Julia during the party.

Aaron started mulling over Tipu's sketches. Nabeezath stood befuddled, not knowing how to play hostess to the American lady. Probably Julia was the first foreigner to step inside her house. Before Nabeezath's bemused eyes, Thankayamma made her presence with a cup of black coffee for Julia. There was no confusion in Thankayamma about how to treat the foreign guest. Julia happily sipped the coffee and praised her for the exquisite taste of it too! Nabeezath stood utterly bewildered wondering how that old woman had mastered such niceties. Where was it written down that American guests should be offered black coffee? Even if it was, there was zero chance of Thankayamma being aware of it.

Aaron liked the picture of the itch-provoking nettle the most. He, too, had once been a victim of that stinging nettle.

Though he was not Julia's biological son, Aaron was more like Julia than Noel. Julia was his mother, and no one could recognise that Aaron was her stepchild. In such cases, the belief that peculiarities of character and form were transmitted exclusively through genes was proven wrong. It was not through 'nature' but through 'nurture' that many of Julia's qualities had been imbibed by Aaron. In common words, those were habits which were picked up by close observation and imitation. Julia's poetry, music and love for nature manifested so naturally in Aaron.

Julia wished to camp inside the serpent grove that night and had come to seek Nabeezath's permission for taking Tipu along. Nabeezath pointed out that Thiru-Nilam house was lying vacant and that there wasn't any need for camping in the grove. Everyone knew that Julia camped in forests; but Nabeezath could not see a possibility of that happening inside the grove. Besides, Julia had seen the foremost forests of Kerala and wasn't much enthralled.

It was no small matter of pride for Nabeezath that Tipu had impressed a *madamma*, a foreign woman, in such a short period! She realised later that it had been her own shortcoming, being used to seeing foreigners as mere tourists. Tipu had the open-mindedness that came from having grown up familiar with different languages and different skin colours in his neighbourhood. The teacher at school was Indian, the worker at the shopping mall was from the Philippines, the domestic help was from Bangladesh, the server at his favourite restaurant was a pretty lady from Lebanon, the person who washed their car was from Sri Lanka… How many nations walked past him in human forms every day! He had seen the myriad differences of the world more than Nabeezath and consequently, nothing surprised him much. However, the mesmerising wonders he had observed in the grove and the experiences that the Herbarium had granted him were ineffable.

Julia and Aaron reached the grove with the camping material by 6 pm. Julia erected the scaffolding of the tent in a jiffy. It was a triangular contraption in blue. Thankayamma, who had come to watch, liked it a lot. With a few differences, it was similar to her own home. The truth was, she felt that her hovel was a luxury. It was said that the old woman had a son. But nobody had seen him around. Even if he had been around, Thankayamma would not have liked it; she preferred a solitary existence. She ate properly cooked food only at Nabeezath's home. Typically, Thankayamma consumed vegetables, fish and meat either raw or after sautéing them over embers. Tipu had been under the belief that only those in Dubai knew the art of the barbecue. Thankayamma had totally toppled that belief! She ate birds, crows, fishes, straight off the smoldering coals. And she never showed off about having had a barbecue either.

Tipu had discovered that human beings exhibited different attitudes after eating different food. While eating *kanji*, rice gruel, one's face took an innocent expression. While chomping on KFC, a victor's preening flashed on the face! When chomping on a pizza, the person's mannerism is akin to an Italian. Well, while slurping on noodles, it seemed as if all the world's problems had been sorted out! But Thankayamma maintained the same expression irrespective of what she ate!

Julia had packed supper for the night stay in the blue tent. Thankayamma was curiously watching everything, as if evaluating a child at play. Tipu was yearning for the night to fall. He was wearing his favourite T-shirt captioned 'Trust me, I am a gamer'. When Aaron asked him if it was true, Tipu slipped into deep thought. He had been feeling rather strange wearing that T-shirt for a while now.

Aaron always carried headphones with him. His studies, play, sleep and meals were carried out in tandem with the music. He took them off now to talk with Tipu. Aaron could understand a little Malayalam and also managed to speak a few words. Tipu's knowhow of Arabic and Aaron's knowledge of Malayalam had much in common.

'Do you come here often?' Aaron was gauging Tipu's intimacy with the serpent grove. Tipu told him about Ammalu and how she could not join them because her mother hadn't allowed her to. Sita had forbidden her, saying that she was a girl and she could not stay overnight at a strange place by herself. Although Vineet argued that it was not a strange place but Sita's own house, and that child abuse cases happened more by day than by night, Sita remained adamant. She believed that mothers of daughters should be like hunting dogs, able to sniff out dangers from a distance. The reality was that she kept even her husband away from their daughter. It had been a while since Vineet had given a bath to Ammalu or helped her change her dress. It was possible that after seeing the flood of child-abuse incidents perpetrated even by caregivers, Vineet could empathise with Sita's wariness in matters of their daughter's safety.

Aaron handed a book to Tipu—*Endangered Species of the World*, a book created by National Geographic. It spoke of plants and animals that were slowly going extinct. It was full of pictures of the 'Red Listed' creatures and plants identified by international organisations working on conservation. Tipu knew that red meant danger. In case such a list was made for humans, Thankayamma would figure in it. After her demise, the chances of seeing another person like her were almost nil.

The book had almost 3000 species in it, both plants and animals. Tipu searched for the Missing 10 amidst them. He found out that two or three of them were in the book but were already extinct. That made him very unhappy. Tipu could not believe his eyes when he saw the elephant, giraffe, leopard, tiger, monkey and rhinoceros in the pages. How could such strong and smart animals disappear? If this was the condition of the kings of the forest, then what would happen to the minions? There was a tortoise too, in the depictions! Tipu thought of Anku and felt miserable.

When Tipu was starting for the camp, Anku had been foraging among the plants in the yard, searching for insects. He had raised his head to glance at Tipu. The child wondered whether the creature would be alive when he returned after his adventure. How come such innocent creatures like his Anku were becoming extinct? Who did they disturb in their habitats? Who felt threatened by them?

On reading further, Tipu realised that extinction did not happen overnight. He jotted down all the precautions he had to undertake to ensure that Anku lived long. Anku should have offspring and should be fed food properly. Now, how could Anku become a father? What was the easiest way to create some tortoise babies? Tipu's head was muddled with dilemmas.

Tipu flicked the pages again. Ah, the penguin was there! How sad! Tipu had seen penguins not only in cartoons but also in the Dubai Zoo. What was more wondrous than its body, seemingly draped in black? Tipu used to mimic the way the penguins strutted around, waving both hands. Ummudu used to tease him, saying that the way Tipu used to walk as a toddler, with his legs apart after his circumcision rites was akin to a penguin's waddle.

Tipu knew about both the black panda and the one-horned rhino mentioned in the book. Their Science teacher had forewarned them that the one-horned wonder would not be with them for long. Tipu was a fan of the cartoon show, *Rhino-Season*. He had taken solace in the fact that the rhinoceros would continue to live on at least as a cartoon character.

He had never seen dodo birds. They resembled swans, but he was intrigued by the name 'dodo'. It was true that dodos were an extinct species. Along with the dodos, the Calvaria trees in Mauritius had also disappeared. When dodos feasted on the fruits of the Calvaria, their excrement carried undigested seeds from which new Calvaria saplings would sprout. With the extinction of the dodo, the Calvaria vanished too, the trees not knowing any other means to distribute their seeds. Both had been destroyed together. Imagine a bird taking a tree as a companion to its coffin!

The book opened Tipu up to these startling facts. If Thankayamma disappeared like a dodo one day, what all would she take along with her? If only she would leave Anku behind!

Apparently, chimpanzees were endangered too. What fun would a zoo be without monkeys and chimps? Tipu vowed that he would never visit a zoo in case such a thing happened.

The book had pictures of both African and Asian elephants. Tipu had seen elephants a few times after returning to his maternal home. Once, when he had accompanied Ammalu to a temple festival; another time, when he saw a tusker who was being used to lift heavy logs in a wood mill; finally, the elephant that was tied up in Khadeejumma's neighbour's front yard… Perhaps these were the only remaining ones of this endangered species.

In the last pages of the book there was a picture of a red wolf. Tipu remembered *Little Red Riding Hood*. The little girl who had set off with a cake for her ailing grandma, the wily wolf who had misguided her… Ah, what a trickster he was! Yet he could not survive for long on this planet. If this was the situation with the smart alecks, then…?

In Chicago, there was a museum for dinosaurs similar to the one shown in *Jurassic Park*. In his nine years, the only creature to catch Tipu's fancy was the dinosaur. Asif had promised to take him on a visit to the Chicago Museum one day. But something else was troubling him now! If these dinosaurs, which had reigned over Earth crores and crores of years ago, remained only as fossils, what would happen to the 3000 animals and plants shown in the book? Tipu felt suffocated at the thought. Imagine Anku's skeleton and shell being displayed in a museum! The child covered his eyes instinctively.

There were 10 missing plants now; in a decade, it would double or quadruple in number. Their fossils, too, would appear in museums. Like Tipu's dream, the Earth would become devoid of green. Banished greenery! Only the Herbariums would remain in the world to commemorate their memories. Tipu became aware of one fact—of all his possessions, the Herbarium was the most precious.

It was night. Tipu had read most of the book. Darkness spread all around, the silhouettes of trees were visible, and insects were swarming around lights. Tipu started seeing them with a different eye. The insects were ghosts which infested the lights, and the ancient trees were erstwhile dead people. Tipu became afraid. He walked towards Julia. She was seated outside the tent, smoking a cigarette, while Aaron was lying nearby, listening to music.

Julia was sighing about how it could be the last night for all the trees. Tipu understood what she meant. But he could not comprehend that the building would come up so fast. There was nothing that could stop Rashid Ali, he was so rich… What could he not conquer?

Tipu closed his eyes. The night in the grove reminded him of Tilapia. The sounds of birds at night were different from the day; even the trees and the grass took on a different guise altogether. The wind seemed different too. Everything seemed to be enthralling. He listened to the way the wind shuffled around, without awakening the leaves. Even the aimlessly meandering bugs had different habits at night. The night changed everything. Even those who obstinately refused to change, the night transformed them completely. The moistness of the soil felt different. Tipu gathered a scoop of mud and put it on his palm. A pleasant chill crept up his arm. Was it a chill or his hair standing on end? He occasionally felt that the two feelings were different.

All natural creatures were excellent actors. Their roles however, changed drastically from day to night. The usual daytime characters like ants and butterflies left the stage temporarily. But the play had to go on. And so, some new characters took over the stage. How did they know when to play their roles, and that too with such perfection? Who ushered them in such a timely manner onto the stage? Tipu was caught in a bewilderment cast by his own ruminations.

An owl hooted from some tree. It was Julia who informed him about the owl.

'Human beings are terrified of bats and owls,' Julia explained. 'They are heroes because they travel fearlessly at night,' Tipu responded, and Julia agreed with his evaluation.

Tipu had heard that his Ummudu used to be scared of their round glaring eyes on flat faces. When Fatima was a child, the owl had come in handy for scaring her into finishing her dinner quickly!

'Unlike other birds, Tipu, only the owl has two forward-facing eyes; the rest of the birds have eyes on their sides. Maybe the fear is triggered by that,' Julia elucidated, and Tipu agreed.

Only if they searched in the night would these birds find their favorite food; it was tough to hunt mice during the day. Let the owl sleep and wake at its convenience, why be concerned about it? Tipu abandoned the topic. But Julia again offered another tidbit from the Owl-*Purana*.

'American folk stories say that owls swoop in and take away the brats who bawl at night,' she smiled, looking at the tree from where the hooting ensued. Rarumma had told Tipu that a bird lived in a tree-hollow inside the grove. Perhaps it was the residence of this owl.

'This ruse is for persuading the recalcitrant kids who do not come home at night and those who vex their mothers with unwanted obstinacy,' Julia laughed. Tipu was thinking of his Rarumma with awe; when had she read all those American folk tales? Not just Fatima, Tipu too was afraid of owls. But he liked bats. Since the hero of the *Batman* movie was a bat, Tipu found himself fascinated by that creature.

A firefly flew in from somewhere and landed on Julia's arm.

'Wow, this is one torch which I can carry confidently,' Julia chortled in glee. Battery-operated torches did not last long around her. The reasons would remain unassailable. The fireflies had light in their tummies. Nabeezath renounced those with no light in their heads as fools and praised those who had it as intelligent! So what would be the term for someone with light in their tummy?

'If they could produce electricity from fireflies, it would solve Kerala's electricity issues,' Julia cracked a joke. Tipu pondered over it and found himself agreeing to that observation. The fireflies could not bite anyone surreptitiously like mosquitoes, neither could they hide anywhere. Wherever they went, their light would shout, 'I am here, I am here'. But nobody could see their light during the day, so they could play a trick or two then!

Aaron managed to catch a huge butterfly which had landed on their tent using a net. It was the largest butterfly Tipu had ever seen.

'Wow, how pretty! It is so big! Hello, lovely butterfly,' he cried in delight. Its dusky brown wings and wingspan were as big as the book in Tipu's hand. There were white triangular patterns on each of its four wings. The ends of the wings were bent like an umbrella handle. Its antenna was long and full of furry hair.

'It is not a butterfly; it is a moth. An atlas moth,' informed Julia.

As per Julia, such night-fliers were called moths. But Ammalu called them butterflies, stupid girl!

The markings on the atlas moth's wings resembled Sita's vitiligo-affected fingers. After the moth emerged from its one-month stay inside the cocoon, it went on a strict fast. The moths did not have mouths, and the leaves and fruits they had eaten as a grub remained their sole source of energy. Tipu wondered if perhaps Vineet knew all these tidbits, too. But he hadn't had much of an opportunity to learn from Vineet, neither would there be scope for that in the near future. The grove was going to be devastated, what else mattered?

The curved upper corners of the atlas moth's wings bore an uncanny resemblance to a snake's hood. The light green hue of the edges had designs like Nabeezath's saris. But what was the use of all that beauty when it did not have a mouth? After its wings developed, it would die in about a week's time, bereft of any food or water. Perhaps when she muttered how the life purposes of certain lives were unpredictable, Nabeezath had been thinking of the atlas moth as well as Fatima.

Aaron let the moth go free. But after a while, it fluttered back to the original spot. 'Go ahead and catch me,' it seemed to say. Tipu tut-tutted that these creatures had no intelligence at all. He crept inside the tent and lay down. Through the transparent blue surface of the tent, he could see the shadows of the vast wings of the atlas moth. Wouldn't the space where it sat, at least the space beneath its wings, belong to the creature?

Rashid Ali's hands, extending all the way from Kuwait, were casting its shadows over the grove. His fingers would entrench themselves under the earth and uproot all the gigantic trees. They would be dethroned forever. Poor creatures, like the atlas moth, born without mouths or sounds, would end up losing their ground.

Crickets chirped all around Tipu. That was perhaps the only sound he hadn't heard at Tilapia. At least the crickets could chirp away now. It was really sad when even that was not possible. There was a Talking Cricket in the story of *Pinocchio*. Fatima had told him that it made the sound by rubbing its wings together. The Talking Cricket, who had lived for over a century in carpenter Geppetto's house, had been the first to warn Pinocchio that his pranks were going beyond tolerable limits. 'You are a puppet, and what's worse is that you have a head of wood,' it says, and an annoyed Pinocchio throws a mallet at the Talking Cricket, killing it immediately. But he reappears in many parts of the story, and saves Pinocchio from many dicey situations as a ghost.

'Trouble awaits boys who rebel against their parents.' 'My boy, don't trust those who promise to make you rich overnight.' Wise words of the Talking Cricket. The only philosopher whom that naughty puppet ever met in his life was the Talking Cricket. When *Pinocchio* was made into a movie, Walt Disney had renamed the Talking Cricket as

'Jimini Cricket.' Fatima was vehemently against all such liberties.

'Walt Disney is teaching children falsehoods. There is no one like him to create new creatures, modify the old ones and rejig old tales,' Fatima fulminated. How dare Walt Disney rename author Carlo Collodi's 'Talking Cricket' to 'Jimini Cricket'?

Perhaps one day, the crickets would become silent too. Like abrupt blindness or sudden hearing loss, they also might develop a few variations. Their *kurr chirr kurr chirr* hubbub for attracting mates would be rendered useless when there were no mates. When Rashid Ali's fingers dug deeper under the serpent grove, when the greenery vanished bit by bit, the crickets, too, would be scattered widely. They would wander hither and thither, searching for their dispersed mates. Then eventually, they would stop. Silence would lead to a withdrawal and later to extinction. Tipu felt a pang in his heart, and for the next 10 minutes, he carefully recorded the chirping sounds of the crickets on his tablet.

Julia was keenly observing Tipu's actions. She had not moved from her position.

'The sounds for you to record are still to come. Just wait for a bit. The night birds shall arrive when the darkness intensifies; there will be an orchestra in the grove! An orchestra that plays a unique music unheard of before.'

'Rashid Ali shall take away all these sounds. Would the birds come if there are no trees? Would they come to the balconies of the houses? I have never seen a bird singing on our Dubai balcony,' Tipu was baffled.

'I could never bring myself to love the forests of Kerala. Now that I see what is happening to the grove, I think my judgment was correct.' Julia had never before observed the extermination of forests at such close quarters. She was reeling under the shock of the imminent destruction. Tipu could not sleep either. Aaron was lying with his eyes closed. What a night it was turning out to be! Tipu went to sit by the platform of the snake deities. He was seated on a fallen log. Suddenly, there was a rustling amidst the dry leaves. A snake! Tipu watched it slither away desperately into a hole, terrified at the movements around.

It was for the first time that he was seeing a snake in the serpent grove. Maybe the real owner had come to take a look around the place, aware that the property rights were being seized from him. The labourers hired by Rashid Ali for clearing the grove would first murder this original owner. What was the sense in saying that it was deadly and venomous? Look how it was scurrying away at the sight of a small lad like Tipu! Maybe the snakes were thinking that it would have been better to grace the crowns of the Egyptian pharaohs than dwell in the grove. Anyone would think twice before messing with the King's royal crown; even Rashid Ali would be terrified.

The log on which Tipu was seated had been lying there for a long time. He remembered the stormy day when there had been a heavy downpour; that was when it had fallen. He noticed some toadstools growing on the wood. They had fully harvested the opportunity to reside on this branch that had been firmly flourishing on the tree. Had the branch taken a nosedive to provide shelter for the toadstools? Rarumma's wise saying about how everything was predestined might be right. When the toadstools were yearning for germination, the wind had helped the branch descend, transforming it into their refuge. Nature's unpredictable plans!

Tipu peeked beneath the toadstool. Wow, so many seeds were there! The black spores could create a nice cycle wheel.

In another corner, the ants were hollowing inside the log and building a home with the enthusiasm of attending a housewarming function. They had no idea that the first inhabitant of their new home would be Rashid Ali.

All the fungi that Vineet had pointed out to him had spread their web across the decaying leaves. How did these fungi find out about the fallen log so quickly? Who was the go-between here? Tipu had no clue about how this get-together had happened. There were both visible and invisible members among them. No way to count, no way to measure…

To find out whether there would be impending rainfall, an alert would typically be issued by the Meteorological Department. Tipu was yet to meet a human being who could augur the rain, wind and sunshine ahead of time. In spite of the various alerts given by the department, millions died in Cyclone Katrina and the tsunami. But the dwellers of the wooden log did not wait for any climate alerts. The denizens seemed to have waited, fully knowing when the branch would fall. What an amazing sixth sense!

Tipu had observed everything with the help of the emergency lamp in front of the tent. But there were spaces inside the grove where only the moonlight fell. It was pleasantly cool there. Tipu made an effort to spot the owl in the moonlight. Except for the *kkummu kkummu* hooting, he could not figure out where it was hiding. It wasn't in the hollow either. If only he could decipher how the owl managed to camouflage itself in the moonlight, he would use the same trick to outplay Ammalu in the next hide and seek game.

It wasn't just the owl; Tipu was also aware of the hideaways inside the grove. Many amusing escapades occurred whenever Tipu and Ammalu played hide and seek. But that day, what had happened hadn't been much fun.

As Ammalu counted till 50, Tipu was supposed to hide. He had hidden near the fence between the grove and the adjacent farm. He was crouching beside the mud partition, looking out for Ammalu.

He would intermittently peek out to check Ammalu's whereabouts, then retreat to a crouching position. There were a few holes in the mud fencing where the soil had loosened. Those were hollows of vague shapes akin to the vitiligo markings on Sita's body. Above the mud fence was a tattered thatch, bringing to mind toothless grandfathers. One could see the banana plantations through the holes. Tipu started observing the plantation through each hole, and saw different angles and shapes. He spotted a hole which was blocked by a bottle. It was covered with a paper. Tipu opened the bottle; and found it was full of small specks. When he sniffed, it was odourless. Furadan 5g, it said on the top of the bottle.

Tipu opened the paper, but the writing was in Malayalam, so he could not read it. The child knew both English and Arabic, but was still learning Malayalam alphabets from Rarumma. With considerable effort, he could make out a word or two. There had been no other person in the grove except them, so how did the bottle get there? He raced towards Ammalu with the evidence.

Seeing Tipu, Ammalu shrieked, 'Satttt' and galloped towards the tree to register her victory, thrilled that she was on the verge of an easy win. But instinctively sensing that there was something amiss, she stopped half-way.

'What's in your hand? What's inside that bottle?'

'Ah, it says Furadan in English. Full of some powder, I checked!'

'Ayyo, its poison, Tipu! I read in the newspaper. Acchan had purchased some for spraying on the pests in our garden once. He had kept in the shed outside and cautioned us against touching it. If you touch it, you will die!'

Tipu felt scared, and started searching for ways to wash his hands.

'Wash your hands quickly, or else you will end up like the pests!' Ammalu promptly became maternal.

'Read this note,' Tipu said.

'Why don't you read?' Ammalu countered, knowing fully well how ill-equipped he was to do that. These were the rare occasions when she could show off. Ammalu hadn't forgotten how he had teased her with the apricot, avocado and kiwi!

'Don't brag, okay! Read fast. Otherwise I shall ask Rarumma. What a know-it-all!' When Tipu grabbed the paper sulkily, Ammalu's bluster vanished.

'If you have two Malayalam alphabets in your name, I have three, okay? Sit down, I will read,' Ammalu clambered atop the platform and started reading, swinging her legs.

Tipu sat under a tree nearby. From a distance, they looked like teacher and pupil.

Ammalu read aloud:

For the information of Dear Agricultural Officer,

Sir, you went out of the way to help me, and I cannot trouble you anymore.

For a respite from my never-ending loans, I am going to take refuge in these specks of Furadan. My house is under legal attachment for defaulting loan payment. The agricultural land I had taken on lease is under loss; my mother, wife and children are in terrible distress and that's why I have taken this decision. You know all about my story, but my parting note is for the larger society which is unaware of it.

Undertaking a loan for agriculture is nothing new. But the farming I carried out on my land was not of a common farmer. My rice, bananas and vegetables, which I had nurtured without a drop of artificial pesticide or pinch of chemical fertiliser, quickly shoved me down a treacherous pit! Following all your advice, using only organic farming methods, I had lovingly brought up my crop. Like me, you are confident about the purity of both my soil and the air above it, since they are devoid of any chemicals. My ladies' fingers, rice and plantains shall not wreck anyone's health. When someone I have never seen eats the rice sourced from my field, he should remember me with gratitude, for not adding harmful elements to his intestines and protecting his children from harm.

Sir, I am a coward. Someone who lacks even the courage to scatter a few specks of Furadan near a plant and adversely affect its wholeness. I am terrified of even walking too firmly on the ground and creating a shift in its structure. But what I did, in spite of all my fears, was very daring. When every other farmer around me resorted to expensive and strong pesticides and fertilisers, I struggled to maintain my produce with tobacco potion, organic compost and items made of neem.

All the pests and insects which were driven away by their powerful chemicals sought refuge in my farm. They attacked in hordes and drank the life-blood of my plants, gnawed the leaves, and weakened the roots. The pests had adapted their own genetic makeup to resist the powerful chemical pesticide, exactly like you said. With renewed vigour, they bred their younger generations and mastered the art of survival.

Only I could not learn that survival tactic. And hence, I am forced to take refuge in the specks of Furadan. The first chemical that I am ever touching in my life, I hereby use on myself rather than on my plants, for the first and final time.

Through this, I am declaring my protest against an ignorant human race which is not lucky enough to eat the organically cultivated food that I have produced. The administration shall not be able to find those responsible for my death. Only my family shall grieve over my death. Or is it my murder? If anyone other than them feels a pang, I hope that the emotion will assume the proportion of a pandemic. If I can be the cause of an agricultural revolution, that would be my victory.

Taking leave with much hope,

Signed,

Krishnan Nadar

'What is all this about?' Tipu asked, utterly bewildered.

'Seems like someone is about to die,' Ammalu replied, feeling uneasy.

The children had hurried to hand over the letter to Vineet. The Agricultural Officer, Sadiq, was Vineet's good friend. They found Krishnan Nadar in the span of a few hours. He had sneaked inside the grove with the Furadan, but the noisy kids had created a ruckus in the vicinity. Nadar had waited for a while, but on realising that the children were likely to be around for a long time, he had thrusted the bottle of pesticide and the note into a hollow of the fence and gone back home.

He must have decided that it was less dangerous to keep the pesticide inside the grove than at home. There were some distressed living beings in his home; anyone could be prone to a tragedy. Though Vineet and Sadiq couldn't solve Krishnan Nadar's problems, they could prevent him from committing suicide. Though it was the children's game of hide and seek which had paved way for saving a farmer's life, the kids themselves could hardly comprehend the real matter.

Tipu got up from the fallen log. The moonlight seemed to brighten. Say, would the moon become a sun if its light intensified? Perhaps that was the goal behind the moon's daily resurrection. He went and sat beside Julia, though they did not have much of a chat afterwards. Julia stayed in that posture all the night. Tipu, however, drifted off to sleep.

While pulling down the tent in the morning, Julia remarked, 'We should meet again.' Tipu did not bother to prod further either.

After Julia's return to the house, she and Janardhanan ended up bickering. Usually, Julia kept away from interrogations and squabbling, but this time, she was the one who started the fight.

'You are very sleepy,' Janardhanan quipped.

Julia merely hummed in reply. Janardhanan was getting ready to go somewhere.

'Everything happened as per plan. Rashid Ali is a smart fellow, we definitely need more business men like him! See, he will end up changing the very face of this village,' Janardhanan was full of zest since the business deal had come through.

'Yes, that is most certain!' Julia replied sarcastically. Hitherto, she had never interfered in the issues of his family property.

Janardhanan was aghast at the sudden change in her attitude.

'Look, what's the point if that house and land are left desolate? Neither Aaron nor Noel are ever going to settle down here. Since it is not a tourist destination, one cannot build a resort either. Rashid Ali is a son of the soil; he shall manage well.'

'Tell me, which land do you belong to?' Julia queried.

'You know that I can adapt to any place, Julia. My village has never given me anything valuable. My wife, job, home, kids—everything was given by a foreign land. The only person with roots here happens to be my father. And he is more than willing to live with me anywhere. So why should I have any connections with this land?'

'You said this land never gave you anything. What have you given to your land?' Julia's question was acerbic.

'Julia, you will not be able to understand that. See, you won't be able to appreciate the societal environment of this place. You know that Sita's marriage was a huge shock to father.'

'Of course Father could never accept it. How could he accept that after being in the elevated position of a headmaster who taught students at the school for 30 years, he would get downgraded to being the father-in-law of a man belonging to scheduled caste, eh? No average Keralite can handle that feeling.'

'That's why I said you cannot understand! I am the one who saved my father from the degradation of his daughter marrying a scheduled caste Thandan boy. When father cried, lamenting that he could no longer face anyone in the village, I was there for him.'

'Indeed! You are a very good son. Your father has hatred for Sita who married a scheduled caste man and adoration for you who married a foreigner. He feels shame at a *thandan* becoming his son-in-law and awe at a *madamma* becoming his daughter-in-law! Going by that logic, my parents should have sentenced me to hanging for marrying a guy from a developing country, right? Janardhanan, you shall never change!'

'Julia, you don't know about the olden days. Vineet's father Shankaran used to climb our coconut trees. He was never allowed inside the house. There are categories of people who are allowed inside and kept outside one's residence. It is not just untouchability, but there are certain family heritages and customs behind such things…'

'Is it so? Of which family branch is Rashid Ali a member?'

Janardhanan seethed, but did not deign to reply.

'Father wanted me to sell the property and I followed his advice. That is all.'

'You might know the area and the value of that property perfectly well. But I know much more about those sixty cents of land than you.' Julia said.

'Don't teach me about the land I was born and brought up on.'

'What's the use of all that? There is a world there, unknown to you. You don't need a microscope to see it; you don't even need eyes. Just open your mind with generosity.'

'Oh, an epiphany after spending a night there, I suppose!'

'No, it was because of an epiphany that I went there. That was revealed by two children, Ammalu and Tipu, who barely reach your knees.'

'Oh, is that the way the wind blows? Nabeezath is against selling the property. Is she behind all this brouhaha? Has she come with a tenancy suit, eh? Let her son-in-law, the Dubai-*wallah*, purchase the property, what's the need for all this jealousy? He entered the scene after burying his wife in the sand, right?'

'Please, don't hesitate! Come on, say that Sita is behind Ammalu's rebellion. Let your accusations flow. Have you seen the mushroom circles of the grove or ever observed the owl inside the tree-hollow? What about the ants under the dried leaves? The eggs they carry? Do you know what the earthworms eat? Do you even know that they exist, tell me! Are you aware that Krishnan Nadar was trying to commit suicide by eating Furadan?' Julia raged.

Rajasekharan Nair was sitting nearby, listening to the war of words. What left the son speechless silenced the father too.

'You cannot see the world that a nine-year-old sees clearly. And you are not in the least aware of the global disaster that they are foreseeing. The land where you were born indeed!'

Janardhanan went out without saying a word. Perhaps because he did not have another place to go, Rajasekharan Nair continued to sit at the same spot.

Nineteen: Hope and Despair

Ammalu was quite woebegone. Sita hadn't allowed her to join the night camp adventure in the grove. Though she hadn't been there, Tipu had enjoyed the camp. Ammalu had assumed that he wouldn't go either, since she wouldn't be there for company. Tipu failed to understand why girls thought with their hearts! On hearing that the sights in the grove at night were starkly different from the day, Ammalu couldn't bear it.

'You are a boy. And so is Aaron. You guys can go anywhere.'

'What about Julia? She's a girl!'

'She is a *madamma*!' Ammalu made a wry face.

'Julia is very friendly. You could not talk much with her, could you? She told me many stories about the forest. Aaron gave me a book too. Want to see?'

Tipu extended the book. Ammalu pondered over the pictures in the pages. Tipu explained the portions he had read.

'Look, a tortoise is here,' Ammalu pointed out. Tipu had known that it would catch her attention.

'Hmm…poor Anku. You thought of him too, right?'

'Hmm…poor thing! He is not aware of anything at all.'

However, it was their misconception that Anku the tortoise knew nothing. They had no idea that Anku was dragging a shell on his back by himself, bearing the loneliness of long, desperate years. The heaviness of his shell increased with his solitariness. Anku was again and again relegated as a slowpoke. None of the changing faces in that vicinity could resolve the problem of Anku's endless wait. Every one of his days passed by in the relentless wait for a mate or a companion. Though he was in good health, the fact that death was far away, had proven to be a curse for the tortoise.

Anku's childhood was spent in the forests of Wayanad. His species was the foremost among the tortoises. Mating during the rainy season and laying eggs inside the deep forests, Anku and his pals had enjoyed their days without facing any adversity. The days had gone by within the deep forests where sunlight hardly entered, snapping up buzzing insects and indulging on the moist, tender shoots of grass.

They would traipse off as a rambunctious group to drink water from the small ponds in the vicinity. Submerged under the water, many happy hours would be cherished. The pond would transform into a gathering of tortoises during their mass-bathing expeditions. During the rains, it would be like a festival; groups venturing forth in search of sprouting mushrooms. On sighting any such sumptuous growth, the tortoises would give out a blaring sound, much like a horn! They would encroach into any land for their unending feasting.

Thankayamma never knew that Anku loved mushrooms. He hadn't hunted for mushrooms for a long time. When mating season approached, young males like Anku developed a darkish pink hue near their eyes. Many female tortoises would fall for that charming colour. Innumerable little tortoises had been hatched in the forest. In the security provided by the forest, the tortoises caught insects, laid eggs and slept with utmost comfort.

In those days, Anku had been unaware about the world outside the forest. But there was a wizened old tortoise amongst them who was familiar with the ways of both the forest and the world outside. It could barely move its limbs. If a snail or a bug was offered by another, it would chew at it listlessly, else stay hungry. Grandfather Tortoise vouched that he was 150 years old. He would challenge the sceptics to count the rings on his shell. Growth rings of old tortoises were akin to the annual rings on the trees! The old fellow had made many trips outside the forest. He had worked closely with intelligent scientists too.

He would narrate the tale of being caught by a wildlife researcher to the little ones around. In the cages, there were other experimental subjects like rabbits and mice. They would be taken out intermittently, given some injections, and then put back inside. Though they were fed regularly, the food had tasted bitter. The drinking water was bitter too, mixed with many powders. Every morning, the bespectacled, white coat-clad man would crouch near the cages and scribble in his book. Some days, all the humans came together, but they all looked the same. They would gaze at the tortoise and the hare as if they were magical creatures. Every day they measured the weight, length and growth by checking their heads and limbs.

For a few days, they had allowed a female tortoise inside the cage. Those days were fun. Afterwards, they removed her and placed her in a cage nearby. Though he had been a bit saddened at the time, now, the Grandfather Tortoise was totally indifferent. After a long time in the laboratory, the same men had returned him to the forest, back to the same spot they had taken him from. But they had attached some instrument beneath his tail which had stung him sharply for a while. Gradually, he had become accustomed to it.

Anku had heard many yarns like these from his forebearers. But what had happened to him was very different from the stories of his predecessors. Once, when Anku and his friends were returning after a dip in the pond, they saw that their homes were on fire. The flames reached the skies.

Grass and trees were spluttering and cracking, and the stench of burning flesh wafted around. Tortoises, hares, snakes, deer, buffaloes—all burnt to death. Even the fastest runners were chased by the flames and were consumed. How could the slowpokes escape then?

The tortoises had started shambling away at the first touch of heat, but the poor creatures couldn't really flee, let alone from a wildfire. Nobody could predict which way the fire would surge. Anku and two of his friends had somehow made their escape. After a long time, the sight of smouldering embers and the fierce heat of the fire disappeared. Both Anku's friends were missing. He had looked around for quite a while, making urgent noises, but they could not be found. But hearing his sounds, a duo had come closer. They were not tortoises, but humans.

Anku had heard about the men who took away tortoises, not to laboratories, but to be cooked and eaten. He had even felt a twinge of pride when the old gaffer said how highly priced tortoises were! But Anku had been seized neither for the lab nor to be eaten. The forest dwellers had handed him over to a driver visiting from the mainland. Anku had first stepped outside the forest in an open jeep with his buyer.

The man was smoking endlessly and singing loudly as he drove. Anku mistook the smell of cigarettes as the smell of human beings, and thought that their voices were mellifluous.

The driver stopped the vehicle twice. Whenever the jeep became still, Anku stirred inside the sack holding him. The man would tie the sack firmer. But the sack became loose due to Anku's frequent movements. After a long trip filled with song and smoke, the man stopped near a river, wanting to go for a refreshing swim. Anku wriggled inside the sack, and after a while, the knot came undone. When the man had sauntered off with his soap and towel, he had forgotten to close the back door of the vehicle. Anku crawled his way out and landed on the ground with a plop.

Creeping along the sides of the river, the tortoise reached a cluster of grass. He snacked for a while to satiate his hunger. After gulping down a locust and three grubs, he felt a little respite. The forest blaze was heating him from within. Moving from the grass, Anku clambered onto the sand. It was night, and darkness had fallen all around. The tortoise kept crawling until he saw light. He did not know that the old woman seated near a hurricane lamp in front of her hut was going to be his lifelong companion, Thankayamma.

When the old woman came near him, Anku crept into some shrubs. She offered him some fruits and leaves. Then, she lifted him up into her arms and took him home. That night, she snored away with Anku on her grass-mattress. Anku sat staring at Thankayamma's open mouth. What sort of a creature was she? Definitely not the scientist that Grandfather Tortoise had warned them about; nor the wicked man who roasted tortoises alive! The place wasn't a zoo, since there were no other animals around. Then, what place was this?

In the course of time, the tortoise got a new identity and a home. Since dogs pounced on him at sight, Thankayamma either locked Anku up or took him along on all her sojourns. In fact, she had heaved a sigh of relief after entrusting Fatima with Anku's care. She was very averse to sharing her home with anyone. Human or tortoise, made no difference in the matter.

It was Fatima who gave him a name. Though he did not know why she had addressed him as 'Anku', he reckoned that the name held something deeply friendly within. Anku had the same fraternal feeling for Fatima that he harboured for his pals back home. Sometimes, he wondered whether Fatima was a tortoise, too! She would crawl with him on the ground, keep watch as he slept and was ready to hunt for insects with him. When Anku foraged for insects amidst the plants, Fatima would join the melee. Their joint expeditions were full of fun.

Fatima would lie on her cot, dangle snails tied to her long hair and tempt Anku. When Anku would approach with his gaping mouth, she would lift her head, and the snails would dance like puppets before Anku's bemused eyes. Fatima had been a girl of a mischievous disposition. She would take Anku along when she shuffled to the grove with her books. Staring at her open books, she would stroke Anku's shell. Anku would cuddle with her. After some time, Fatima would keep her books aside, lay on her back on the dried leaf bed and start talking, mostly to Anku. Perhaps he had wished to acknowledge her prattling at least once. Although Anku could hardly understand what Fatima was chattering about, he would sit next to her until she closed her eyes and dozed off. But Fatima had unexpectedly vanished one day. A vanishing act where she had not even left behind the burden of a goodbye.

After Fatima's marriage, Thankayamma had to take back Anku's ownership with full responsibility. Anku the tortoise always had mentors and protectors around him. People who loved him, and offered him food. But the tortoise felt restless without the familiar environs of the forest where he was born. He could not feel at home anywhere else. Tipu and Ammalu were his friends, and they had endless love for him too. But they were not tortoises, though often he wished they were.

What fun it would be if Tipu Tortoise and Ammalu Tortoise would accompany him on trips to the pond and the pit, searching for bugs and grubs! If so, he would make them his best friends and turn into a Grandfather Tortoise himself. He would regale them with tales of the forest fire, the jeep trip and his stay with Thankayamma. Besides, he would plan his journey back to the forest along with them.

Like Fatima, Tipu too gazed into Anku's eyes while chatting with him. Anku felt that both Fatima's and Tipu's eyes had spoken the same stories. But where was she now? Maybe someone had hijacked her, like he himself had been kidnapped from the forest. Of course, one day she would be back to have fun with him in the grove again. Anku the tortoise wished that his hopeless existence extended until Fatima returned to him.

Who was there to talk to? What was there to think about? What was there to see? What fascinating sights were around? His only relief was the daily trip to the serpent grove, and he patiently bided his time for their daily adventures.

Ammalu was flicking the pages of the book. The temple elephant, the hornbill from the *HerbaRush* game, the firefly and the tiger were all getting ready to depart forever. She remembered visiting a railway station to bid goodbye to Vineet when he had to take a train to attend a seminar in Thrissur. Thinking of her father going away from her, she had wailed ceaselessly until he had returned. The image of waving goodbye to all these animals who were being packed away in a similar train flashed across her mind.

'If only we could morph Anku into some other animal!'

'How is that possible?'

'A species which is not on the verge of extinction. Maybe he, too, wishes for a change!'

'We don't have Aladdin's magic lamp with us, do we? No genie, no spirit to appear at our call either.'

'No BenTen, no Superman, no Batman,' Tipu added.

The plants in the book cast her into misery. A few from the Missing 10 of their Herbarium were featured here; the sandalwood tree, too! Unbelievable!

'Didn't you know that they are going to clear the serpent grove, Ammalu?'

'Yes, I got to know. But I am dreading that one of the plants that would disappear might happen to be the last of its kind on earth!'

'Really?' Tipu became eager.

'Why not? When they destroyed our 10 missing plants, did anyone know that those were the very last of their kind?'

'Could this be the last *jamun* tree?' Tipu caressed the *jamun*'s trunk.

'Is this the last Indian coral? The very last mango tree?' Ammalu wondered.

'No way! I have seen lots of mango trees in Dubai too!'

'What about the *ashoka* tree? Have you seen it outside the grove?'

'Not at my house.'

'Neither at mine, nor at my school. There is no *ashoka* tree at Acchan's old home too. But there is one at his college.'

'I cannot believe this! Where will the earthworms go now?' Tipu sat on his haunches wretchedly, his hand clutching his head.

'What about the ants?'

'The seeds under the dry leaves waiting to germinate?'

'Yesterday, I saw a snake. He crawled inside a hole. They will first scare him off. Everybody's afraid of him, right?'

'But he never bit us, Tipu! When the grove disappears, he might crawl inside our houses...'

'Of course he will! Where else would he go? You were the one who told me about the leopard which was prowling in the village.'

'Would the wild animals come to attack us one day?'

'Why wait for wild animals? If all these ants were to raid us, what then?'

'There are man-eating ants too!' Ammalu must have heard it from Vineet. As if recollecting something else, she added, 'Ah, what can be done now? Let us collect the seeds of all the plants before the grove is destroyed. That is the only thing left for us to do.'

'You and your collection! Everything is about your hobby, huh!' Tipu was irritated.

'I mean that we should try and grow the seeds elsewhere!'

Tipu thought it was a sound idea.

'But which place is as vast as the grove?'

'Not just a single place—in all possible places! In our homes, in the neighborhood, at our schools...'

'Hmm...plant the grove in multiple places, good idea indeed!'

'But we can't accomplish this work if it's just the two of us. I will tell my friends at school and distribute the seeds. You do the same in your new school. Let everyone plant a few in their homes.'

'Right, a *jamun* in the place of the missing one; a *gulmohar* in the place of another; a *peepul* in the place of a *peepul*.'

They high-fived each other and unanimously passed their new resolution.

There were only three days left for the reopening of their schools. Asif arrived to take Tipu to their new city flat. Nabeezath would stay with them for some time. Asif had agreed that every weekend, Tipu would visit Njarakkadu. Ammalu would get busy with school, and since the grove was being destroyed, all games would be relegated to Sundays...no fun in staying there now. Both Tipu and Ammalu were unhappy about Anku. Both kids cried while handing him over to Thankayamma.

When they were stacking their luggage in the dickey, a commotion was heard near Thiru-Nilam and inside the grove. Tipu took a peek. There was a crowd thronging the place. Most looked like manual labourers. When he watched them sharpening their saws and shovels, Tipu's heart started throbbing in his chest. Every tree in the grove would be spliced with that sharpness! Tipu yearned to be the monster in *Minecraft*. He would assume a gigantic shape and lurk like a shadow above the serpent grove. Whoever crossed his shadow would be blasted to dust. The saws and shovels would fly away from their hands. He felt angry with himself for not being able to grow into a giant.

If only he knew how to play cricket like Anwar and Asgar, he would have aimed a ball at each labourer, felling them ruthlessly. Tipu started strategising guerilla war tactics. If they were characters in a children's adventure story, they would have immediately deployed an effective strategy right then! He wished that some children's author would adopt him and Ammalu to star in his or her fantasy novel for a few days.

Tipu climbed into the car after seeing the labourers enter the grove with their weapons. Rashid Ali, dressed in a blue T-shirt and jeans, was all over the place, issuing instructions. He was beaming proudly. The man waved at the sight of Asif. Seeing Asif shake hands with Rashid Ali, Tipu disembarked. Rashid Ali and Asif were meeting each other for the first time. After the initial chit chat, Rashid Ali asked with a sly grin, 'You had an eye out for this place, right?'

'No way! Who told you?' Asif responded.

'I heard something along those lines. Just wanted to check with you.'

Bending low, he chucked Tipu's chin and murmured, 'Smartie pie, aren't you!' Then he started blabbering all the Arabic words he knew. He tried to confound Tipu by asking him the meaning of some words. Tipu turned his face away and stood silently. Rashid Ali went on showcasing his knowhow in the Arabic language. But Tipu's rebellious stance seemed to annoy him a bit.

'Smart boy, but I suppose ever since his Umma went away, he has been this way…or was he like this earlier, too?' Rashid Ali questioned Asif.

Asif wanted to leave the place right then. As they turned, Rashid Ali called out, 'Keep an eye out on this place when you can… We are going to be neighbours now…haha!'

Tipu turned on his heels and threw a blistering look at Rashid Ali's face.

'What are you going to build here?' The intensity of his gaze and the sharpness of his question wiped away Rashid Ali's grin.

'What do you wish to see here, dear? Maybe we will build a huge building, like the one in Dubai?'

'Certainly not Burj Khalifa!'

Rashid Ali staggered a bit, wondering whether the boy was poking fun at him.

'No, we'll build an amusement park for children instead! You can play in the water, ride a bike; I will even import some dolphins if needed!' Rashid Ali was exaggerating his motions and pulling faces to amuse Tipu.

Tipu entered the car and shut the door noisily, before sitting down with his head bowed.

Twenty: Tipu's School

The best thing about the new school was that Tipu did not have to wake up at wee hours of the morning. In Dubai, the bus would trundle by at a quarter to six in the morning. In the winter, he would have to step out in pitch darkness. By the time he reached school, dawn would break. But he had rather liked wearing his woolen gloves, cap and sweater. Showing off his uber cool 'yo yo' look, eh!

The classes in the new school started late, but ended only in the evening. There was no air-conditioning in the school bus either. It was very hot and there were a lot of children, too. There were no seats specifically allocated to any child, unlike Dubai. Many kids stood during the entire journey, and those who got on at the final stops often stood on the footboard of the bus! Tipu's stop was the second one and so, he had enough space to keep his bag and get a seat.

Those who stood leaned over the ones who sat; never before had Tipu experienced such physical proximity with his schoolmates. Back in Dubai, there were fixed places for every student in the bus as well as the classroom. There was no need for heckling each other, and they existed as 'separate countries' in the class. There had been students from different states of India, but unified by the common tongue of English they were all alike. The only one to stand out was the Punjabi boy Krish Gaur; he had a knot on his head, tied with a cloth.

In the new school, students did not have separate tables, and they sat brushing against each other on the same bench. Tipu had shivered while sitting alone in the air-conditioned classes in Dubai. Here, as he sat snuggling against his friends, he felt warm. Tipu understood how relationships became firmer when the warmth of someone's body was transmitted into one's own. He started to like the close-seating arrangements for students here.

The teachers were all very affectionate by nature in the new school. He started warming up to the teachers who spoke to him in his mother tongue. He was starting to understand that the purpose of language was not merely communication. The teachers in Dubai were good, too. But they were just 'teachers.' Over here, they had different aspects to their personalities.

He knew that his Rarumma had been a teacher once upon a time. He yearned to sit in her class. Fatima had been Nabeezath's student for almost two years. When Tipu would ask Ummudu if she would become his teacher, Fatima would warn him, 'Whew, there is nothing more boring that having your mother as your teacher at school! Imagine seeing the same face at school and at home. You can't even move around freely anywhere. One is expected to come first in everything. Responsibilities pile up, my dear. How much I struggled to uphold the "teacher's daughter" label!'

At school, a big bonus was that Tipu could play in the school playground during the lunch break. He would wait for the bell to ring before racing to the vast playground. In Dubai, the ground was in the premises of the school building. But due to intense heat, nobody was allowed to play. There was a garden in the new school; it was not very big, but pretty. No child was allowed inside the locked enclosure of the garden. You could only gaze at it from outside. The girls would make fervent pleas to the Security Uncle who watered the plants, 'Uncle, please give us a red rose…one dahlia please…'

One day while Tipu was playing, he saw a boy sitting in a corner of the playground, looking thoroughly exhausted. He seemed very familiar. Tipu identified him by the wheezing sound emanating from the boy as he moved closer. It was the boy he had met at the hospital, Jobin. It was really sad to see him struggling to breathe, fatigued after running only a little. Jobin recognised Tipu too.

'Haven't you recovered yet? I didn't know that you studied here,' Tipu said.

'Sometimes it is better and sometimes it is bad. I am sick of taking medicines. Pills and inhalers all the time... People say that it is not good to consume so much medicines, so I have stopped most of it.'

'Is that so? I hate taking medicines. It's remarkable that you handle it so well. Hats off!'

'The doctor said that there was one way to get cured. We should live in a place far away from the city.'

'What's wrong with this place? It is good.'

'It is full of dust and smoke and vehicle fumes, right? Those are not good for me. When I inhale polluted air, my lungs shriek—that is the high-pitched whistling you hear.'

'Jobin, where will you go then?'

'I need a peaceful place to stay. Where the vehicles don't make a din. Few people, fewer houses; somewhere like that. A place with lots of trees and plants. In the flat we have here, there is not even a front yard, forget about trees or plants.'

Tipu's mind started a massive search for a place suitable for Jobin's residence. He had transformed into a Google Map!

'Eureka! I know the perfect place for you!' Tipu cried.

He told Jobin about the serpent grove. Where else would they find such a perfect place for his asthmatic friend? If he stayed in a tent there for 10 days, all his sickness would vanish! His lungs would never lament after that, but laugh in delight instead. But that possibility was becoming remote too. Imagining the sights when he visited the grove the forthcoming weekend, Tipu covered his face in sheer horror. He narrated the fate of the grove to Jobin.

'Can I come along to see the grove with you?'

'I do not know if there will be anything left in that place. But you should definitely come with me.'

Jobin noted down Tipu's phone number.

'I want to see that thing too…what was its name?'

'Herbarium.'

'Yes, that!'

'I have told you about Anku the tortoise, right? Thankayamma has him now. But she has promised to bring him along when I reach home this Sunday.'

'Wonderful! I have never touched a tortoise before. Can I pick him up?'

'Why not? He is quite friendly.'

'I can meet Ammalu too. Would you show me that book with lots of pictures?'

Everyone in school was by now familiar with Tipu's tortoise, his Herbarium and his grove. Many students wished to visit Tipu's house in the village. His schoolmates talked with awe about how the boy from Dubai was an expert in matters of the local flora and fauna. When their mothers dropped them to school in the morning, they would point out Tipu through the window of the classroom, 'Look, that is the new boy I was talking about.' However, for the first three weekends after Tipu joined the new school, he could not visit Njarakkadu because of Asif's hectic work schedules.

This was the fourth week and Tipu was moping around, displaying his displeasure with Vappu. Nabeezath also wanted to check on her home and yard; there were a lot of activities which needed to be entrusted to Thankayamma. Finally, Tipu's obstinacy won.

They had to cross the grove to reach Nabeezath's house. Tipu's heart started beating madly as they neared the place. The unpleasant sight ahead would shock him, perhaps even devastate him. Tipu lowered the car window and peeped outside. His eyes were tightly shut. What happened to the cool breeze which used to caress him when he passed by the grove? A dry wind came and cast a fiery heat on his face. Tipu almost thought that he had returned to Dubai. Usually, there was a darkness all around the grove. Today, although his eyes were squeezed shut, a penetrating light was fighting to enter his eyes. How true were the words of the book! *When there were no trees, the sunlight would bombard the earth ruthlessly*! Could the sun have come down and taken over the area since the grove was no longer there?

'Tipu, Ammalu was waving at you near the grove. Didn't you see her?' Asif wondered at his indifference. Ordinarily, he would have leapt down after spotting Ammalu.

'Have you forgotten her after making new buddies at school, kiddo?' This boy who had handled his mother's sudden absence so courageously, could he have forgotten Ammalu on getting new friends? Asif had his misgivings about the way children adapted so easily to new circumstances.

Tipu did not reply that his closed eyes had prevented him from seeing Ammalu. If someone asked why he had closed his eyes, he had no answer for that either.

Ammalu came to them, huffing and puffing.

'Come, don't you want to see?'

Clutching his hand, she started racing to the grove.

As soon as he stepped inside the grove Tipu was dreadfully shaken. Half-hacked trees, stripped branches, some trees with chopped-off branches, some merely stubs… Huge ropes wound down from some tree branches. They looked disoriented, like a teenager contemplating death. When the sunshine had entered the serpent grove, all the mushrooms had vanished. Instead of dried leaves, the floor was covered with fresh green leaves. There were no crunching noises of the past; in fact, all the old sounds had retreated from the place. There was the sharp smell of wood everywhere; that tree-chopping odor. It was like smelling blood in a battle field. Tipu felt dizzy.

The child sat on the stump of a *peepul* tree. The *jamun* tree across them was merrily swaying in the breeze, resplendent with fruits, oblivious to its imminent destruction.

What did a tree say to a stump? No, it was the stump which spoke to the tree. It was the corpse of a tree—the shuddering body after a beheading. The stump and the roots. The roots of the decapitated tree struggled towards the roots of neighbouring trees, quivering, yearning for their embrace. Pleading for some strength from their compatriots. The degradation a tree stump endured was that of a human stripped naked in the streets. With their annual rings exposed, they opened up about their agonies of being born and living on the earth. Their stories of woe included the pain of every woodpecker's effort to drill a hole in the tree trunks. A forest area which was lopped off, resembled a battlefield where all the warriors were lying dead. Their dead bodies were buried where they had fallen while fighting.

The stump on which Tipu was seated still bled. If that murder were to be prosecuted in any court in the future, the first evidence would be the chainsaw. The sap-stained saw would be exclusive proof of the atrocity. It would bear the blood of the murdered victim and its shrieks of anguish. When it hacked another tree, yet another wail was added to the stain. The accumulation of such shrieks turned the chainsaw into a instrument of torture. Due to continuous use, the serrated edge of the saw lost the sharpness. It soon turned into a musical instrument played by ruthless hands.

The insects, microbes and moss which crept near the tree stumps gave them companionship for a while. They, too, would leave finally, after absorbing everything they could. The stumps would not be left behind for long; soon they would be uprooted.

Tipu started searching for earthworms. The workers had desecrated the mud with their stamping feet. The earthworms must have been vanquished. Stuck on the footwear of strangers, their corpses would have travelled to far-off places. The tree with the hollow, where the owl resided, was lying on the ground. When their homes were devastated, the inmates became blind, deaf and mute instantaneously. These thoughts about homes made Tipu remember the fire.

It was the day a building near their flat in Dubai had caught fire. The embers from a barbecue on the third-floor balcony had been the root cause. Some whispered that it was the blazing remnant of a cigarette thrown away carelessly. The flames leapt high, engulfing all 18 floors of the building. Even the glass doors of Tipu's flat had heated up. All of Fatima's plants had shriveled and died in the insufferable heat. Everyone had been evacuated from the neighbouring buildings. The residents stood across the road, staring at the inferno. They must have been picturing their belongings, precious documents, favourite dresses being burnt to cinders. They sighed with relief that they had escaped with their lives at least.

Tipu's classmate Suhair was a resident of that apartment complex. Tipu had visited Suhair's house. It was a beautifully decorated home, as Suhair's mom was an interior designer. Tipu had felt disappointed that his Ummudu wasn't a designer too, after seeing Suhair's lovely house. Red and orange flames were licking that house now. Only the frames of the photographs would be spared. Suhair's guitar, which had been hanging on the wall, melted in that blaze.

Suhair and his family had stayed in Tipu's house that night. Since his books were all burnt, he hadn't attended school the next day. They had to buy everything from scratch. Not even having a spare dress to change into, Suhair's father had gone to the nearby shopping mall to purchase clothes for his family.

The saddest part of the story was Suhair's pet parrot. Chunnu was left in a cage which hung from the attic. When the fire alarm sounded, everyone had rushed out. When the thick plumes of dark smoke entered their houses from the air-conditioning duct, everyone had started coughing and choking. His mom was pregnant, and there was only a week's time left for the baby to arrive! Everybody had been concerned about Suhair's mom when the smoke spread.

Since the lift was not functioning, they had to climb down many flights of stairs from the sixth floor. There was a mad rush on the staircase, where people were hurrying down with bags. Some carried small suitcases while others were fleeing with just the clothes on their bodies. Some were in their bathing attire, with towels wrapped around them. Seeing a shrieking woman, whose face was slathered with a green face mask, Tipu couldn't help but grin.

In that melee, Suhair had forgotten to open Chunnu's cage. Neither had he remembered to carry her along. In the tension of getting his mom downstairs, everything else had been left behind. Suhair was deeply disturbed after seeing his house on fire with his parrot still inside. His pet parrot used to chirp Tipu's name very sweetly.

The administration had readied temporary tents and food for all the apartment residents in a nearby park. Everyone had been aghast at turning into refugees overnight. While resting in the tents, they watched their burnt flats. The same situation was being faced by the owl in the grove now, after losing its home in the tree hollow. Could he be around in the hope of building yet another nest in the fallen tree?

Were birds believers in miracles? One could not help but believe that there was some magic that the birds seemed to know. Suhair's parrot had miraculously escaped the conflagration. The fire department officers had recovered her safely when they were checking the premises the next day. Her body was ridden with soot. She could not chirp or make any sounds due to the impact of the heat. Could it be that she had shrieked out so loud that her voice had finally given away? Had her personality been affected by the terror? The newspapers had flashed the news of Suhair with his pet parrot. He was smiling in the pictures, something he had done after a long time.

Since it was Sunday, there were no workers in the serpent grove. Ammalu started gathering something from the ground into envelopes.

'What are you doing?'

'Seeds, see!' Ammalu showed him her collection.

'Is it your new hobby?'

'I had told you that day about collecting seeds and replanting them.'

'Ah, right. How many different varieties have you collected till now?'

'Lots. I come daily and collect seeds of all the plants they chop down. Acchan asks me to collect saplings of certain trees. I have planted those in plastic bags filled with mud. Come home with me, and I will show you.'

'Have you found a place to plant all your seeds?'

'That is the big problem, Tipu. Nobody is ready to give me space for these seeds, because they will grow into huge trees.'

'Give me some seeds. I'll distribute them among my friends.'

'Did you know, they killed eight snakes in the last three weeks?'

'So many were here? We never knew, did we?'

'I heard they got snake eggs too.'

'Thankayamma would have fried them for dinner. I am sure they got birds' eggs too. Don't you remember that cuckoo's nest which had fallen in the wind? All those broken eggs?'

'Yes, I do. The workers found many creatures which we had never seen. We never saw a mongoose, did we? Civets too! It seems that many animals leapt out of their holes.'

'Did you see them?'

'No, I was at school.'

'What if I stayed here on a week's leave?'

'Huh! As if you are some bigshot, to take a leave of absence from work!' Ammalu laughed mockingly. 'We read so many adventure stories, but we could never think of a plan to save the grove!'

'Ammalu, they were concocted tales. Those things never happen in reality. Can you become Tom Sawyer? I cannot become Huckleberry Finn either.'

'What's the use of reading all these books then, except wasting our time?'

'Yes, the superhero books are useless too. Aaron's picture book was much better.'

'Can I borrow that book for a while? I want to show it to my friends.'

Tipu did not hear Ammalu's request. His attention was diverted to Thiru-Nilam, whose roof had been removed.

The children entered the house. It was very bright inside. The sunrays were rushing into every nook and corner, hidden from them until now. There were no dinosaur lizards around. Some cobwebs were dangling here and there. How much effort must have gone into making those spider webs! Homes built without any architects or blueprints.

'We need engineers to build our houses. But all spiders are engineers. No one needs to teach them anything,' Tipu commented.

Some termites were scattered on the floor, stunned after falling from the attic. They would slowly move into the door frames now, and after those were destroyed, they would be homeless. Rats were screeching and running all over the place. Hearing noises, they fled the scene. There were no more foolish rats in this house, like the ones who had accompanied the Pied Piper. These were intelligent ones!

'This house is another Herbarium, isn't it, Tipu?'

'Hmm…a museum, rather. Let us hang a board outside saying that once upon a time, a horrible man called Rajasekharan Nair and a demon called Janardhanan lived here.'

Tipu forgot that he was speaking about Ammalu's grandfather and uncle.

'Amma says that in the olden days, people were afraid of even picking up a twig from the serpent grove. They had never eaten *jamun*s or mangoes from here in their childhood, like us. They were afraid of the wrath of the gods! The snakes were the guardians of the grove; so nobody touched anything.'

'What happened to all that fear now?' Tipu asked.

'Now, everybody wants to own houses. They need shopping malls… Amma says people have too many desires… that is the reason behind this lack of fear.'

'I don't think so. Maybe the gods have lost their powers. That's why nobody is afraid anymore,' Tipu countered.

'Perhaps you are right. I prayed so hard that they would leave the grove untouched. But look what happened eventually!'

When Tipu reached home, Thankayamma arrived with Anku.

'Has Anku become thinner?' The 'mother' in Ammalu reared her head again.

'Not at all. He is looking very smart. I feed him very well,' Thankayamma pitched in.

'But he is so languid in his movements,' Tipu agreed with Ammalu.

'Ah, he is pretty old. Must be nearing his deathbed,' Thankayamma delivered that barb and went away to the kitchen.

'As if! You are nearing your deathbed, not Anku!' Ammalu hollered after the old woman.

The next day, on his way to the school, Tipu glanced at the grove. He could see it only next weekend now. There was an earth mover machine standing near the grove. Earth diggers brought to uproot the stumps. Fanged creatures who would gnaw their way to the heart of the earth. By the time he came next week, the grove would be reduced to a pile of debris.

After two days, Tipu got a call from Ammalu. She had had a dream! Ammalu normally never had dreams. Dreams were the rarest of rare occurrences in her life. Aaron dreamt with his eyes open; Jobin's dreams had been nipped by asthma, and Anwar dreamt of impossible things. Tipu's dreams were all tied to the grove; in other words, he had started dreaming after finding the grove.

But Ammalu's dreams were starkly different from all the others. In her dream, Ammalu looked crazy, a street kid with soiled, ragged clothes, her face filthy and sooty. She was wandering through the grove. Suddenly, a mountainous heap of seeds sprung up before her. It was an assortment of different seeds which kept increasing in size by the second. A growing seed mountain!

Abruptly, there was a sound behind her; the sound of waves. A huge sea was attempting to swallow her. Ammalu tried to scramble up the seed mountain. As she struggled to scale the heights, the seawater rose to catch up with her. It had reached almost halfway up the seed mountain. Terrified at the rising waters, Ammalu cried out, 'Grow, dear seeds!' Hearing her shriek, a few seeds sprouted. Some grew into huge trees quickly. Ammalu sought refuge on a tall branch. But the sea was not subsiding; it kept rising further. Ammalu wished that the tree would grow sky-high! She chanted, 'Tree, please grow, please grow!' The earth was swallowed by the sea, now the only way out was the sky. 'Please, dear tree, grow fast and reach the sky!'

Sita and Vineet had woken up with a jolt at their daughter's shrieks. Vineet understood the reason behind her befuddlement on hearing about the strange dream. Ammalu was sobbing ceaselessly, hugging her father and mother alternately.

'I keep warning her not to collect seeds from that grove. They are destroying the sacred place, of course there will be fallouts! Besides, there are male labourers thronging that place, and she is such a litle girl, walking amongst them…' Sita fumed.

'Don't worry, Acchan will find a way out,' Vineet consoled his daughter. She slept cuddled up on his chest that night.

In the morning, Vineet got ready to take Ammalu out. She was asked to pack all the seeds and saplings she had taken from the grove. He put gardening implements in the car dickey.

'Have you taken all the saplings, Ammalu?' Vineet cross-checked. Sita assumed that they were going to visit one of Vineet's friends or Tipu. Due to her nightmare and consequent lack of proper sleep, Ammalu hadn't gone to school that day.

After driving a long way, Vineet reached a rather desolate stretch of the road.

'This is a national highway, *chakkare*. What you are about to do is something iconic. One of the greatest activities you will ever do in your life. Come on!'

'I know this road. You took this route to fetch your friend from the airport,' Ammalu quipped.

'Smart girl! You remembered, although it was five months ago.'

'That day you told me that many trees were cut down to make way for the road,' Ammalu pointed out.

'Yes, and my darling Ammalu is going to fix that,' Vineet grinned and tossed her into the air playfully.

'You will never forget this road again. Run along and get your seeds and other stuff from the dickey.'

In every hole that Vineet dug by the roadside, Ammalu planted a sapling. At a specific distance from each other, on both sides of the road, they planted the saplings, and made an enclosure with sticks, like a tree-guard. Having arranged for water from a nearby tea-shop, Ammalu watered every plant. Vineet took pictures of Ammalu planting the saplings and watering them on his phone. He sent them to different news channels and print media immediately.

On seeing the strange activities of the father–daughter duo, many curious onlookers, including those from the shack and the houses nearby, started gathering in the vicinity. Vineet explained the state of affairs to them in detail. When they returned, Ammalu reminded Vineet to inform Tipu. Though Vineet told her that Tipu was most likely in school, Ammalu became impatient to see her friend. How could she keep the secret all to herself till evening? She became fidgety. On the way back, they visited Vineet's college as well. They planted some seeds near the area of his experiments. Vineet advised Ammalu to safely keep the remaining seeds with herself.

How quickly news travelled! After watching the afternoon news featuring Ammalu planting saplings on the roadside, Nabeezath called them up. When Tipu called her on Vineet's phone, Ammalu was astonished. Multiple news channels started reaching out to Vineet, seeking an interview with Ammalu. The next day, even newspapers carried Ammalu's pictures.

'Ammalu, everybody knows about your collection hobby now! It was fun to see you in the newspaper,' Tipu warmly congratulated her. How could he not congratulate her, seeing how smartly she replied to all the questions, nodding her head happily as the aunty from the news channel interviewed her. She looked so adorable!

The media evaluated that little Ammalu's sincere efforts were a slap in the face on the hypocrisies exhibited by many ministers and high-society show-offs who 'planted' trees in public places for a spot in the limelight. Vineet got Ammalu a whole new wardrobe. She was in high spirits now, since everyone knew her at the school and the village. There were fans at the bus stop where she waited for the school bus. Students trooped in from other classes to meet her and talk to her. The school principal made her stand on the stage during the assembly session and praised her heartily! Ammalu became a heroine overnight.

Rashid Ali was also watching the news. Ammalu told the story of the serpent grove and the seeds that she had collected from there, in her TV interviews. He was concerned that he would have to stop his work halfway. If someone complained, he would be in a big mess, especially since many organisations took up issues without rhyme or reason nowadays! Rashid Ali decided to suspend the work for some time. There were many political parties willing to 'adopt' Ammalu as their mascot, and Rashid Ali was afraid of what would follow. And thus, the clearing of the grove was suspended indefinitely.

Twenty-One: Groundwork

There was hardly a week left before Julia and Janardhanan returned to the US. Janardhanan thought that Rashid Ali had no reason for stopping his work.

'Do serpents and groves scare Muslims? What drivel!' He scoffed.

'Snakes have been revered as the incarnations of natural forces since ancient times. They didn't ask to be considered godly, did they? They do not differentiate between Muslims or Christians!' Julia's rebuttal was forceful.

'Religions arose due to man's fear,' Janardhanan countered Julia.

'Just fear, you say? His never-ending desires, avarices, have contributed to creating many gods. His crop would be impacted if the sunlight was either too harsh or too weak. He felt hungry, and to be able to get food regularly, he started worshipping the forces of nature. Then he tried to influence yet another powerful source so that the natural forces wouldn't act against him and stay under his control. A self-created god! God, please give me good rain this year; God, please save us from floods... Such fervent prayers became part of his routine.'

'Nature itself taught us to bribe our way to results, eh?' Janardhanan found himself in agreement with his wife on certain points.

'Nature did not teach us that. Man tried to entice a greater force, to teach nature a lesson. Utmost stupidity!'

After a while, Julia herself stopped the argument, since things were getting out of hand.

'I want to see Sita and Vineet's little girl. After seeing her on the TV with her planting adventures, I have decided to meet her once before I leave. Need to get her a gift too.'

'Since when have you started watching Malayalam TV channels, Julia? Seems like a conspiracy. I have to go somewhere. Ask the driver to take you.'

'She is your niece. You should have congratulated her for doing such a good deed, at least by giving her a call.'

'This is unnecessary melodrama for seeking fame. It is pretty common in these lands. Especially after reality shows became a hit. Poor Rashid Ali, he is in a soup! What was the ultimate outcome of this hullabaloo except the suspension his project? Big deal, planting saplings! I am not coming with you.'

Julia did not argue any further. She disliked conflict.

Sita was taken aback at Julia's unexpected arrival. Vineet's presence at home reassured her. Julia had purchased a Herbarium file for Ammalu.

'Go ahead and paste all that you like,' Julia wished, while handing her the gift.

'What shall I collect to fill up this file? I plan to accumulate a hundred plants not known to Tipu!'

'Do try! We will see who wins in the end. You might end up discovering a new species too!' Aaron high-fived her.

Vineet and Julia were talking properly for the first time. It was surprising for Julia when Vineet told her that he followed her blog and found her poems similar to those of the Malayali poet D. Vinayachandran. Julia warmly praised him for guiding Ammalu on such a noble venture and said that the drawbacks of nature lovers being solely restricted to poetry were rectified through such efforts.

'If you were to look at this from another perspective, superstitions also have a significant role in society. See, there was a time when people were afraid of serpent groves. Look at what happened when that fear abated!' Vineet spoke from his heart.

'Yes, indeed. In my mother's time, there would be regular worship at the grove. I have never eaten even a tiny mango from that place,' Sita jumped in.

'Humans are greedy now, and that's more dangerous than any fear! Westerners believed that India was the land of snakes. Serpents symbolising the rays of the sun was ubiquitous imagery. Until I married Janardhanan, I, too, had similar beliefs.'

'Hopefully, all your misunderstandings have been cleared now. Snakes have been used to symbolise both the sun and the rivers. Haven't you seen engravings of the egg and the serpent? The egg stands for the earth and the serpent is responsible for guarding it. The sinuous rivers have been metaphors for snakes as well.

'There are communities which worship the snake as the giver of rain. Though we might dismiss it as a foolish belief, in the olden days, people thought that the clouds were once rivers. Humans had sighted serpents for the first time in rivers. The rivers which were carried to the skies showered rains. All these beliefs point to a principle that any dynamic energy resource is symbiotically related to serpents.'

When Julia paused, Sita interjected; with the remembrance of Vedas that she had studied.

'Vritra is a wicked serpent who stops the rain from falling on earth. He is a black serpent and Indra had to fight a war with him to free the clouds from his grasp.'

'Not just snakes; in ancient Egypt, they worshipped birds, too. The crow, the cuckoo, the woodpecker—they were all worshipped as deities,' Julia added.

'Oh, I know that brat of a cuckoo! Tipu and I chased her away! Else, she would have laid her eggs in a crow's nest!' Ammalu jumped in. She was playing chess with Aaron.

'Haha! Why blame that poor bird, Ammalu? The cuckoo lays lots of eggs; in fact, she is very busy laying eggs all the time. One mother to take care of such a large troop of baby cuckoos! No maids, nor playschools to help her. That is why she lays eggs in the crow's nest, as those eggs look similar to hers. She wants her children to grow up under the care of some kind bird,' Julia opened Ammalu's eyes to a new truth.

'Ah, at least she does not destroy her eggs. By using a ruse, she manages to ensure her baby lives well, right? Cuckoos are smart!' The empathetic side of Ammalu raised her sensitive head again.

Julia requested them to meet her at the serpent grove once more before her departure. Ammalu and Tipu were both invited for that get-together.

On Sunday, Ammalu was waiting for Tipu to join her. Jobin was yet to come to Njarrakadu, although he had got all the details of the village. His mother did not allow him to move around much due to his sickness. But this time, the children were determined to have Jobin with them. Tipu reached the village by Saturday evening. Jobin somehow managed to convince his mother, and arrived on Sunday morning.

Khadeejumma and family were visiting too. Anwar was travelling after a long time. Ever since he got a wheelchair, the rooms of his house were the only tourist spots for him. All of them getting together was a rare occasion, but it finally happened that Sunday. It was also special because the Van-Mahotsav (Forest Festival), a series of events to commemorate forests, was starting that day. It was the sole festival for forests that was celebrated all over India. Nabeezath reminisced that in her time, school students used to plant saplings during that celebration. But Tipu and Ammalu hadn't heard of any such thing in their respective schools.

'It is an auspicious day. Ammalu, fetch your seed collection! Let's go to the serpent grove.' When Julia suggested this, no one could understand what she meant.

'Julia seems to be planning something in the grove,' Vineet said.

'Oh, please don't! That Rashid Ali might take affront and oppose us!' Nabeezath became wary.

'Let him oppose us! We will do what we have to do!' Julia stood firm.

'Are we going to plant saplings again in the grove?' Ammalu bubbled with enthusiasm.

'Of course! How can we let go so easily? I was born and brought up here too! I also have some rights over that property. It is not just my father and brother who get to decide things. Let us plant saplings in the serpent grove. Next to each chopped tree, let us plant another sapling!' When Sita piped up, Vineet was stunned. Where had she gathered the courage from? Perhaps this was the moment when all her previously dammed-up feelings about years of suppression were able to finally shatter the restrictions and flow uninhibitedly.

'Wow, look how smart my Amma is!' Ammalu cooed.

'But still, to do this on someone else's property…?' Nabeezath hesitated.

'Don't be afraid. Rashid Ali stopped the work because of the TV interviews of Ammalu. He will be hesitant to act now. This is the opportune moment for us to strike!' Vineet bolstered everyone.

Ammalu and Jobin started separating the seeds. They were chalking out where to plant the mango, jackfruit, *jamun*, *ashoka* and *peepul* saplings. Ammalu suggested that they should try planting them in different spots, away from their forbearers.

'Why create any artificial pattern? Let us recreate the grove exactly as it was. Through the decades, the trees flourished without any issue whatsoever. The grove thrived all by itself, and that naturalness is its uniqueness,' Vineet explained.

'Ammalu, blueprints and designs are for Rashid Ali and his ilk. We shall endeavor to create a grove without any models,' Julia said.

Vineet, Sita, Julia and Nabeezath, accompanied by Tipu, Aaron, Ammalu and Jobin entered the serpent grove. A revolutionary re-entry into a forbidden place! Anwar did not go with them; he was at home with Khadeejumma.

Tipu used his hands to dig holes for planting the seeds. This was the first time in his life that he had stepped into the soil without footwear. Quintals' worth of microbes collected in his mud-filled nails. Julia was inhaling the scent of a foreign land for the first time too. Just because one had given birth to a foreigner's child did not mean that one connected with his land or his identity. When you knew the soil, you appreciated the land better. Julia was entering into the womb of another country. She was morphing into an embryo there, and it was beginning to grow. Perhaps she would be able to understand Janardhanan better after this experience. The differences between them might dwindle. Scraping off some mud that stuck to her feet, Julia inhaled its scent. Was this the real scent of her husband? The original scent, which he himself might not have known until now? Was something coming to life from within?

There was nothing new in this venture as far as Vineet was concerned. He was born as the son of Shankaran Thandan, for surrendering his soul to earth and tree. Vineet had become a total devotee of the earth after his higher studies at the Agricultural College. During their field assignments, many classmates had been averse to getting their hands stained with manure and slush. After their practical projects of rice cultivation, which sometimes extended for hours at a stretch, many had complained of Athlete's foot caused by fungal infections, but Vineet had been immune to all of that. While digging the soil to make the earth ready for planting bananas, tapiocas and coconuts, Vineet had never collapsed in the heat, unlike many of his classmates. He had graduated in Agriculture with full confidence. It was almost a proclamation: *This is my space and my calling.*

Sita had mastered many lessons after becoming part of Vineet's life. Though she could not adapt to microbes and microscopes, she was well-versed with water and earth like her husband.

Jobin was sitting on the fringes cautiously, afraid of an imminent asthma attack. Without the inhaler, he always felt full of trepidation. Vineet firmly pulled him into the mud. Though he was not assigned any heavy tasks, Vineet entrusted him with small jobs.

'Try to inhale as deeply as you can,' Vineet advised him. Shutting his eyes, Jobin took a deep breath in, his nostrils flaring. His lungs expanded—never had they known such flexibility, such fullness, such expanse…

'Wow…so much fresh air! It's like my chest is filling up with the breeze, I feel like it'll break open now… Amma!'

'Your chest is not going to break! It is expanding. The same amount of air goes in and out of our lungs every second, okay?'

'I feel like I have enjoyed a delicious feast…'

'Take a deep breath in, Jobin! Until your tummy is full! Devour the air…let your lungs expand.'

Jobin's thin nasal tubes and narrow airways started opening up. Again and again, he inhaled deeply through his nose and exhaled through his mouth.

He relished the taste of the life-giving fresh air.

'You all breathe like this normally, don't you? How wonderful it feels!' Jobin remarked. His jutting bones, affected by the asthmatic wheezing, seemed to swing up and down in his exertions. Jobin was in the mood to settle down permanently in the grove.

'How lovely the breeze tastes! As if I am gulping down water after eating a gooseberry!' He sang delightedly.

Jobin sat with his eyes closed. Nobody disturbed him. The workers had cleared up certain areas which used to thrive with grass earlier.

The group prepared to plant vegetables there by piling up the soil and making layers. Ammalu planted some seeds. Aaron was busy examining an earthworm which was wriggling in his palm.

'Looks like a robot!'

Tipu borrowed it for a while. He felt relieved that the earthworms were still around. Rashid Ali's army of labourers hadn't caused any irremediable damage to the grove as of yet.

By the time they had planted the seeds and saplings and watered them, Anwar arrived in his wheelchair, rolled by his Umma. He wished to see the grove too. Anwar took a bit of mud sticking to his wheelchair and slathered it on his lifeless feet. Smearing wet earth all over his ankles, he joked, 'See how arrogant I am! Would you say these are the legs of a cancer patient? Let some sludge coat my legs too, right, Umma? As the saying goes, a trace of manure left behind where the elephant once lay!'

Anwar's mother's eyes filled with tears at his self-mockery. 'Umma, why are they struggling so hard? Ammalu looks totally exhausted. Tipu is bathed in mud. This place will be crushed by an earthmover machine in a few days' time. All their work shall go to waste.' Ever since he had fallen sick, Anwar had become pessimistic. He would have a cynical view about almost everything. A sort of rebelliousness and disbelief towards any activity. He had started contemplating about death.

'No, you are wrong. What if Rashid Ali decides not to create a building over here? Won't it be shameful if the television channels were to broadcast everything? No one knows how he weaseled his way into all that money either! That wife of his belongs to some Arab's family. If his deals are brought to light, he shall be exposed!'

'None of these hacked stumps are ever going to sprout again. Just because you plant another in its place, the loss of the tree cannot be replaced. Can this wheelchair take the place of my legs?'

'Don't depress the kids with your wayward talk. They are innocent children. See, your Umma is offering *dua* for your health daily. You shall get well soon with my prayers.'

Anwar's Umma took him away, not wanting to upset him further.

Everybody felt tired after a while. Nabeezath came with refreshments: lemon juice and biscuits.

'How are the Van-Mahotsav celebrations going, kids?' Julia enquired.

'What an *adipoli* festival!' the children shouted in unison.

'Tipu, why don't you show the Herbarium to your teacher?' Vineet asked.

'Well, all my friends have seen it. They really liked it.'

'That won't do. You should show it to your class teacher too. If possible, show it to the school principal. You should request for the Herbarium to be exhibited at the next school assembly. Let every student prepare a Herbarium!' Vineet asserted.

'Vineet, will it be practical? Children are overwhelmed with homework as it is! I even heard that parents were doing it for them nowadays,' Nabeezath objected.

'Let the parents join them in this assignment. If this project can be included in the syllabus, that would be great! The children will get to know some plants, trees and grains at the very least,' Vineet smiled.

'It could be tough for a child to do all this work alone. Better to make it a team project!' Julia suggested.

'Let the school authorities decide the implementation. Anyway, Tipu, get ready to introduce your Herbarium and your adventures at the serpent grove to your school. You should not delay any further.'

Tipu gave Vineet a thumbs-up.

Twenty-Two: Inspiration

Considering Tipu's limited knowledge of his mother tongue Malayalam, Vineet had prepared a speech for him. It was the school assembly the next day. Tipu had been rehearsing the speech the entire week. Nabeezath and Asif had to repeatedly train him to pronounce certain words. Yet there were words which were too tough for him. But Tipu had a sharp memory and hence, Nabeezath was sure that he wouldn't forget anything when he stepped onstage.

The school assembly was held twice a week. If any child wished to present something scientifically or culturally relevant, he or she was given an opportunity to showcase it. Tipu had volunteered early on, and submitted his topic of presentation as well. Another student would stand next to him and display the pages of the Herbarium as he spoke.

More than his speech, Tipu was flustered about the newly planted saplings in the grove. He had given instructions to Ammalu to keep a daily watch over them. Any day, Rashid Ali and his gang could encroach into that area. The first thing he did after waking up each day was ring Ammalu, and the last thing he did before going to bed was ring her again. Ammalu was the security guard of the grove; in fact, she was the secret camera.

Ammalu and Vineet visited the grove daily to water the plants. There were no signs of Rashid Ali visiting that compound. He was probably getting updates through his many spies. Rashid Ali was a wily man, and would probably come that way only after all the agitation had died down. Except for birds taking off with some cowpea seeds, Ammalu mentioned that nothing amiss had been observed in the serpent grove.

Both Ammalu and Vineet had been invited by Tipu to listen to his maiden speech. It did not matter to Ammalu that she would miss one day of school. The last time she had missed her classes was when she had gone to plant saplings by the highway. That day had been more important than any usual school day.

When Tipu stepped onto the stage, her heart started beating faster. Would he blurt out something foolish? Ammalu felt that they should not have forced him to speak in his mother tongue. Jobin was beaming away in the assembly. He was whispering to his neighbors, 'That's my friend. I have visited his home.' He waved at Tipu cheerfully.

Tipu looked very serious. He seemed to have suddenly grown older by ten years. The peon adjusted the height of the mic. Tipu started to speak. His friend was standing nearby with the Herbarium, ready to show the pages to the audience.

'Respected Principal, Vice Principal, teachers and my dear friends, today I am standing in front of you with a special showpiece. This is a book of remembrances, carrying the remnants of plants, as you can all see clearly. This book is called the Herbarium. First, we dry the plants—either partially or completely—and then, without destroying their shapes or colours, we paste them onto specific papers and create the Herbarium file. On the right side of the page, we note down the scientific name of the plants, its common name, place of origin, date of finding it, the place, and other details.

The Herbarium is useful for understanding different varieties of plants and identifying them. Not only that, but we can also study the changes and deterioration a plant faces in a particular area over the passage of time. If we examine these plant records every year, we can determine whether any species have become extinct. Of all such records, the Herbarium is the most important. For the climatologists who study the alterations undergone by humans and plants due to climate change, Herbarium files are of utmost relevance.

Statistics show that the number of animals facing extinction due to climate change, poaching and deforestation is growing every year. Plants are facing the same situation. Due to the heavy air pollution, extraordinary growth of the human population, destruction of their natural habitats, and natural disasters like wildfires, most plants are vanishing from the heart of earth. Global warming, destruction of the ozone layer, water and air pollution have grown into monstrous dangers, causing the elimination of different animal and plant species on earth.

Our earth shall soon be reduced to a wasteland. Barren, with soil that grows nothing; air that carries deadly contaminants and germs, and poisonous, polluted water, the earth shall no longer be habitable. In a class of 40 students, 35 will be chronic patients. Tomorrow's generations are doomed to days filled with floods and thunderstorms!

Our scientists are working hard to search for habitable planets in outer space. Friends, do you think this desire to escape after devastating the earth by drinking up her very life-blood is a worthy thing to do? Instead, shouldn't we be trying to protect the sources of life on this earth which had been taking care of us for all these centuries? Does a dutiful son or daughter abandon their sick parents? Never! It is our solemn duty to take care of them and cater to their needs. Our nature is turning sick now. Hence, we have to work together to protect her, to sustain her...

Let me conclude my speech now. Just another thing… Let our future generations not see plants as corpses inside a Herbarium! Let them not become extinct like the dinosaurs of the Jurassic Age! I thank one and all.'

There was a thunderous applause. Teachers surrounded Tipu with their warm adulations. Everybody asked him about the writer of his speech. Ammalu hugged Tipu and gave him a high-five. Whenever she was overjoyed, her eyes would well up with tears.

Vineet shook Tipu's hand.

'You were brilliant, Tipu! You did forget some data which I had scripted in, but no worries!' Vineet winked at him. It was true that Tipu had forgotten to quote some statistics. But he had spoken with great passion.

The school principal spoke after Tipu.

'Dear students, you must have listened carefully to our young friend. Tipu's Herbarium shall be kept in the Teachers' Room. Anyone who is interested can go and take a look during the lunch break. You might have understood how nature influences human life, and how the environment allows us to thrive. Each of you should be aware of the environmental issues around you. It is up to the younger generation to bring about a revolutionary change in society. Our time is about to set. Nature and all its forces and resources belong to you children! So you should not take this matter lightly.

I'm going to contribute what I can to this cause, as the principal of your school. For that, I would like to pass on this assignment to each one of you. Along with your usual academics, I am entrusting another task to you all. You are free to take help from your parents for this.

Every class teacher shall divide the class into four groups. Each group shall be given a Herbarium file containing thirty sheets. Each group shall collect a particular category of plants. Food crops, weeds, medicinal plants and cash crops. Group members can do their work either individually or collectively. So in every class, we shall end up collecting 120 plants through the efforts of four groups. Considering the number of divisions we have for each year until Class XII, imagine the number of Herbariums that the school shall create! But keep this in mind: you must not destroy a single plant under the pretext of this assignment. You shall collect your specimens without harming the plants.

After the annual examinations, we shall conduct a science exhibition at the school using your Herbariums. The best among them will be awarded. The winning group members will also be appointed as the Nature Club representatives of the school! There shall be special marks for those who collect rare plants. For further details, contact your class teacher. I believe that each of you will feel more connected to nature after all your efforts.

My dear students, now I shall see you exploring plains, forests, meadows and rivers, chasing the green! I wish you all the best.'

After the prayers, the students trooped into their classrooms. Heated discussions ensued from each.

Saumini of Class 7B to her friend Sheena: 'You have a huge backyard in your house. Shall we choose edible plants? We can collect all 30 from your place.'

Minu of Class 8A to Anita: 'Weeds, you said? Are you nuts? We will go for ornamental plants.'

Shanth of 5B to his pal Sudheesh: 'What do you mean by food crops? Rice and wheat? Let's stick to that. Nothing is more important than food.'

Ani of 10C to Sareena: 'I shall visit my grandmother's place and pluck the plants. They have a huge plantation there.'

Thomas of 11D to Sekhar: 'Where do I get a plant in my flat, I ask you! I might have to, I guess.'

Anoop of 6C to Sarita: 'I am not going to do it. Will ask my sister instead. Let that lazy bones get a bit of exercise, eh?'

Krishna of 1A to Derek: 'I have vases and plants in every single room of my house. But they are all made of plastic. Will that do?'

Shiny of 8C to Sangeeta: 'My late grandfather used to request us to have a thriving garden full of plants and trees. We have many acres of farmland. After my grandfather passed away, there was nobody to take care of them. Everything is lost now. How easy it would have been for me to build an Herbarium in his time.'

Shruthi of Class 6C to Meera: 'I pulled out a "communist *pacha*" just yesterday, you know? It is a weed! I'd have never dreamt that it would come of use someday.'

Amrita of 9A to Vinod: 'Listen, we don't even have time to finish our studies. Where will we find time for all these things? Still, we have to try hard and win that prize.'

Such were the apprehensions of the students. The parents had a different set of peeves and heartburns! The Parent Teacher Association meeting was in an uproar. There was many a Doubting Thomas around. Some parents were going quite ballistic.

Saumini's father: 'This is highly objectionable! You have implied that the kids should be stealing from their neighbours' compounds! Who has time for all this at home? How can we be at peace after sending our children wandering about for plants? We'll be forced to accompany them.'

Minu's mother: 'Are we sending our kids to an English-medium school for such a charade? Sending them to scour farms and yards! My daughter said that even weeds have to be collected. Who is answerable if they end up finding some snake pit, eh? You don't care about such things, do you?'

Shanth's mother: 'Who shall provide the names and details of all these plants? That is part of the task, right? I have no clue about these things. We are from a business family. In our childhood, nobody let us step into clay or slush! Now you are forcing us to make our children do all this?'

Ani's father: 'Tell me now, do they get special marks for all this work? Will you be adding these scores to the annual examination results? If so, we shall send her to our family home in the village and uproot some plants.'

Thomas's mother: 'This is the age of computers. Are you trying to convert them to Adivasis? These kids are supposed to take up jobs in multinational companies in the future. Technology is evolving day by day. And here comes this ancient Gurukul style of teaching!'

Anoop's father: 'What's all this, sir? If you want to make them do physical exercise, try some yoga or aerobics! This is too much. My son is sickly too. If I get a medical certificate from a doctor, can he get out of this task?'

Krishna's father: 'At least avoid involving the small children. Make it mandatory for Class V onwards. My child does not even know of any creatures except the hen. And here come all these plants.'

Shiny's mother: 'Until my father died, we were respectable farm owners. We thrived because of our farm. In fact, we were able to study and eat well because of what we earned from the land. But sir, is it practical nowadays? What will we gain by training them in farming, eh? What use will it be in the future?'

Shruthi's father: 'My daughter is generally lazy when it comes to studying. Now she has a new excuse! Though this project is not expensive, it entails a lot of effort. Shouldn't they just study something and pass the exams? Why add onto their woes? I enquired in all the nearby schools. No one has changed the syllabus in those schools like they've done here! I'm seriously considering changing her school.'

Amrita's father: 'Will we have to arrange tuitions for this too? Or maybe hire some labourers or self-help group workers from Kudumbashree?'

There was a plethora of reactions in the same vein. Among the crowd, a few parents responded positively to the assignment. But such voices were few and far between, easily overwhelmed by the naysayers. Many people started calling Tipu to get more updates. Some people visited the grove too. Tipu's Herbarium was venerated like a holy book inside the Teachers Room, where it was kept on a stool. The visitors were mostly parents. How could they explain what the whole thing was to their children without taking a good look for themselves? There were some who even cast nasty glances at the boy, almost accusing him of creating this hullabaloo.

The parents of the students studying at St. Thomas Missionary School had one single topic of discussion during their comings and goings now. Tipu's unique project became a talking point for everybody. People started thronging the serpent grove since it was the reason behind this complex, inspiring project. Vineet joked that they could have minted money if they'd start charging for entry tickets! Most people were hearing of the term 'Herbarium' for the first time. But the children reacted very differently, unlike the parents.

The students were highly enthusiastic about their mission. The idea that children should be brought closer to nature through the Herbarium was a success. Every child carried a plant in their hand as they traipsed to school daily. They would keep it tucked away in the pages of some magazine or book. Many kids tried to identify new plants with the help of friends and teachers. By the evening, classrooms filled with flowers, leaves and fruits—a green world! It was as if a garden had come dancing into the classrooms. How quickly had the enchanting nature flowed inside the school rooms! Each child showcased their plants with great pride before their friends.

The Biology teacher got a new shot of vigour. The students were learning at a rapid pace; and even without pictures in the text, were absorbing facts more quickly. It was like entering a flourishing vegetable garden. Even the lazy ones were stirring with fresh energy nowadays. Everyone seemed refreshed. Every new plant was being approached as if meeting a new friend. There were spies too, who sneaked around trying to find out the achievements of the competing groups. Some small-scale thieving happened during the lunch breaks. The school had a festive air about it. The bubbling energy which used to suffuse the school during the sports day and annual day seemed to have become a daily affair.

While the Herbarium Fest was going full throttle, Tipu's English teacher made them write a composition. The topic was: 'My pet'. It was but natural that Anku the tortoise made it to Tipu's essay. He described the entire series of events, starting with Anku's entry, in a very funny manner. The special bond of Anku and Thankayamma also featured in his narrative. His teacher read Tipu's composition out in front of the others. His was the best of all the submissions.

Nirmala, the English teacher, started showing a keen interest in Tipu from that day. She would sit next to him in the bus. Since his stop came much after her own, Nirmala would keep talking to him throughout the journey.

She would offer him books to read. On Friday, she asked him for his Njarakkadu house address and phone number.

'Tipu, Nirmala Teacher will be coming to your house this weekend.'

'Where? Why?' He asked.

'I need to see someone.'

'Who? Vineet Uncle?'

'Who? Not him. Tipu, you don't know this person.'

Tipu thought that he should inform Rarumma about Nirmala Teacher's imminent visit immediately. His Rarumma typically got flustered with unexpected visitors.

'What will you give me when I visit your house, Tipu?' Nirmala wheedled.

'Rarumma cooks many delicacies—*pathiri, pazhampori*… You can eat whatever you want!'

'Is that so? Then I shall most definitely come. I'll bring my brother along, okay?'

'Little brother?'

'No, he is a university student.'

'Hmm.'

'Will you show me your Anku tortoise?'

'Sure, Thankayamma will bring him.'

Tipu got down at his stop. He told Nabeezath that his teacher, Nirmala, would be coming to their house because she liked his composition.

'I think it is because of all the stories related to the serpent grove,' Nabeezath murmured.

'No, Rarumma. She became so friendly after reading my English composition.'

'Let her come. We shall give her many nice things to eat.'

On Saturday, as soon as he arrived, Tipu called Ammalu on the phone. The two of them went to check on the plants in the grove. All the seeds had sprouted. Ammalu had sowed new seeds to compensate for the ones that the birds had flown away with. There was no news of Rashid Ali. Tipu thought that he must have been feeling intimidated. He realised that even the so-called boisterous ones easily shrank away in fear.

'Now we have turned into real superheroes!' The children high-fived each other.

'Tipu, your school's Herbarium project is becoming very famous. Everyone in our school knows about it too. Some parents were asking the principal to introduce it in our school as well. My friends are all eagerly waiting for it to start in our school, you know?'

'If so, you should win the first prize. Carry the whole grove to your school!'

'Hmm... Nobody can beat me at collecting things. Not even Tipu, the Arab from Dubai, could do that, haha!'

Tipu poked Ammalu's cheeks.

'My Amma says that I should stop making friends with boys.'

'Your Amma is strange! You better listen to Vineet Uncle like me.' Tipu stood on tiptoe, with his collar turned up.

'Aha! Look at him preening away,' Ammalu laughed.

As they stood chattering, they saw Nirmala Teacher and her brother passing by the grove on a motorbike.

'Come with me, Ammalu. Let me introduce you to Nirmala Teacher. I wonder why she came today, when she was supposed to come tomorrow?'

Nirmala had brought many gifts for Tipu. Her brother Karthik looked serious. Though nattily dressed in jeans and T-shirt, his overall body language and style of speech gave him a conservative air. Tipu disliked men with beards. He believed that there was a false face hiding behind the shagginess: perhaps a wily fox, or a cat; or even a lion! Karthik wore round, black-rimmed glasses. Tipu did not bother to cast another glance at him.

Karthik was looking at Tipu's sketches. From behind the bushes of his beard came a voice: 'Good!'

Nirmala Teacher began to gush, 'How can it be not good, I say! Tipu is the smartest boy in my class.'

Tipu thought that his teacher was fibbing. How could she forget Vinayak who always scored full marks in every subject? Nabeezath liked the garrulous Nirmala who seemed to fawn over Tipu.

It had been two years since Nirmala had married; but she and her husband were separated. Though not yet divorced, matters were heading that way. She was living with her mother and brother in her maternal home now, and she had no children. Though not very well-off financially, her family had fixed a good marriage for her. Her husband Abhishek was an engineering graduate, who preferred working in his father's business. They had a cashew factory and other medium-sized enterprises. Abhishek did not really need a job, as such. His wish was that a bride from a slightly weak economic background would help his mother with the household affairs; and since she was educated, be of aid in his business too. Abhishek had married Nirmala with these hopes.

But things had gone awry. If it was Abhishek's snoring which troubled Nirmala on the very first day, the next day's issue was his bad breath! The third and fourth day saw bickering over the number of hours he spent in his shower. Her major peeve on the fifth day was about the bass in Abhishek's voice! Then it graduated to finding faults with the weird sounds Abhishek made while chewing nuts, the way spittle flew as he spoke, the crunching sounds made by his slippers, and the way he clapped hands while watching a film. Though Abhishek tried to pacify her storminess with expensive gifts, these did not solve Nirmala's problems.

Abhishek's mother ran a small enterprise where she sold homemade snacks. There were four women to help her with this work. She would provide catering services for marriages and parties. Abhishek's mother had been doing this work for a long time now, and would not hear of stopping it for any reason whatsoever. In the holes of the *acchappam*, in the bald head of the *unniappam*, in the twists and turns of the *murukku*, she must have seen some shapes invisible by others. Her cheeks would become round like *neyappam* as she fried these up, and her lips would redden like *jalebi*s as she deftly tossed them in oil…

'Look at that old woman's avarice in spite of all her wealth!' This was Nirmala's barb towards her mother-in-law's business endeavour. One day, when one of the maids was absent due to a fever, the woman had asked Nirmala to help her make a round rice snack. That was the last day that Nirmala had stayed in her husband's house. When Abhishek had come home, Nirmala was pouting, her bag stuffed like a round snack. As Nirmala was whining away about her life—which had been apparently destroyed by a food item—someone had procured a school job for her. She was determined never to return to Abhishek's house again. On seeing any round rice snack, Nirmala would eye it with abhorrence. Fortunately, there was nothing of that genre among the variety of delicacies that Nabeezath offered her.

After sipping some tea, Karthik whispered something in Nirmala's ears. Immediately, she asked Tipu to come closer.

'Tipu, where is your Anku tortoise?'

'Come with me, I will show you,' Tipu invited them to the backyard. Thankayamma was washing vessels, seated on her haunches. Tipu had once sketched a picture where Thankayamma was depicted washing plates with a *beedi* clenched between her lips. Of course, she had never actually done anything like that.

Anku was searching for something in the water which Thankayamma was throwing away after washing up. Karthik sat near Anku, and started examining his limbs. He measured the span of his shell. Lifting him up, Karthik peeked underneath, and then started clicking a flurry of pictures on his phone after placing him back on the ground. In one photo, Tipu was also present. However, Tipu observed that Karthik immediately deleted that picture.

Meanwhile, Nirmala was engaging Nabeezath in a never-ending conversation. Her tales were about the 'torture' endured at the hands of her wicked spouse. Nirmala was assuming that Nabeezath would empathise, since she once had a daughter of her own age. Nirmala pretended to open a treasure chest of her secrets before Nabeezath!

Karthik was asking Thankayamma several questions about the tortoise. Where had she found him, how long had it been with her...so on and so forth. He was circling Anku, and showed no indication of backing away. After taking pictures, he was sending them to someone via WhatsApp. He took out a scale from his pocket and measured Anku's body. He reminded Tipu of his pediatrician. Peering into his stuck-out tongue, poking into his throat, opening his eyes and shining a torch into them, opening and closing his fingers, examining his nails, tapping against his palm… Fatima had explained the logic behind those actions, 'The doctor cannot peep inside your body through your open mouth, Tipu. He is deducing the disease by examining the symptoms shown by various organs.'

Karthik's assiduous examination would beat even that of a pediatrician. It went on for a very long time until Thankayamma took Anku away. Karthik looked disappointed, as if Thankayamma had taken away the gift he was expecting to be offered.

'Yes, sir. It is the same species we saw that day. A good specimen,' Karthik was speaking to someone on his phone.

Keeping Anku safely inside the house, Thankayamma muttered softly to Tipu, 'Thieves! Beware of that fellow!'

Tipu did not understand anything. Karthik started whispering into Nirmala's ears again.

'Tipu dear, can we borrow Anku for two days?'

'For what?'

'Oh, Tipu, are you such a selfish boy? We shall return him after playing with him for a bit, okay! Today is Saturday; we shall return him by Monday evening. What do you say?'

'Nobody is taking this tortoise away. He belongs to me! I have just loaned him to this lad to play with. That is because I am close to the child and his family. I will not let anyone carry my tortoise away from here!' Thankayamma shouted furiously.

Tipu was flabbergasted.

Thankayamma had seen many people who had been eyeing Anku. She did not know why Karthik needed Anku. Perhaps he wished to give him away as a pet; perhaps hand him over to a lab; or even smuggle him away to another country? Specimens of Anku's species were rare indeed. Imagine finding an almost-extinct tortoise in a mofussil panchayat, when there was no trace of his type even in the Wayanad forests! It was Tipu's English composition which had brought Karthik to his house. Nirmala Teacher never came to his house after that incident, and she stopped showering him with her unmitigated affection soon afterwards.

Tipu yearned Anku to grow wings. Poor thing, let him fly away and escape! He felt a terrible anxiety about Anku. Should he ask Thankayamma to lock him in a cage? But how would that be different from Karthik's laboratory or a zoo? Tipu consoled himself that Anku was safe in the superhuman custody of Thankayamma.

The Herbarium project was quite the success at school. Tipu's group was assigned 'Weeds.' The labourers had hacked away the touch-me-nots, the Siam weeds and the grass in the grove. Since most of the children had well-maintained gardens in their homes, there were no entrypoints for weeds there. Weeds were the first to be banished from human habitations. Destined to sprout only in exiled spaces!

Tipu entered Thiru-Nilam and started looking around. Since the roof was dilapidated, sunshine, fog and rain had a heyday in that place. The corners and edges of the rooms, usually made smooth with human interactions, were rough and frayed. The claws of the mice needed coarseness, and snakes needed desolate corners for laying their eggs. The centipede and the leech needed ruggedness in the environs. Nature had taken the lead and made the place habitable for all those creatures.

Grass was sprouting from the splinter of wood that had fallen from the beam, as well as the crevices of the cement floor. Tipu had no idea how plants grew from rooftops and fissures of walls. Hiding away in secret recesses inside the walls, they would suddenly spring forth. He had mostly seen banyan saplings growing in that manner. Compared to the magnificent banyan tree in the grove, such Peeping Toms were embarrassing indeed. Shameless brats! In Tipu's opinion, such secret plants were hiding in every building. But they never emerged. These mysterious walls were hiding many such lives!

Tipu liked to analyse such 'secret' growths through a different perspective as well. Whenever someone left his house, or forgot about his house while living there, such 'secret' plants extended their necks. Imagine that people devoid of any love for where they live, are living in a house. The walls would not get even a word of appreciation, a truthful caress, or the moistness of love. Then they would start cracking up. Through those fissures, the plants would stretch their heads. Thiru-Nilam had turned into such a house. Though Nabeezath had difficulty wrapping her head around Tipu's innovative theory about plants which grew from crevices, she magnanimously agreed with him.

Tipu gathered six weeds from Thiru-Nilam. The house held much more variety compared to the time that humans lived in it. Though these rogue weeds were of no use to anyone, Vineet had stated that they used every potential gift endowed by nature. Which place was free from their encroachment? They would do their utmost to establish a foothold in any place. It was irrelevant to them whether the place was a rubber plantation or a paddy field. They needed no fertiliser, no water, nor care. Unsolicited, they would just spread around. Thankayamma's nature rather matched the weeds.

It was night, and Tipu was having his supper. An owl hooted in the front yard. Tipu raced to the foyer. Rarumma chased after him. They were having *kanji* and boiled green gram for dinner. Tipu disliked eating *kanji*, since he associated it with fever. Only feverish people ate rice-gruel! Nabeezath stood near him with a bowl of *kanji*. An owl was perched on the electricity line, rolling its eyes.

'See, the owl came because you were not having your *kanji*. Better hurry up!'

'Hey, trying the same trick you used with Ummudu, are you? Rarumma, please don't try to fool me!'

Tipu slapped away Nabeezath's arm. The rice-gruel toppled over and scattered on the floor.

'You just watch out, you naughty boy! The owl shall take you away tonight! It is waiting to flee with scamps who don't listen.'

'As if! The owl moves at night because it has lost its home. Not to catch me, okay? What happened to his tree-hollow? His serpent grove?'

'Whatever...' Nabeezath emptied the rest of the gruel inside the sink. Chewing on some boiled gram, Nabeezath sat next to him.

'That poor creature is complaining to us. Where shall he go now?' Tipu pressed his face against the window bars and stared at the owl. Did Ummudu get scared at the sight of this poor chap? Tipu couldn't believe it. Maybe the owl had been a villain in those days! Now he had no home, no neighbourhood, no friends, or even sufficient food... Tipu felt that the owl sitting on the electricity line and the wandering girl who came begging for food were very similar to each other.

In one and half months, Tipu's group got their Herbarium ready. Some lazy bones were busy ironing leaves beneath newspapers! Teachers were catching them red-handed too. Ironed leaves gave off a different scent; their colour became a yellowish-green, and they resembled a mosaic floor. The watery portions remained green; the rest would dry up and die. But the parents who lamented that the project would take up too much of their time had been grumbling in vain. The teams of 10 students could easily handle the project.

It was the time of Onam examinations and everyone had kept their Herbarium projects on hold. Tipu approached the principal with the matter of the Missing 10. With her permission, the details of the missing ones were displayed on the main notice board. Their scientific names and other information was exhibited along with the pictures of the 10 plants. Exactly like the 'Missing' columns in newspapers. On seeing those advertisements, Fatima used to rage, 'Missing? Who thinks they're missing? Why do they insist that these people should be seen in specified places? They will be somewhere, visible to some eyes. Can people ever really go missing?'

It was no wonder that Fatima, who used to speak about such things, went missing one day. Tipu knew his Ummudu well. He wondered whether he should display Fatima's picture, too, with the Missing 10. Tipu had come to understand that the rarest of the rare lives were likely to vanish fast from the earth. His Ummudu belonged to that category.

The next day, another picture appeared on the notice board. It was that of Anku the tortoise. It was a picture that Karthik had taken that day. There was a note beneath the photograph.

This is the picture of the endangered species Indotestudo travancorica, also known as the Travancore tortoise. Breeding these tortoises illegally in homes and keeping them captive are punishable under the Wild Life Protection Act, 1972. Whoever finds this missing tortoise is hereby requested to contact the Forest Department.

All those who read the notice board went running to find Tipu. 'Isn't that your tortoise? Will the police catch you? Nirmala Teacher has pasted that notice, she will hand you over to the cops... Better give her your tortoise...' A barrage of advice hit him from every corner of the school.

Tipu refused to go to school the next day and insisted on reaching Njarakkadu right away. Asif stood his ground that trips during school days were not allowed, and that he had too much work. Tipu protested in the balcony for a long time. He held this stance for hours. When the 'hunger strike' carried forward from breakfast to lunch, Nabeezath intervened. On the suggestion that she and Tipu could catch a bus home, the protest was called off. Nabeezath wondered whether the child was trying to find his mother through the tortoise and the grove, given his deep attachment to both.

'Rarumma, let us bring Anku back with us. We have to take him away from Thankayamma.'

'How can we do that, dear? We are going by bus, remember!'

'Let us tie him up in a sack.'

'What if someone catches us midway?'

Tipu became afraid.

'Let us ask Vineet Uncle for help.'

Tipu called Vineet. It was Ammalu who picked up the call.

'I shall take care of Anku. No need to take him to your flat,' Ammalu said.

Vineet took the phone from Ammalu.

'What's the matter, Tipu? Let us give him to the Forest Officers when they come.'

'No, I won't! I want him. I will take care of him.'

'Listen, dear, Anku should not be living with us. Let him go home. The Forest Officers will set him free in the wild, where he can be with his friends. That will make him happy.'

'But, but… I will miss him,' Tipu started sobbing.

'Don't cry, my child. Anku isn't like your other toys. He wasn't born to do as we dictate. Let him go, Tipu.'

'Are you all part of Nirmala Teacher's team?'

'Haha...not at all. Nirmala Teacher wanted to make some money by selling off Anku. You protected him. Frustrated at the failure of her plans, she has raised this complaint.'

Tipu was miserable. He had hoped for a solution from Vineet. But his response had stumped him. The child became silent. Nabeezath tried to chat about the owl, but he stayed where he was. This was the saddest day for him ever since his arrival at the Njarakkadu house.

'Tomorrow your Vappu shall come. We will take Anku back to the flat with us,' Nabeezath hugged him.

Tipu silently went off to bed. After some time, he slipped into slumber.

Asif arrived the next morning to take them back. Tipu climbed inside the car first. His face was dark. He ignored the sweets which Asif had purchased for him.

'See, I have Anku with me,' Nabeezath called out from the back seat. Anku was sitting on top of a newspaper. Even after they had driven for miles, Tipu had not given a single backward glance at Anku. Asif understood one thing—the same strategy that Tipu had adopted to forget Fatima, he was now trying with Anku. He was training himself to forget the tortoise.

Representatives of two different species were travelling in the same vehicle. Whenever Anku tried to scramble up the seat with his forelimbs erect and head extended, Nabeezath would forcefully make him return to the seat. In the unexpected jerks and stalling of the vehicle in the city's traffic, the tortoise toppled off the seat too. Yet, Tipu did not look back. Anku was making weird noises. He was very rattled. Intermittently, he clung to Nabeezath's sari tip. Perhaps he was remembering another life-changing jeep trip. The discomfort exhibited by the hapless creature highlighted his inner turmoil. Rolling his eyes in all directions and thrusting forward with his limbs, he tried to crawl as fast as he could. After trying to make sounds, Anku finally relapsed into stillness, like someone who had lost the ability to move.

It was Asif who carried Anku to the flat. Seeing Anku on the drawing room carpet, Tipu felt pity welling inside of him; the creature looked so pathetic. Anku was like a child coming to a new school for the first time. Tipu took him away to his room. Anku crept under the cot. When Tipu stretched his neck and peeped under the cot after some time, he found Anku asleep. The way he slept, with his long neck and head on the floor, made Tipu miserable. He lay on his bed and wondered: where were Anku's parents right now? Anku was waiting for another Ummudu just like him. But the waiting had stretched for years on end.

Anku had been solitary since Fatima's schooldays. Wouldn't he have wished to chat with his friends all this while?

The only language he could relate to had been Fatima's. They used to converse with each other for hours. They would argue with each other sometimes; and Anku would retreat into his shell. To cajole the cry-baby out, Fatima would jingle her anklets and circle the shell. Anku would pretend to be miffed with her just to listen to Fatima's tinkling anklets that scolded him ceaselessly.

Though Tipu and Ammalu always tried to include him in their games, nobody knew whether Anku found those amusing. Tipu fell asleep while contemplating such matters. Even when he woke up the next day and got ready for school, Anku was fast asleep. 'What sort of sleep is this? I have never seen this before,' Tipu said.

'Please go, dear, the school bus will come now. I shall take care of him,' Nabeezath consoled him.

Tipu had gone to school hesitantly. His mind was wandering even in class. He was punished for making mistakes in the arithmetic class. Nirmala Teacher had stopped talking to him, and pretended that she had not seen him. What a trickster she was! Tipu felt infuriated. Whenever he thought of the plight of his tortoise, he grinded his teeth thinking of her role in it.

During the lunch break, Tipu did not venture into the playground. He wished to sneak back into his flat. He didn't even taste the fried rice which Nabeezath had prepared for him. He shut his lunchbox and returned to the class room. Tipu once again read his composition, 'My favourite pet'. He felt sure that Anku was going to vanish like Fatima.

When he raced back to the flat after disembarking from the school bus, Tipu was met with a strange sight. A group of kids and a befuddled Anku in their midst! Tipu was still panting due to the exertion, and now he felt a boiling anger. It became an emotion which was indescribable. A few cabbage leaves were strewn in a plate kept before the tortoise. The children were staring at the tortoise with open mouths. One of the kids was adding plastic leaves to the cabbage. Another was balancing a paper weight on top of the poor creature. He was also prodding Anku from behind, forcing him to move forward. They were trying to make Anku walk on two limbs and balance stuff on his shell, as if he were an elephant in a circus. They were calling him funny names. As Anku crawled with the paper weight on his back, they were clapping their hands and yelling hoarsely. What a hullabaloo!

Tipu yelled with utmost fury, 'Get out, you stupid folks!'

Hearing the uproar, Nabeezath came running from the kitchen. The woman next door had come to pay a visit, and her son had come along. While Nabeezath was talking with the lady in the kitchen, the boy had amassed an army of children who had come to 'see' Anku. She had no idea that a group of little monsters was thronging her drawing room.

'Rarumma, you failed to look after a small tortoise, then how will you take care of me?' Tipu shouted.

Hearing Tipu's anguished question, Nabeezath became upset, but she remained silent.

Tipu took Anku to his room, deciding to lock him up during school hours. Or should he buy a cage and keep it in the balcony? He couldn't bear to see Anku languish inside a cage! It would be downright cruel if he were to be locked up when he was already lonely. Tipu felt contempt for himself on even thinking about caging Anku.

Tipu took Anku with him when he entered the bathroom. Filling the bathtub, he deposited Anku inside. Nabeezath understood that Tipu no longer trusted her with Tipu's safety. After swimming about for some time, Anku tried to clutch at the sides and emerge from the water. Since he could not find a grip on the slippery surfaces, he again slipped back into the water. Tipu had to pull him out finally.

'Anku might not be familiar with the chlorinated water available here, Tipu. He is only used to the riverwater.'

'Shall we get a bottle of mineral water for him then? Or should we give him water mixed with cutch tree barks—the sort that we drink, Rarumma?'

Unable to eat or drink or swim, without his favourite tidbits to gnaw on, Anku started looking lost. He would sit in a place listlessly and lie down wretchedly, as if his neck was broken. Tipu often wondered if Anku was lifeless. He would crawl towards Tipu, rub his head against his ankles and then crawl under the study table. When Tipu peeped beneath, Anku would raise his head as if he yearned to say something. His eyes seemed to ask, 'Aren't you seeing my plight?' It was the same expression in the eyes of the owl which had perched on the electricity line.

When Tipu went to school, Anku would be placed on the balcony so he could bask in the sunlight. After some time, he would make his way back to the room. Without walking on the carpet, he would make his way to Tipu's room. Whenever Tipu deposited him on the carpet, he would scramble off to plain floor in a hurry. Anku exhibited acute discomfort when placed on carpets, mats, sofas or in the bathtub. He had stopped eating properly and looked lethargic.

Anku's inertness seemed to seep into Tipu. He lost his enthusiasm for life. When students called him regarding Herbarium project, he would be impassive. In class, too, Tipu remained unresponsive. Nabeezath understood that the root cause was the tortoise.

Asif was determined that Tipu should never get affected by Fatima's absence. He was willing for any compromise to avert that pain. He wondered whether he should let Tipu stay with Ammalu for a while. Asif believed that Tipu was acutely experiencing the lack of his mother. The house was redolent with a depressing silence. It had turned into a house of mourning.

Tipu was apprehensive that the officials from the Forest Department might come searching for Anku anytime. Nirmala Teacher knew about his flat and whereabouts.

Anku wandered around the balcony and the hall, unaware of the goings on. Nabeezath suggested showing him to a vet. But Asif warned against exhibiting Anku publicly. Nabeezath concluded that old age had caught up with Anku. Tipu searched the internet to discover a tortoise's life span. Google gave him solace by spelling out 400, 300, and 170 years.

Anku had much to tell Tipu. Of course the lad did not know how the water in the bath tub had stung his body! When he had swallowed few gulps, his throat had burned too. Anku wished to warn Tipu against bathing in that water. Tipu's skin was so tender compared to his own. How was he not getting affected?

Anku's legs slipped on the marble floor. When he tried to lurch ahead, it felt like someone was pulling him from the back. How hard he had to struggle to move even an inch forward!

Tipu would sometimes listen to Anku's breathing. He would try to measure both their breathing rates. Tipu would always win the game! While Tipu managed to inhale and exhale 10–15 times in a minute, poor Anku could hardly manage three or four times. One could almost watch the air travelling inside his throat. He moved his head and forelimbs while breathing. Tipu realised later that Anku's lot survived for centuries due to this peculiar habit. He informed Ammalu about it. While Anku 'chewed' the air, Tipu 'gulped' it down. Tipu had no idea that those who breathed less air lived longer. Indeed, Anku would nudge his feet occasionally to tell him all of this.

When Tipu became furious, he would speak in a high pitch with Nabeezath. His rate of breathing increased noticeably. 'Breathe slowly, deeply,' Anku would yearn to teach him that philosophy.

Once, Fatima had smuggled Anku into her room without Nabeezath's knowledge. Soon, irritated by the *kurr, kurr* snores emanating from him, she had shoved him outside and shut her door. Only Anku knew how he could not sleep that night due to Fatima's own snores vexing him through that door.

When Tipu placed him on the balcony for basking in the sun, Anku found it objectionable. The sun was so cool over here! Only whatever sunshine the concrete shades regurgitated reached the eighth storey balcony. Why should he keep waiting for these measly bits of sun? He would clamber back into the room irately.

Anku the tortoise was flummoxed; he couldn't tell Tipu that the food was not to his liking. The tortoise had been born in the forest. He knew the taste of grass and fruits very well. In the Njarakkadu village, he somehow managed with the food he was offered. But in the flat, it was becoming deadly! He could not bear the smell of the cabbage leaves Nabeezath gave him, forget about eating them.

Once, Nabeezath had sliced a watermelon and offered the pieces to Anku and Tipu. Anku had spat it out due to the bitterness while Tipu relished it while watching television. He would eat anything while engrossed in the TV. But the fact that Tipu suffered from loose motions the next day affirmed Anku's belief in the noxious quality of the food.

Asif was complaining that the tortoise wasn't eating well, breathing well, rejecting the sunshine, and hence should be shown to a vet. He did not know the real state of affairs. Nobody in that flat really understoof Anku's problems.

Eventually, matters worsened and Anku could hardly move an inch. Tipu was in a silent, melancholic mood. One weekend, while readying to go to Njarakkadu, Tipu told his father, 'Vappu, let us give Anku to the Forest Officers.'

'Why?'

'They will take him to the forest, won't they?'

'Maybe. Or hand him over to a zoo.'

'No, not that!'

Asif brooded for a while.

'Tipu, let us go on a trip. We will free Anku and send him back to the forests. In his home at Wayanad.'

'What will happen if the forest officials come?'

'We will tell them the truth. Don't worry. Let's get ready for a journey to Wayanad. You can invite Ammalu too.'

Twenty-Three: Journey

The journey to Wayanad became a reality. Vineet, Sita and Ammalu accompanied them. For Anku the tortoise, it was another adventure just like his first jeep trip. He sat in turn in the laps of Tipu, Ammalu and Sita. Throughout the trip, they fed him with leaves and fruits. Though he had no clue about the destination, there was a lively sparkle in his eyes now as compared with the dullness in the flat. The sounds he made sporadically made Tipu recollect the DH Lawrence poem he had saved on his tablet. He recited it from memory to Ammalu.

"Tortoise Shout"
I thought he was dumb,
I said he was dumb,
Yet I've heard him cry.
First a faint scream,
Out of life's unfathomable dawn,

Far off, so far, like a madness, under a horizon's dawning rim,
Far, far off, far scream...
Worse than the cry of the new-born
A scream,
A yell,
A shout,
A paean,
A death agony,
A birth cry
A submission,
All tiny, tiny, far away, reptile under the first dawn...'

'I remember only that much...' Tipu said.

'Very interesting poem. Aren't you feeling sad, Tipu?'

'Yes, but I feel sadder when I look at him.'

'What shall we tell Thankayamma?'

'She protected him from enemies and took care of him. But even she did not think about what Anku himself wanted, did she?'

'True, he will be happy in the forest. Perhaps he will reconcile with his old pals!'

'We should leave him in the inner forests, or else people will catch him again.'

The deeper parts of the forest were far off from the hotel they stayed at in Wayanad. The hotel itself was surrounded by a small forest. But Vineet wasn't ready to let Anku walk away in that vicinity. It was a reserve forest, and there was a busy road nearby. Anku would struggle to survive in that area. Vineet had once worked in Wayanad and had acquaintances in the region.

When he heard the decision that Asif and Vineet would free Anku in the inner forests while the rest of them stayed in the hotel, Tipu protested vehemently.

'I will come… I want to see!'

'Me too…' Ammalu joined in.

'Look at this girl's clamour for hiking inside the forests. Don't forget you are a girl,' Sita reminded her with her favourite warning. But Ammalu was adamant.

Vineet's friend Sumesh, who worked as a guard in the Forest Department, came to pick them up in a jeep at 4:30 in the morning.

Tipu and Ammalu were dressed in warm clothes. Having fought with her mother, Ammalu's face was frosty.

'Are you taking the family along? It is an open jeep, and taking children will be risky. You might have to trek in between,' Sumesh said. Ammalu started weeping copiously on hearing the words. Tipu sat on the verandah, totally despondent.

Ammalu kept crying.

'Acchan, take me along… I want to come…'

Both the children sat in protest in front of the jeep. Finally, the adults had to change their decision.

Anku was travelling back home to the forests in the same way he had travelled away from them, in a jeep. Sumesh was singing ceaselessly and smoking non-stop. Asif had to intervene to make him stop smoking. 'There are kids here, and a tortoise too,' Asif told him.

The throbbing movement of the jeep, the cigarette stink—Anku knew perfectly well what these two things had ushered into his life. The sheer coincidence that both his arrival and departure were in the same settings! Nobody knew whether Anku actually understood all of this.

When they entered the deep wild, the essence of odours changed perceptibly. The density of air decreased. It became truly life-giving air; the oxygen content was optimum. Anku's lungs—used to breathing polluted air with meagre amounts of oxygen—yearned to expand in spite of his thick shell, exhilarated at the pure oxygen reaching his nostrils. There was an elephant somewhere near; a strong gust of elephant musk billowed in.

It is said that when vipers lie with their mouth open, the smell of boiled tapioca wafts by. A viper was certainly out there lying in wait for a rat with the final requiem; because the boiled tapioca odour was in the air again.

The fragrance of *gulmohar* was also present. There had been a *gulmohar* in the serpent grove too.

'Ammalu, if we were to view the grove with 3D glasses, it would be like this forest,' Tipu commented.

'But there are no animals in the grove. This area is dangerous,' Ammalu warned. She snuggled close to her father. Tipu observed that the trees in the forest were majestic; a sense of pride and grandeur was palpable in their presence.

The glares that the trees bestowed on them were similar to that of the burning looks that security guards shot at the trespassers inside the state assembly building. The trees were arrogant: the way their roots went deep into the earth and the manner in which their chests puffed out…! The deer hiding behind the shrubs leapt at the sound of the jeep. Rabbits were bounding away too, sometimes crossing the vehicle's path.

'Is Anku asleep? Isn't he seeing this hare? Is he ready for another race?'

No one smiled at Ammalu's jest.

Anku wasn't sleeping. He was listening and inhaling it all; the forest, the trees and the soil.

Sumesh halted the vehicle near a boulder.

'From here, we have to walk. The vehicle won't go beyond this point.'

There was a stream nearby. Everybody splashed water on their faces and refreshed themselves.

They sat on rocks by the side of the stream and had their breakfast of sandwiches. There were thin leeches glued onto the rocks. No one would suspect them to be bloodthirsty. But a leech was possibly the slimmest Dracula around.

Dawn was breaking. It was time for birds to leave their nests.

'Tipu, look at the birds in that tree. If only the grove had so many of them…'

'I wish there was a stream like this in our grove,' Tipu responded.

His impossible, wistful wishes!

'Definitely! A stream big enough to drown Rashid Ali,' Ammalu cracked another witticism. She had the expression of a child looking at a teacher about to distribute the examination paper. Ammalu was troubled by two questions: what would happen the moment Anku took their leave? And what would come after that? All these lighthearted jokes were her conscious effort to keep the anxiety at bay.

Sumesh stepped into the stream for a bath; he seemed to be crazy about water. He was singing full throttle even while bathing. But nobody could make out exactly which song he was singing: it wasn't a poem, a movie song or a hymn… undecipherable indeed!

Ammalu started filling her frock's pockets with yellow flowers growing nearby.

'See, I collected 20 flowers.'

'Huh! Is this your only job? Let us feed Anku, come on…'

The children walked towards the jeep. Sumesh had forgotten to shut the back door. Anku was lying on the ground;

writhing on his back. He was struggling to get himself upright again. The tortoise was spinning around and kicking, his limbs moving frantically. Tipu ran to restore Anku to his normal posture.

Anku lifted his head and took a look around. Then he snapped up few shoots of grass nearby. He elongated his limbs and stood up as tall as he could. He looked back at Tipu, and rolled his eyes at Ammalu. Now he was moving as fast as he could, with his body erect. Anku was racing away quickly. Tipu was reminded of those vehicles in Dubai which moved forward despite the red signal. They would intentionally flout the traffic rules and dash away before anyone could rebuke them. Anku the tortoise was rushing away, ignoring the red signal. Beneath his limbs, the grass bowed at first, then was crushed.

'Wow, look at that speed! Did he compete with the hare like this?'

As the children looked on, Anku ran through the meadow and entered the stream. Hiding amidst the rocks, he observed the flow of the water. His neck was stretched out as long as it could go. Crossing the rivulet, Anku disappeared inside a shrub. Tipu followed him to the other side of the stream. From the shrub, Anku made his way into the deep forest, where huge trees clustered in tight groups. Ammalu and Tipu were astonished that he did not pause to cast a backward glance. Why should he? He had so many things to look forward to!

The creature which had seemed to be on its deathbed inside the flat had scurried away in great speed. Tipu waved at him. Marks left behind by Anku's limbs were visible on the moist earth. Like Tipu's Ummudu, who had gone deep into Tilapia's mud, Anku merged with the trees. Tipu knew that he would never ever see the tortoise who had been gulped down by the forest. But he was still hoping to see his Ummudu whom the desert had swallowed. *For some time, the serpent grove was his Ummudu; intermittently, Anku was his Ummudu. Ummudu would come to his side again, in some other form.*

'He galloped away so fast!' Ammalu's eyes were full of tears.

'His home, his friends; of course he is eager. Let him go!'

'He was looking so sickly yesterday. But did you see him run? He is absolutely healthy!'

'Sickness? We were the sickness that troubled him. The forest is his doctor. It shall remove all his ill health now,' It was Vineet who spoke. He and Asif were observing everything from the rock.

'Tipu, I was so wonderstruck! Think of a butterfly trapped in our hands being set free.'

'You are right. It was exactly like that… We are cruel people, Ammalu.'

'Hmm...' Ammalu lowered her head.

The imprints of Anku's limbs remained as the postscript of his lost days. On the trip back home, the children were imagining Anku's fabulous return journey. Anku swallowing fat snails and creeping amidst the grass, making a *kupp* sound; Anku's eyelids turning pink on sighting his mate; Anku sleeping near the tree roots... Tipu decided to sketch the images as soon as he reached home. Ammalu asked him to draw the picture of Anku and his friends swimming in the lake.

The grown-ups had expected the children to cry when Anku departed. But it did not happen. Sometimes, children displayed great maturity, to an astonishing degree.

Twenty-Four: The Eleventh Pit

The Missing 10 on the notice board continued to be a legend. They remained enigmas that were untraced, though nearly 3000 school children had forayed into forest, meadow, city and village searching for them.

'No point in looking for those plants any more, children. I don't think you can find them anywhere on earth,' Vineet said firmly.

Julia and her family returned to America. Rashid Ali was preparing to restart his deferred activities in the grove. When the din died down a bit, he became full of alacrity. It was Thankayamma who informed everyone that Rashid Ali and the engineer had visited the plot of land again.

The saplings which Ammalu had planted by the sides of the National Highway were knee-high now. There was a furore in the area for watering them; every vehicle would pause and make the children participate in watering the plants. Many parents scored brownie points by posting pictures in social media of their kids watering the saplings by the roadside. Why ignore easy opportunities to become popular? It soon became a selfie-point. Slowly, tender-coconut sellers and balloon sellers shifted their business to the vicinity. The only thing yet to happen was the granting of a suitable name for such an attractive spot on a national highway. There were folklores and poetry in praise of the 'children's plants'; many a drama and movie were created; research and studies were conducted.

Jobin's sickness abated a bit. He shifted houses and travelled long distances to reach the school. Next year, he planned to attend school near his new house.

At the grove…

Rashid Ali was there. Accompanying him were three or four labourers. An earth-moving machine came grunting behind them. Rashid Ali dispatched the men in different directions of the serpent grove. He waved to the machine driver, beckoning him to follow his footsteps. Rashid Ali and the huge, yellow monster started moving forward, forward, forward—devastating the grove.

Suddenly, Rashid Ali stopped. So did the giant machine.

The way forward was being obstructed. It was a lad swinging on a creeper hanging from the banyan tree. His shriveled legs were swaying in the breeze, in tandem with the creeper.

'Where are you off to?' Though the voice was not commanding enough to intimidate Rashid Ali, it was rebuking in tone.

'Who are you?' Rashid Ali asked.

'Ha, ha. Am I not everything? I am everything.' His contemptuous laughter rang out in the grove.

'Don't make trouble here, come on, get down… Get him down now!' Rashid Ali demanded, looking at Tipu. The child ignored the instruction and kept pushing Anwar's creeper-swing. Anwar's wheelchair was lying orphaned near the white ebony. White flowers scattered on the dark seat of the huge machine, like those which had fallen on Anku's shell.

'What? Are you trying to scare me? Who do you think you are? Where are you from?' Rashid Ali was incensed.

The machine driver got down, and whispered into Rashid Ali's ears, 'He is a sick one, belongs to the other party.'

There hadn't been much improvement in Anwar's condition. He was nearing death day by day. The boy was very thin and fragile, and had lost his hair. His eyelids were dark and he had lost all interest in cricket. The doctors suggested giving him what he liked, saying that it would help him conquer pain better. There was no more treatment left to be done. His loved ones could only watch haplessly as he held on.

Most days, Anwar insisted on visiting the serpent grove and they would oblige, and he would return with a new enthusiasm every single time.

Anwar's face was very serene. He kept swinging on the creeper. The breeze he loved was blowing in the grove. He had no worries; having overcome the anxiety of death a long time back. Death had become a bosom friend; someone who walked with his hand draped around his shoulders.

'I don't care that you are a sick boy. I'll tear you apart…!'

When Rashid Ali raged, Anwar gesticulated, making the man look down. There were eleven small graves for corpses, dug beneath the creeper. Tipu was the one who had made the pits. A baby mouse could have been buried in each.

'What's that? Has some dog dug up those holes?' Rashid Ali baulked.

'Great simile! Do you know where those 10 plants are? The Missing 10 from Tipu's Herbarium?'

'How am I supposed to know? Get down and scram!'

But Anwar kept on swinging; with his shrunken feet, he reached to touch the pits.

'These ten death-pits are meant for the 10 missing plants from Tipu's Herbarium. Now, to turn them into death-pits, we need at least one dead body for each. Here, we have none; not a single corpse to vouch for their souls. No point in keeping these waiting, is there?'

Rashid Ali looked around gravely when he heard those words, staring at the trees and plants in the grove. There were tender leaves sprouting on the newly planted saplings. A few of Ammalu's vegetables were on the verge of flowering. Grass had grown again on the ground which had been cleared by the labourers, akin to springs of hair on a bald head. The huge trees that had escaped the chainsaw were entranced by the new growth on earth. 'Grow, grow fast, cover the earth,' they seemed to cheer. Due to the regular watering by Ammalu and Vineet, the soil was moist. The earth oozed water, and softened and succumbed at a mere touch.

The saplings were at Rashid Ali's ankles, and small plants had grown to his knees. Shrubs were reaching his waist, and trees towered over him. He had seen them all, yet Rashid Ali took another look, as if seeing them again.

'You haven't asked for whom the eleventh pit has been dug, have you?' Anwar pointed to the eleventh death-pit on the ground.

Rashid Ali was silent.

'Vineet Uncle's Herbarium captured the entire flora of this region. It was a Herbarium made exclusively using the plants which thrived in the village during his college days. Ten plants have gone missing from that collection. Where are they? A whole school searched with Tipu to retrieve them. Where are they indeed? Even if the whole world were to search for them, they shall not be found. Do you know that?'

Anwar paused, and then continued. By that time, the wind in the grove had changed its direction and held a different intensity.

'This eleventh pit is meant for you and me. Maybe one day, that too shall lie without anyone to occupy it,' Anwar swayed on the creeper. The wind swung along with him.

Rashid Ali turned to look at the earth mover machine. It was right there, behind him.

Anwar looked at the machine and queried, 'How's that chum of yours?'

It was Tipu who shared a short narrative about the chum.

'Doesn't he resemble a monstrous dinosaur? That humungous body, an unquenchable tummy, elongated neck, sharp fangs…Stegosaurus, Triceratops, Tyrannosaurus, Allosaurus… They were all greatly formidable creatures. None of them exist now. Now, only earth-eating monsters shall remain on earth; in fact, they alone shall forage over the earth like dinosaurs.'

Rashid Ali's monstrous machine slowly started moving forward. In the moist earth of the serpent grove, its wheels made deep imprints like the clawed feet of the dinosaurs. Its gigantic body shaking and heaving, it reached the vegetable bed. Spinning its long neck and opening its mouth with deadly fangs, it lowered itself. The teeth hooked onto the twine of a flowering cow pea plant, filled with blue blossoms. Along with it, many vegetable saplings were uprooted by the gigantic machine. The remains of the plants dangled like noodles from the mouth of the monster. In the next dive, the machine devastated the last of the cow pea saplings. Everything was crushed by its fangs. It was turning its head, trying to plan the next move.

The machine turned its gaze at Tipu and Anwar. Again, turning leftwards, and lowering the neck, the giant opened its mouth. It was aiming at a tree stump. Well, here was a corpse. The monster machine did not distinguish between the dead and the living. It reached the stump with the same ferocity as before. Now it was consuming the tree-stump with its fearsome teeth. The enervated roots appeared from the hiding place under the earth. The leviathan spun the tree stump in the air once, and the bits of earth from the roots fell on Rashid Ali.

Removing the carpet of dried leaves, the giant machine was digging underneath. Earth worms thrashed about in the soil; the ants were frantically racing; the leeches and centipedes were petrified; but the yellow demon was emotionless.

The second earth mover machine, too, reached the grove. Both the giants were ploughing and furrowing their way through the serpent grove. How many groves had they murdered in their adventures till now!

Flicking away the earth which had fallen on him from the dead roots, Rashid Ali raised his right hand at the machines. Abruptly, the long neck and open mouth froze in the air. The grove looked askance at the machine, wondering where its next dive would occur. An anxious look towards the future. Such an agonised look! The gaze held everything in it—much like the dinosaurs which wandered aimlessly without any refuge in an earth devastated by floods and cyclones, these hideous machines were wandering all over the earth. With their open mouths full of monstrous fangs, they would keep stretching their necks and spinning their heads, searching for a hill of mud, and the thrashing of a root. In the world where these yellow ogres reigned, only their roars would resound; the roars of avarice!

Tipu covered the death-pits meant for the 10 extinct plants. But the eleventh pit, he let it stay open.

Acknowledgements

I owe my heartfelt thanks to my translator, Ministhy S., for her meticulous work, which has opened a wider new world for my novel. This work would not have been possible without her genuine interest, and I truly appreciate the rapport we shared throughout the process.

I am also profoundly grateful to the editorial team at Niyogi Books for their invaluable suggestions and insights. I sincerely thank Mrs Tultul De Niyogi and Shri Nirmal Kanti Bhattacharjee for their unwavering support and encouragement.

A special note of love and thanks to my spouse, Muhammed Rafeek, for being by my side throughout this journey. To my son, Raihan, who has been an inspiration in shaping the main character, Tipu, through his own traits as a young boy. Thank you for being the spark behind this character!

SONIA RAFEEK